CAPTIVATED
SOULS

USA TODAY BESTSELLING AUTHOR
ELLIE WADE

For Anna Brooks, who is one of the most amazing supports I have in this industry. Thank you for being my friend, my sounding-board, and my therapist. lol Your love and support mean more to me than you could ever imagine. Love you!

QUINN

I CLUTCH the front door handle and pull in a fortifying breath. I don't know what to expect when I enter my best friend's house, and that terrifies me.

I'm not good with death, nor being with people while they deal with it. Perhaps it's a major flaw, but it's the reality of who I am. I *want* to be good with it. I'd love to be the person who knows what to do in awkward and heartbreaking situations. There's always that one woman, we'll call her Sue, who's a life saver at all events. Sue's the one who shows up to funerals with a giant purse containing literally everything. She pulls extra packets of tissues out of her bag for all who need it, and painkillers for those with horrible tension headaches from too much crying, and snacks for those who've been so lost in misery that they forgot to eat. If there is a need,

Sue will reach into her magic bag and pull out the solution.

I want to be a Sue, especially for those I love the most, and have the remedies my friend needs, but I'm not a Sue, not even close.

I'm the girl who walked down the aisle at her grandmother's funeral years ago, not realizing the skirt of my dress was stuck in the waistband of my nylons, revealing my hot pink "Tuesday" panties to the church full of mourners. To make matters worse, my grandmother's funeral was on a Saturday. Moments later at said funeral, I got a tickle in my throat during my uncle's eulogy and was trapped in one of those never-ending coughing fits while he was up at the podium pouring his soul out for all those who loved my grandmother. I know that whatever he said was beautiful; I just wasn't able to hear it while hacking up a lung.

The story of my grandmother's funeral is typical Quinn. I have the best of intentions, but I often fail to execute them correctly in awkward situations.

Sure, anyone can have a bad day. The unintentional peep show and coughing fit could've happened to anyone. But they aren't isolated incidents. A co-worker's mother died a couple of years ago, and during the funeral service, someone's loud and obnoxious cell phone rang out during a moment of prayer. I kept my eyes closed, silently chastising the inconsiderate fool who didn't silence their phone for a funeral until the person to my right nudged me with their elbow, clueing me in to the fact that the inconsiderate asshole was indeed myself.

Later at the reception for that funeral, I asked my co-worker's sister when she was due as she appeared to be about eight months pregnant. Her red and offended face huffed in anger before she rolled her eyes and stormed off—far away from me. I knew better, too. I've never asked a woman if she was pregnant unless I was a hundred percent sure that she was. I'm normally a very kind and considerate person, but the sister and I were talking about her late mother, whom I had never met, and it was awkward and uncomfortable. I had wanted to lighten the dark moment with a brief conversation about something a little more positive. What is more positive than a new life entering the world, a perfect little baby? Maybe my change in topic would've worked if the sister had indeed been with child. But alas, I'll never know because the sister hates me, and I'm pretty sure my co-worker hates me now, too. We were never the same after that, and she's now transferred to another department.

There are other incidents of my grand inadequacies when it comes to dealing with death over the years. I'm pretty sure I've blocked a lot of them out, too. I mean, who wants to remember the worst parts of themselves?

My friend Amos texted me to let me know he had a work meeting he couldn't get out of and suggested I pop by our mutual best friend Alma's house to keep her company, seeing that she buried her husband, the love of her life, two days ago. Amos is a Sue, at least when it comes to Alma. He always knows what she needs before she needs it. Though, I'm wondering if his intuitive abilities might be slacking a bit since he thought it wise to send me.

No, I'm not a ten-year-old girl at her grandmother's funeral. I'm a grown woman, and my best friend needs me. I can do this.

I plaster on a smile and open the door. *Wait.* A smile definitely isn't appropriate. Dropping the cheesy grin, I attempt to appear concerned and helpful...whatever that face looks like. *This isn't going to go well.*

"Alma, it's me," I call out in the large foyer to no response. Stepping farther into the house, I follow the sound of the television to the living room, where Alma sits cross-legged on the sofa staring at the screen.

She looks awful, and I don't mean that in a cruel way. She simply doesn't look well. Her long brunette hair hangs in tangled strands with part of it matted to the side of her head. She has dark bags under her eyes, making it appear as if she hasn't slept in days. *She probably hasn't.* The skin around her eyes is swollen from crying, and my heart breaks for her.

"Hey," I say gently as I close the gap between us. She doesn't pull her gaze from the television. Turning toward the screen, I notice there's an infomercial for a vacuum airing. "Is this what you want to watch?" I sit beside her, grabbing the remote from the end table. "Alma," I say more forcefully.

She slowly rotates her face toward me as if just realizing I'm here.

"Hi," I say with a sad smile. "Can I find you something else to watch?"

"Okay," she whispers.

I flip through the guide to the streaming service currently airing *Friends*. Alma and I spent many nights in college watching this show. It's one of our favorites.

"You can't go wrong with *Friends*, right? Can I get you something to eat or drink? Do you need anything done? I could do your laundry. Oh, or I could load the dishwasher or paint your nails?" Nonsense explodes from my mouth. *Paint her nails? Shut up, Quinn.*

Alma looks at me, her expression blank.

"I'm sorry," I say, moving closer to Alma on the couch and wrapping my arm around her shoulders. "I'm not very good at this stuff. I just want you to know that I'm here for you, and I love you. If you need anything, just ask. Okay?" I squeeze her shoulders.

She nods and turns back to the TV.

Ross, one of the best characters, is on the screen talking about the importance of Unagi, and I chuckle. Alma's body starts to shake as a flood of tears leaks from her eyes. *Shit.*

"Alma, it's okay. Oh..." I lean my head against hers. "I'm so sorry."

I want to say so much more, but I leave it as a simple apology because I am—so sorry—for her. It's not right that someone so young has to lose her husband in such a horrific way. I'm sorry I don't know what to do to help her through this. I'm sorry there's nothing I can do to heal the pain in her heart.

Grabbing the pillow to my side, I set it in my lap and pat it, urging Alma to lie down. She complies, laying her head in my lap. I throw the small blanket on the back of the couch over her and run my hand across her head, smoothing down her hair as she sobs against the pillow.

"Shh, it's okay," I say again. "You'll be okay."

Alma's sobbing drowns out the show, so I mute it.

No other words are spoken. Alma cries while I go through my head trying to figure out how I can help her, only to come up blank. Eventually, her sobs cease, and her breathing steadies as she falls asleep.

I've never been so happy for someone to fall asleep in my life. She clearly needs the rest, but beyond that, I can't mess this up.

At Alma's husband Leo's funeral, I held it together for the most part. Amos was there, of course, so he was able to attend to all of Alma's needs. I spent a lot of my time with Alma's parents, who were stoned, to make sure they didn't do or say anything to upset Alma. I don't think I could've ruined that day anyway. I could've shown up to that funeral in just a thong, and I wouldn't be what people remembered from that day.

The funeral was at Leo's estranged parents' mansion. Alma wasn't happy about the location, to begin with, and while Leo's father delivered the eulogy, she stood, yelled, and called the father out on his treatment of Leo over the years in front of everyone. It was a nightmare, the whole ordeal. Not Alma—she was brave. Her loyalty and fierce love for her husband shined through her tears as she spoke. But everything else, from the way in which Leo died to the stories of his past abuse, was so heavy.

The air in this house, the complete sadness, the utter heartbreak Alma is going through is heavy, too. It's suffocating.

I watch *Friends* on mute and sit as still as I can while Alma naps with her head in my lap. I swear I hardly breathe, too afraid that I'll wake her. Six episodes and a little over two hours later, the sound of the front door opening is music to my ears.

Amos enters the living room with bags of reinforcements. *A total Sue move.* He sets down a bottle of Gatorade that I know Alma needs desperately. I can tell by her chapped lips that she's dehydrated. I'm not sure what food he brought, but it smells delicious, and I hope it's good enough to tempt even the saddest of hearts.

"How is she?" he asks, voice low.

I just shake my head.

He nods in understanding. "Do you want to stay for dinner? I have plenty."

"No. I should go." I slide out from under Alma's head, setting the pillow against the couch cushions.

"Are you sure?"

"Yeah," I reassure him. "I'll touch base soon. Call me if you need anything." This last sentence makes me cringe.

With a weak hug, I excuse myself and bolt out of the house. As I close the front door behind me, I pull in a deep breath, my first one in hours. I get into my car and shut the door. Draping my arms on the steering wheel, I lean my forehead against it and cry—full-on, back-shaking sobs.

I hated seeing Alma like that, so broken. She's always been so strong and full of life. Leo ruined her life, and I'm devastated for her. How will she come back from this? My heart shatters for my friend, and I wish I could take her pain away, but I can't even be helpful for two hours. I'm inept with all this. She needs help, obviously. I've never seen someone so sad in my entire life. I just don't know what to do to make it better. The fact is, it will never be better because he's gone.

A knock on my window pulls me from my thoughts, and I lift my head. Amos peers in and opens the door.

He reaches his hand out to me. "Come here," he says, pulling me up out of the car and into a hug.

I cry against his chest. "I'm sorry. I couldn't do anything to help her. She's so sad, and I didn't know what to do. She just cried and cried, Amos. It was horrible. She's not okay."

He rubs my back. "I know, but she will be."

I shake my head. "She won't. Her heart is broken, and I'm useless. What can I do?"

"You're not useless. You did everything you could. You made sure she knew that she wasn't alone, that she is loved. That's all we can do. It's going to take time. She'll get better, Quinn. I promise."

"I'm so worried about her." I take a step back and look up into his eyes.

"Give her time," he reassures me. "She'll be okay."

"I hope you're right," I say on a sigh.

"I am. Are you okay to drive home? You can stay a while?"

I pat his arms. "No, not everyone's a Sue, Amos."

"What?" He chuckles.

"Nothing. Just...she's lucky to have you."

"She's lucky to have you, too. Your love and support, just as you are, is enough."

I attempt a grin. "Thank you. I'll call tomorrow."

As I pull away from Alma's, I'm overcome with a crippling fear. I'm sure Amos is right and that Alma will bounce back from this, but I know for a fact I never could. I'm a mess in all situations involving death. I'd be completely useless and beyond help if death came for someone I loved as much as Alma loved Leo. I'll never put myself in a position to lose my love in the manner in which Alma lost hers. I need a love that's incredible but safe.

If I loved someone as much as she loved her

husband, and then I lost him—it would destroy me, and no amount of time would make it okay. I've always been tough, and fear has never held me back. Yet with love, I can't take the risk, especially now seeing the fallout first-hand. Maybe it's another personal flaw, but I'm just not that strong.

CHAPTER 1

QUINN

PERFECTION IS relative with boundaries so infinite it's impossible to measure. I could step outside of myself in this very moment, become a fly on the wall peering down with utter cluelessness, and think—she's reached it. *The life.*

Beau, my beautiful boyfriend, is rubbing my feet at this very moment because the Louboutins I wore all day at work were not kind to me. And when I say he's beautiful, I mean it. He's as gorgeous as they come, kind, successful, and good in bed. Let's face it—all those things matter, or at least I thought they did.

Now, I'm not so sure.

I'm the middle child, born directly between two older and two younger sisters. Yet the middle child syndrome that everyone jokes and posts memes about on social media couldn't be further from my reality. I was too busy being seen to ever be ignored. Meek and quiet are two adjectives that have never been used to describe me, of that I'm certain. I've gone after what I've wanted and chased my dreams since I could remember.

At twenty-seven, I've built an incredible life for myself. I took a fashion and business degree that qualified me as nothing more than a glorified fitting-room attendant and worked my way up to the top. I'm now the district manager at the biggest department store in our area. I make good money and love my job.

I've nurtured the relationships in my life that matter and have incredible friends who are like family to me. I live in a city I love, in an adorable little house that I bought on my own.

All the boxes are checked, and the dreams achieved, yet there's this unsettling truth that invades every part of me, telling me that I'm not there yet.

"You okay, baby?" Beau presses his thumbs into the spot on the arch of my foot that makes my back bow in a heady mix of satisfaction and pain. "You're quiet tonight."

"I'm good." I give him a soft smile as I lie to his face —his stunning face.

In terms of checking off the boxes of my partner wish list, Beau checks them all. The moment I met the savvy businessman in his tailored suit, looking like he just stepped out of a romance novel, I knew I wanted him. He's everything I've dreamed about. He's as close to perfection as they come. The fly version of myself looking down at the scene would agree.

Taking into account this evening alone, Beau has prepared stuffed shells, one of my favorite pasta dishes. The entire house smells of garlic and Italian spices, and my stomach growls just thinking about the meal he's made for me. He's responsible for the candles lit around the living room and for supplying the glass of wine at my side. He fills the silence with interesting conversation. Most importantly, he loves me. And I can't deny that I love him, but I don't know if that's enough anymore.

Last night, I dreamed of someone else.

Someone I can't have.

His ocean blue eyes, shining from the sun's reflection, came to me in my sleep. He stood there, his toned forearms reaching toward me, and I remember the dream so clearly as if it were real. He didn't say a word, but the need was evident on his face. The desire was palpable, and as much as he wanted me, I wanted him more. But I couldn't touch him. I yearned to reach out and run my fingers through his disheveled hair and press my lips to his. He was just there beyond my grasp. All boy next door meets sexy surfer—charming and free— the combination irresistible.

All at once, he started crumbling and drifting off into pieces, vanishing to dust until he was simply gone. I called out his name, over and over again, each time my voice more frantic. He was no longer there as if he'd never existed at all.

I woke to a racing heart and a pillow soaked with tears, gasping for air that wouldn't fill my lungs.

I've thought about him all day, unable to forget the dream and the way it made me feel. The truth is, I think about him a good portion of most days. We've never touched or kissed, yet I crave him. All. The. Time.

Instinct tells me to go to him and get what I want, but fear holds me back because he's not an option. He'll never be an option for me, and that hurts. I'm not the type of person to bow to fear, never have been, yet with him, it cripples me. I'm strong and determined in all aspects of life, but this one, for I know he could ruin me. I may be a risk-taker at heart, but I can't risk myself, and I'm terrified he'd destroy me. I vowed years ago to never put myself in a position to be ruined, and that still stands.

Besides, I have Beau, and I love him.

I mean, I do love him?

He lowers my foot to the ottoman and sits beside me on the couch, snuggling into my side as he wraps an arm around me and kisses my temple. "Dinner has another half hour or so. Do you want to watch something?"

I tilt my face to the side and hold his gaze. Beau is safe and comfortable, but he's not my forever. He'll never elicit such raw emotion from me as the man who visits me while I sleep, and though I can't have my care-free surfer boy, I can't settle for less. There has to be someone out there who will make me wake up sobbing with need.

I don't dream of Beau. I don't crave him or need him so desperately it aches. I never have, and sadly, I never will.

Perfection is overrated, and I want the ache, a love so deep that it consumes me. Beau provides everything a healthy relationship should be, tied neatly with a bow. He's the whole package, but it's not enough. All at once, I realize it's not enough. My decision is crystal clear, and though it comes to me seemingly out of nowhere, it fills me with resolve, and I have no choice but to listen and act.

Pulling in a breath, I scoot back from Beau and turn my body to face him. "I'm so sorry. I don't think..." I shake my head and continue with more finality to my words. "This—us—isn't working for me anymore. It's nothing you've done or haven't done. You're near perfect, and I love you, but I don't want to lead you on if we're not meant to be together for the long haul."

He blinks several times, looking at me in shock. I'm certain he can't believe he heard those words just come from my mouth. I can hardly believe them myself. This is not how I saw the evening going. "You don't see us together? Married?"

I frown, hating every second of this. "I don't. I'm sorry. I wanted to, and maybe for a while, I did, but something's missing for me. I can't describe it, but something just isn't here, a feeling."

"What feeling?" He furrows his brows.

"I'm not sure, but it's not here, and I can't force it. I

literally just figured it out, and I don't want to waste any of your time."

He forces his fingers through his hair. "Waste my time? Jesus, Quinn. We've been together for a year. I thought things were great. I love you, and I thought you felt the same." Standing from the sofa, he raises a hand and kneads the back of his neck. "I can't believe this," he whispers.

My eyes fill with tears, and my heart aches to hold him and take it all back but for all the wrong reasons. I yearn to comfort him because I care about him, and he's hurting, but my mind won't change. So I owe it to him and myself to be strong. "I'm truly sorry, Beau. I am."

"Quinn." My name is a plea.

"You were the best boyfriend, and I mean that." I stand and step before him. "I wanted us to work, but it's...but it can't, and I'm sorry."

There's nothing else to say because the truth is this was inevitable. Some relationships just aren't meant to be, and someday when Beau is with his true love, I'll be just some girl he used to date, and all will be right.

He looks at the ground. "I just..." He sighs. His eyes don't find mine when a dejected whisper leaves his lips, "I gotta go."

I don't try to stop him as he walks away, and I don't say anything because no words will make this better. I can't risk giving him hope for us where there is none. This breakup came out of left field, and we both need time to process it. As he disappears into the hallway, he snatches his car keys off the foyer table, and seconds later, the front door is closing behind him, and I feel lighter. It's hard, but it's right. I know it.

I crave an epic, soul-mate-level love. And I'll wait for it.

Turning on the TV, I flip through the channels, stopping on an old episode of *The Office*. It's hard to focus on the show as my mind races with all the possibilities. Perhaps my mental list for a life partner has been wrong. Sometimes, I feel it's not so much about what someone does or doesn't do. It's more a feeling, a connection.

Beau was perfect but not perfect for me. The deep connection wasn't there.

The aroma of garlic and spices is replaced with the undeniable scent of burning.

Crap!

I hurry to the kitchen and pull Beau's dinner out of the oven. The bottoms of the large shells are blackened, but I dish them up anyway.

Scooting against the back of the sofa, I take a sip of wine before putting a forkful of crispy burnt pasta into my mouth, and it's the best charred pasta I've ever eaten.

It tastes of possibilities, a better future for myself than I know to dream for, and I know—deep down—that it's all going to be just fine.

CHAPTER 2

QUINN

I CAN'T WIPE the smile from my face as I watch my best friend, Alma, dance with Amos, an expression of true joy on her face. It fills my heart with happiness to see genuine contentment in her expression. She deserves it. We're a month shy from the four-year anniversary of her husband's death, and though her daughter brings her joy, a part of her has just been going through the motions these past few years. She's great at hiding it, but I can tell she's been forcing one too many smiles.

Not now, though. The grin on her face is real.

Alma and Amos shocked many people moments ago when Alma thanked Amos for her surprise twenty-eighth birthday party with a kiss, but not me. I've always known something was between them. Well...perhaps I believed Alma's insistence that they were nothing more than friends at the beginning of freshman year when I dated Amos.

Gosh, that seems like an eternity ago.

Okay, I will say that after my short fling with Amos, I sensed something between them, a deeper than friendship connection, especially in the way Amos has been here for her these past four years. He's a gem, a true saint if you ask me. I don't know how Alma would've gotten through everything without him. Perhaps, Alma's feelings are just emerging for him, but there's no doubt in my mind that he's loved her forever. Regardless, I'm thrilled that they're dating.

"She looks good. Doesn't she?"

His voice causes me to freeze, and I pull in a startled breath. I'd know that voice from anywhere and the gorgeous man attached to it.

But the thing is, I don't want to know that his eyes are a rich blue, the shade of the deep, infinite ocean. I hate that I know his dirty blond hair is going to be brighter than usual from the July sun. When I turn to take him in, his olive skin is going to be darker than normal, having been kissed by the summer rays.

I've memorized all his features, and I hate that I have.

It's impossible to forget anything about him when he visits me in my dreams almost every night. He's my secret obsession. I haven't told a soul about my real attraction to him and never will because it doesn't matter. I can't do anything about it.

I grip the stem of my wineglass as if it's going to ground me in some way and slowly turn toward him. He pulls out the seat next to me and sits down at the table.

I swallow and force a smile. "Yeah, she looks really happy."

"Right? It's awesome." He grins, and my heart stutters.

My gaze drops to his mouth and full lips, and I bite the inside of my cheek. *Pull yourself together, Quinn.* I take a sip of wine and look back toward the dance floor.

"She deserves all the happiness in the world."

I can see Ollie nodding in my peripheral. "She does."

Oliver Hale was Alma's late husband Leo's NA, Narcotics Anonymous, sponsor for about five years when Leo was still here. He and Leo were close, and Ollie became a part of the family. Alma has a way of making all the important people in her life more like family than mere friends. She's built this sense of community with the people most important to her, and Ollie Hale is one of them. So it makes sense that he still comes around and is still included in events even though Leo is gone.

But it's hard.

I met Oliver about eight years ago at Leo and Alma's old house in Ypsilanti, across from Eastern Michigan University's campus, and I felt this immediate attraction to him. I blew it off as a mere crush, of which I'm very familiar with. I'm a flirty person by nature and have had many crushes and short flings that didn't lead anywhere. I've never acted on my attraction toward Ollie.

At the beginning, it would've been awkward because he was there to support Leo and help him stay sober. It simply wouldn't have been appropriate to fool around with him. Now, after seeing what loving an addict can do to a person, there's no way I can go there—no matter how insanely irresistible I find him.

There's something about him that leaves no doubt in my mind that Oliver Hale could never be just a fling. If I let him in, he'd take hold of my heart and own it forever. There'd be no going back. Yet the more I attempt to push Ollie from my mind, the more he takes up residence in my dreams. I hate the control that he has over me. The funny thing is, no one knows about it but me.

Sure, Alma's known since the beginning that I think he's cute, but I've always played it off as nothing serious, a simple attraction. I'd be blind not to recognize how handsome he is. So no one suspects anything.

I'm afraid giving voice to my feelings—my real feelings—would somehow make them a reality, and I much prefer my current state of pretending it's all in my head.

"What've you been up to since May? Last time I saw you was at Love's third birthday, where, oddly enough, this song was playing on repeat." He chuckles, looking toward the speakers where Angela Lansbury sings *Beauty and the Beast* from the Disney cartoon's soundtrack.

His comment makes me laugh. "I'm sure Love

requested it. She has a mild obsession with this movie," I say of Alma's three-year-old daughter.

Ollie shakes his head, and the side of his mouth tilts up. "Someday, when I have kids, they're going to request Green Day, Smashing Pumpkins, and the Stone Temple Pilots, not this trash."

It's weird to hear him talk about having kids. In all the years I've known him, I've never seen him in a relationship. He's never once mentioned a girlfriend, and now that I really think about it, that's odd. He's so nice and gorgeous—surely there have been women interested in him over the years. Perhaps, he's really private about that part of his life, or maybe he doesn't date as part of his NA sponsor role. I'm not sure, but I can't deny that hearing him mention his future children does something to me. My insides twist, causing jitters to rise from my belly up to my heart.

"Kids like what they like." I shrug, playing it cool. "My sister's daughter is obsessed with the baby shark song, and I'm telling you that Disney soundtracks are better than baby shark any day."

"That may be true, but I think that kids learn to love what they're exposed to, so I'll pull out all my old CDs and play them on repeat." He raises a brow and catches me in his stare. "What?" he scoffs. "What does your look mean?"

I hadn't realized I was giving him a look, but I've always been told that my thoughts and judgments are written all over my face.

I shake my head. "I don't know. I guess it's weird to hear you talk about your future kids. I didn't peg you as the Dad type."

My statement isn't meant to be negative. Ollie is a free spirit. He reminds me of a stereotypical surfer, out to catch the waves and chill out with his friends at the beach. Were we to live in Hawaii or anywhere near an ocean, I picture him spending his days out on the water. Since we live in Michigan, I suppose his motorcycle is his version of a surfboard. There's also the fact that he would have to be serious with a woman to have children and a family, which I've yet to see, either. One would think that at thirty-eight, he'd have settled down by now if that was something he wanted.

"There's a lot you don't know about me, Quinn Kirkpatrick." He raises a brow, and his full lips pucker slightly. His response is weighted, and I can't help but feel he's saying more with that statement than I know.

The way in which my name falls from his lips turns my insides to mush, but as always, I pretend it doesn't. "Maybe." I hold his stare in my best attempt to come off as unaffected.

His tongue pokes out and licks his lips before he absentmindedly pulls the bottom corner of his lip between his teeth. Intrigued attraction flares as my chest swells. I bring my wineglass to my mouth and tear my gaze from his, the intensity in the connection too raw.

I watch as Love dances with her grandma, Leo's

mother, on the dance floor, and Alma sways to the music in Amos's arms.

Ollie taps the pads of his fingers against the top of my hand, regaining my attention. "Hey, are you okay?"

I turn to him, startled. "Yeah. Of course. Why wouldn't I be?"

He shakes his head, squinting his eyes. "I don't know. You seem off, like something's on your mind."

"Nope. I'm good."

He lets out a dry chuckle. "I'm not really buying it. You know I'm good at reading people. It's one of the reasons I'm a decent sponsor. I can tell when there's something under the surface that's not being said."

I raise my brows. "Well, sorry to burst your bubble, but your people-reading skills are off today because I'm fine. There's nothing I want to say." My mouth feels dry with the lie.

He's right. There's so much I want to say and want to know about him, but any information he could give me would only fuel this unhealthy obsession I have with him. My subconscious would take our conversation, his mild interest in my feelings, as a sign of something more. And there's nothing *more*. He's just Ollie, steadfast and friendly, as always. It's who he is and why he is a great sponsor. He genuinely cares about people.

"You don't get paid for being a NA sponsor, right?" The question leaves my lips before I can remind myself that the less I know about Ollie, the better.

"No, of course not."

"So what do you do to pay the bills?"

"I fix bikes." He eyes me, and I can tell my question confuses him.

I've heard him talk about working on motorcycles in the past, multiple times. I guess I thought it was a hobby. It never dawned on me that it was his career.

"Oh, yeah, I knew that. I guess I didn't realize there was money in that. I figured it was a hobby. Sorry." I scrunch up my nose. "Is there money in that?"

"Yeah." He laughs. "I make money."

"Oh, okay." I pause for a moment. "So you're a mechanic for motorcycles?"

He nods. "Yeah, but more than repairs, I do custom work and rebuilds. In Quinn terms, I make people's bikes *fancy.*"

"Ahh," I exclaim. "You're like a bike designer."

"Sure," he agrees, and the corner of his mouth tilts up in a smile.

"That's cool."

"I like it." He shrugs and scans the party before changing the subject. "Where's your guy? Couldn't make it again?" he asks, and I'm reminded of when he inquired about Beau's whereabouts at Love's birthday party a couple of months ago. At the time, the breakup was fresh, and I didn't want to get into it, so I had simply told him that Beau couldn't make it.

I swallow. "No, we're not together anymore."

"Really?" He seems surprised. "Alma had

mentioned that she thought he was perfect for you. What happened?"

"Nothing," I say in all honesty. "He was great. He just wasn't *the one*. You know?" I raise my gaze to meet his. "Do you believe in that sort of thing? Like destiny and soul mates and stuff?"

"Honestly?" He bites the corner of his lip and leans in toward me. "I'm not sure. Most of the time, no. But then every once in a while, I have a moment when I want to believe."

I find myself leaning in toward him, wanting to share the air in which he breathes. My heart hammers in my chest. Separated by a whisper of longing, desire-charged air, and desperate want—the space between us dwindles to almost nothing. He's so close, I can breathe him in. He's all salty, sweet, and intoxicatingly fresh. He smells of wind, and waves, and warmth. His bright blues capture mine, and I notice for the first time, minute gray specks sprinkled throughout his deep blue irises. Our elbows rest on the table between us as our faces inch closer. The draw I feel toward him is all-encompassing.

Without warning, he blinks and sits back in his chair. A chill runs across my skin where his heat just was. I rub my palms over my arms and lean back into my chair.

"But then dealing with what I deal with every day, seeing the lives and hearing the stories of people who are so close to me, I can't believe that something as juvenile as destiny could possibly exist," he continues coolly, making me wonder if I just imagined those last few seconds. "No one is destined to go through some of the horrific shit that many people go through. You know?"

Am I losing my mind? Was that connection in my head?

I clear my throat. "Right. I see that."

"But anyway." His voice returns back to his usual carefree tone. "I'm sorry it didn't work out with you and Ben."

"Beau," I correct.

"That's right." He nods. "Well, I think I'm going to grab some punch and make my rounds. It was nice catching up, Quinn."

"Yeah," I respond before Ollie is up and walking away from the table, leaving me with a severe case of emotional whiplash.

CHAPTER 3

OLLIE

THE CLOCK on the garage wall flashes quarter past six as I set the torque wrench in my hand down and stand from the concrete floor. Tilting my head to the side, I take in the Harley before me, satisfied with my day's progress. My phone buzzes in my pocket, and I know who it is before I check it.

Retrieving my cell from the back pocket of my jeans, I rake an arm over my forehead, wiping the sweat from my brow. Clementine's name flashes on the screen with a message.

Do you want to meet up before the meeting?

I type out my response.

. . .

Sure. Usual spot in 30?

She sends back a gif of some dude nodding excitedly, and with a chuckle, I place the phone back in my pocket and head into the house. I think the guy in the gif is her latest crush from a popular TV show, but I can't be certain. I try to keep up with everyone's interests, but there's so much noise out there between all the shows on the hundred different streaming services, coupled with social media, YouTube, and influencers. I can't keep it straight.

The truth be told, were it not for my role as a sponsor and my clients at the garage, I'd ditch my cell phone. Sometimes, I think I was born in the wrong generation. I like being simple and uncomplicated while living in a world that is anything but.

After a quick shower, I throw on some clothes before grabbing my wallet, keys, and cell. Once outside, I strap on my helmet before starting my own Harley-Davidson. I rebuilt my latest bike, a 1960 Softail Heritage Classic, about a year ago. It doesn't have as much horsepower as my last bike, but I really like the feel of it, especially with city driving. It's just chill, a sweet-ass ride.

It's cheesy to admit, but I credit a motorcycle for saving my life or at least aiding me in saving my own. Back when I was getting clean, I bought an old Kawasaki

W650 from a junkyard. It was in pretty rough shape, a literal hunk of metal. I spent every day in my parents' garage working on that bike.

I knew nothing about bikes then. In fact, my parents had always warned me away from them, stating that they were death traps, and I was never to ride one. But what were they going to say when I came home with the bike at the age of eighteen? I had nearly died of an overdose months before, which put things into perspective. Tinkering with a broken down motorcycle suddenly became a wonderful idea when the idea of relapsing was floating around as a gruesome alternative.

Working on that bike gave me something to do, a purpose. It kept my hands and brain busy, helping me fight through the urges to use again, and it worked. Almost a year to the date of bringing that bike home— countless hours spent in the garage, dozens of trips to the library to borrow every manual and book on motorcycles I could find back before YouTube was a thing, many visits with the local garages and chats with the mechanics, and endless learning by trial and error—the Kawasaki started up.

It had taken a year, but I had done it. I rebuilt that motorcycle, and I hadn't used once.

And I haven't used since. Twenty years clean.

I learned how to drive that bike in the field behind my parents' home. When I finally was able to take it out on the road and get up to highway speeds, I experienced a freedom and sense of peace I can't explain. It was so needed though, and gave me the necessary push to move on from my past and bury the demons that I would no longer allow to haunt me.

I was free.

And I knew that I would never go back.

The garage is my sanctuary, a calming solitude away from a noisy world. Not everyone can say that they get to do what they love day in and day out, and make a living doing it. It's pretty cool that I can.

I became a NA sponsor fifteen years ago after I'd been clean for five. Some might say that it's my way of giving back, but the truth is, I like it. I dig people of all backgrounds. Though I choose to spend my days alone working with machinery, there is nothing like a good conversation with another person. Humans aren't meant to be perpetually alone. We need others.

Back when I was completing the steps fresh out of high school, my sponsor was a sixty-year-old dude named Dwight. He was cool and all, and his intentions were in the right place, but he didn't get me. Sure, he understood what my body was going through and what the immense withdrawal and cravings felt like. But Dwight didn't get what was going on in my head, and I realized...that's the most important part. He was out of touch with my generation.

The truth is, I was a spoiled, entitled, cocky-ass kid.

I was raised in a small, upper-middle-class town where sports are everything and talented high school athletes are gods. In the realm of gods, I was fucking

Zeus. As captain of the varsity football, basketball, and baseball teams, I could do no wrong. I didn't follow rules, and I was never held accountable. I received high marks that I didn't earn in all my classes. Rules were a mere suggestion that I could choose to follow or not.

Junior year, some buddies and I broke into the local ice cream shop after hours because we wanted ice cream. We were caught, and I was told to "please, not do that again." My parents paid for the broken window, and the matter was swept under the rug.

I was the town's golden boy. Why? Because I could throw a ball. Simple as that. I was the starting quarterback in football, center in basketball, and pitcher in baseball. In the three sports that mattered to my community, I was the best.

Football was where I shined the brightest. Everyone knew I was going to a good college on a full-ride scholarship for football with hopes of being drafted into the NFL. Someday, they'd see me playing on the big screen as a starter for an NFL team, and say, "That's *our* Ollie Hale." I'd come back on breaks, and the town would throw a parade in my honor because I grew up in a place that would do just that.

My name and jersey number were painted on each storefront window on Main Street every Friday. Everyone had dreams for me. My parents. My coaches. My friends. My neighbors. I was going to put our little corner of heaven on the maps.

So at the beginning of football season, junior year,

when I hurt my knee, Dr. Shemwell, who was the father of my teammate and a member of our school board, prescribed me painkillers so I could get through the season on a bum knee. I'm sure he felt justified. It was inconceivable for me not to play, so he found a way.

I should've been out, resting my knee and going to physical therapy. Instead, I masked the injury with a prescribed medication. The pain could only be covered up for so long. As I continued to play when I should've been giving it time to heal, I needed more and more pills to get through my days.

I didn't see it happening until it *happened*. I didn't realize Dr. Shemwell was supplying the prescription to make me an addict until I was one. I didn't realize the extent of what I'd become until I was pounding on his door at two in the morning, sweating and shaking from withdrawal, and begging for a prescription refill and higher dosage because I felt as if I'd literally die without it.

After a year of pain pill prescriptions, Dr. Shemwell cut me off, realizing the error in his ways. But by then, I was in too deep. I couldn't stop. I needed more, and if I couldn't obtain it legally, I'd find other ways. And I did.

Heroin is surprisingly cheap and accessible. It fed my addiction the same way as the pain pills had, and maybe even better.

My senior year passed with me shining on the field, a smile on my face as the crowd cheered me on, to hiding in my room withdrawn from those around me, stoned out of my mind.

Until April of my senior year when my parents found me unresponsive and mere minutes from death.

I barely made it to adulthood. My life was seconds from being over before I had the chance to really live it. It's sad when I stop to really think about it because, let's face it, high school sports aren't worth it. Sports, in general, aren't worth it. *Nothing* is worth throwing one's life away for a high.

Nothing.

Yet it happens every day. It's an epidemic few talk about. Teens across this country are becoming addicted to pain meds because of a sports-related injury. Most of them, like myself, never see the addiction coming until it's too late.

Lives are ruined as people continue to be prescribed opioids, which are incredibly addicting. So much so that when prescriptions run out, alternative highs are found. Unfortunately, I see it all the time.

I finish tightening my helmet and start to inch out of the driveway as a neon green Volkswagen bug whips into my drive, halting me.

Releasing a sigh, I turn off my bike and take off the helmet.

Clementine, all five feet, two inches and a hundred pounds of her, circles around the front of her car, holding a root beer float in each hand.

"I thought we were meeting at A&W?" I raise a brow.

She shrugs, handing me a root beer float. "I know, but I was actually already there when I texted. So I figured it'd be easier to just grab our drinks and meet here."

"Right, but remember we talked about boundaries." I put emphasis on the last word.

As an NA sponsor, it's okay to be friends with those I sponsor, but I'm not supposed to get too close or familiar as it can hinder their recovery if they rely on me too much. However, addicts as a whole tend to be needy, and I have an issue with being strict with my expectations. If someone needs me, I can't find it in me to tell them no.

"Boundaries, shmoundaries." Clementine rolls her eyes. "I brought dessert," she says as if that fact alone excuses everything. "Plus, I wanted to see Saki. I'm sure she misses me."

"Alright, come on." I motion toward the house. Clementine skips beside me, content with the fact that she got her way.

I love Clementine like a little sister, and I understand her probably more than anyone else does. Much like me, she was a star athlete. Everyone said she was Olympic bound in soccer until she tore the Achilles tendon in her ankle. Desperate to keep her spot on the prestigious travel team, she was sent back into the sport before she was healed and prescribed opioid painkillers to help with the pain. Her journey took a dark turn, as many do, and now she's here.

"Saki!" Clementine calls when we enter the house.

Saki comes running, and a loud purr resonates from her before Clementine has picked her up.

"Hi, beautiful." Clementine grins into Saki's fur. She turns toward me. "Has she already had her canned food today?"

"Yes."

"Well, can she have more?" Clem's large blue eyes open wide in a plea.

"Sure." I shake my head and sit on a stool at the island in the kitchen.

Clementine sets her root beer float on the counter and Saki on the floor, all the while reassuring the cat that food is coming. Saki whines as if she's starving, pretending there isn't a full bowl of dry food in the laundry room for her. I watch as Clem opens cupboard doors, retrieving a bowl and a can of food while she talks to Saki, and I can't help but smile.

Seeing Clem love Saki reminds me of...me.

I found Saki, a three-legged, one eye-kitten, starving at the dump where I found the Kawasaki twenty years ago. I, of course, don't know what happened to her prior to finding her, but it was obviously traumatic as she lost a limb and an eye. She's never been what one would call a cute cat, and now that she's twenty years old, ancient as far as the life span of cats go, she's more homely as her fur is becoming rough and patchy with age. Her front half is black, gray, and white tabby, while her back half is bright orange. It's as if she got all mixed up in utero and came out this mismatched mess.

Despite her flaws, I fell in love with her the second I saw her hovering beneath the front edge of an old rusted-out Chrysler Reliant, and I had to take her with me. I couldn't leave her in that place to starve to death. I loaded her into the front seat of my dad's truck and the broken motorcycle in the bed. Three very broken things left that junkyard that day, and over the next year, they somehow all became whole—or in Saki's case, as whole as she could be. In reality, Saki doesn't seem to notice that she's missing an eye or a leg. She runs around just like any other four-legged, two-eyed cat would.

Clementine leans her back against the countertop and picks up her root beer float, taking a sip while she watches Saki scarf down her canned food. I pretend that Clem giving Saki extra soft cat food is a treat because it makes Clementine happy to spoil the cat. Yet the truth is the senior feline rarely eats dry food anymore because it's too hard for her to chew. She's an old lady now and gets what she wants.

"How are you feeling, Clem?"

She raises her stare toward me. "Hesitant."

"About?"

"Going to the meeting tonight." She sighs. "It's all so annoying."

"How's that?"

"Fucking Sharon and her bitching about her job. You

know, in all the weeks I've had to hear her complain, I still don't know what's actually wrong with her job. Like, it seems like a pretty low-stress job, *Sharon*." Clementine rolls her eyes. "Then there's Marty who sits there acting like his shit doesn't stink. He comes back with all these condescending comments like he's holier than thou. Uh, no, *Marty*. You're an addict just like the rest of us."

Pressing my lips in a line, I work to keep my face neutral, though I want to laugh. I was an only child, but if I'd had a younger sister, I imagine she'd have been feisty just like Clem.

"We've gone over this," I remind her.

She drops her head back, looking up at the ceiling. "I know, *everyone handles stress and recovery differently*," she says in a whiny voice. Mimicking our past conversations, apparently. "But sometimes I feel like those people don't even need to be there. Like, they think they are just hanging out with friends when the rest of us have real problems!"

"First of all, you know everyone's problems are real and unique to them. You can't judge others' journeys because you don't know what it's like to be them. Right?"

Clementine nods, a solemn pout on her face.

"Why don't you tell me what's really bothering you," I urge gently.

Tears fill her eyes, and her bottom lip starts to tremble. She turns her head to look away from me. "I almost drank rubbing alcohol today." Her voice is defeated.

"Alcohol isn't even my thing, and I saw it in the medicine cabinet when I was looking for a Band-Aid." She turns to me, her pale cheeks now red with emotion and embarrassment. "I wanted it so bad, Ollie. Fucking alcohol to clean cuts, not even the good stuff. I dumped it down the toilet and sat on the bathroom floor and cried." She lowers her gaze to the floor.

"I'm proud of you," I say, and her stare jerks toward mine in confusion. "It's normal to crave a high, Clem, and it's really fucking hard to push through it, but you did. I know it's hard. Believe me, I know. But every time you push past your desire to use, it will get easier. Next time will suck, too, but it won't be as rough as it was today."

"One day at a time," she says softly as tears roll down her face.

"Exactly." I take her in as she crosses her arms across her chest and grasps her biceps. "Do you need a hug, Clem?"

She nods once and takes the few steps until she's falling into my open arms. I hold her tight as she sobs against my T-shirt. "You can do this, Clem. I know you can."

I feel for this girl. At a time when most eighteen-year-olds are getting drunk at college parties, she's dumping rubbing alcohol down the toilet. A freshman at the University of Michigan, she's living alone in an apartment on campus because living with typical college students would carry too much temptation. And though her parents love her, they're in denial and not fully aware of what she goes through on a daily basis to stay clean.

"You are so strong," I tell her, meaning every word.

She hugs me back. "So much for boundaries." She giggles through her tears and takes a step back.

"Just don't tell Marty," I tease. "He would not approve."

"Oh, definitely not." She pulls her cell from her back pocket. "We should go. Can we ride together on your bike?" Her voice is hopeful, eyes wide.

I quirk a brow. "I guess, but be prepared for Marty's side-eye all meeting."

"Oh, I can handle him." She huffs before bending down to give Saki some love. The cat purrs as Clem scratches beneath her chin. "I'll see you later, beautiful."

CHAPTER 4

QUINN

AGE TWENTY

ALMA PLACES the remainder of the cut cucumbers on the vegetable tray, where an array of colorful veggies circle around a creamy white dip.

"Look at you being all domestic." I grin, taking a baby carrot and dunking it in the dip.

"I know. I made the dill dip from scratch, too. It had like a thousand five-star reviews online. You like it?" she asks, a large expectant grin on her face.

"Dill?" I question, the flavorful herbs in my mouth are strong and taste nothing like dill.

She bites her lip, looking off to the side. "Well, I couldn't find dill. I just used cilantro and basil instead.

The little store down on the corner didn't have much in the way of fresh herbs, so I just bought the two they had. I figured it'd be fine. Is it not good?"

"It's not that, it's just...strong. Basil and cilantro have distinct tastes, and I don't think I've ever eaten something with both, at least in such large quantities. It's different." I take a swig of water, rinsing down the herb explosion happening in my mouth.

Alma laughs and shakes her head. "Different is a code word for bad."

"No, not necessarily. I mean, it's edible, just not what I expected."

She walks over to the refrigerator and pulls out a white container of store-made vegetable dip. "I blame Lee-Anne for this. If it were green, she threw it into a recipe. I grew up eating the weirdest combinations of flavors, and I'm used to it. But I'm smart enough to be prepared." She holds up the store-bought dip. "At least I recognize my faults, right?" She chuckles.

"Serve them both. Options are good."

"Well, this was my attempt at cooking today. I have bags of chips, and then the rest of the food was ordered from a restaurant. So that will be good at least." She opens a bag of sour cream and onion chips and dumps them into a bowl.

I take another drink of water, then pick a piece of garlic from the dip out of my teeth. I make a mental note to go use some of Alma's mouthwash as my breath is clearly kicking after that dip.

"Who's all coming?" I watch as Alma sets out serving trays on the granite countertop. It's amusing, the life that Leo and Alma have here in this house that is nicer than my parents' home. Don't get me wrong, I'm totally happy for her. It's just always a little bit of culture shock when I hang out with Alma and Leo in this kick-ass house on campus and eat from real dishes. Most parties I attend, I'm served drinks from a red Solo cup that has more than likely been used by several other people before me. At the same time, it suits Alma perfectly. If there were ever a twenty-year-old who could look natural setting up what are most likely silver serving trays for a college game night, it's Alma. Even when she went to frat parties with me last year, she was never comfortable there. It's just not her jam, and I get that. She's the yin to my yang, and that's why I love her so much.

"The usual. Leo, obviously, and then Amos, Ethan, and Ollie." She rattles off the names of her and Leo's closest friends."

"No Cat?"

"Not today. She's actually in New York City doing a shoot for..." She furrows her brows in concentration. "Skincare, maybe? I feel horrible. I forgot what she told me. But anyway...she's working."

She starts telling me about a new game she got, and I listen for the guys' arrival.

"We were overdue for a game night. Leo's been

working so hard trying to finish up his business degree. I'm just so proud of him."

"Yeah, that's great. Good for him," I say with sincerity. "And the game sounds fun, Alma. The food will be delicious, and it will be nice to hang out with Ethan and Amos. It's been such a busy semester, and we haven't been getting together as much. But you know what I'm looking forward to? What I can't wait for?" I say with dramatic flair and pucker my lips. "I can't wait to see Ollie."

Leo's sponsor is the hottest man I've ever seen. In my life. Period. *Ahh...What I could do with him.*

"Would you stop?" She playfully hits my arms. "We are not doing this again. He's off-limits. At thirty-one, he's way too old for you."

I protest. "Eleven years isn't that big of a deal, Alma."

"It's not the age gap, Quinn. It's the stage of life. He's settled and doing his thing. You're young, in college, and sowing your wild oats. You're not in the same place, so it simply wouldn't work. Plus, Leo needs him. Just don't, please." Concern lines her voice.

I place my hand on hers. "First, I would never do anything with him. I know his first priority is to be here for Leo, and I totally respect that. You have nothing to worry about. The fact is, he's hot, and I just like to look at him. There's no harm in that. "

She releases a breath and a small smile.

"Secondly, are you calling me a whore with your whole, *sowing your wild oats* comment?" I tease.

"No!" Alma huffs out a laugh. "I would never. You're not a whore, Quinn…just free-spirited." I go to open my mouth, but Alma stops me before I can respond. "And no, free-spirited doesn't mean whore, either." She rolls her eyes.

"That's not what I was going to say." *It totally was.*

"Sure," Alma quips as the corner of her mouth turns up.

"What's everyone else been up to? Is Amos dating anyone?" My question is a result of mere curiosity. There are no lingering feelings between Amos and me. He was a fun part of my freshman year, but we weren't in love with one another. Call me crazy—and I'd never say this out loud at risk of making things awkward—but I feel like he's in love with Alma. I could be reading everything wrong, of course, but if Alma wasn't madly in love with Leo, I think Amos would make a move.

"Ethan is the same. He's still living at the frat house and going to school. He's over a lot to play video games with Leo. I don't get the whole video game thing, but they seem to love it." She shrugs. "Amos hasn't dated anyone since you. He just studies and goes to class. You know how he is."

"Yeah." I nod.

"And Ollie isn't dating anyone?" I quirk up an eyebrow.

She throws a piece of celery at me. "Quinn!"

"I'm kidding. I'm kidding."

Leo's voice can be heard from the living room, talking to the guys as they arrive.

Alma grabs my hand and pulls me into the open living room area.

Ethan, Amos, Ollie, and Leo are sitting on the large leather sectional chatting about something, and my skin starts to prickle. I take a deep breath and allow my gaze to roam over to him, where I know he'll be watching me.

His ocean blues hold my gaze, and goose bumps cover my arms. He's so breathtakingly beautiful, it's hard to take. If I didn't know he was a full eleven years older than me, I wouldn't believe it. He has this youthfulness to him. He's not immature by any means, just simple and carefree. It's alluring.

I crave his attention though I know I shouldn't. I meant what I said to Alma. I would never get involved with Ollie, but a little innocent flirtation never hurt anyone. Right?

Walking over to the sofa, I plop myself down between Ethan and Ollie. "What are you guys talking about?" I ask, aware that my leg is up against Ollie's. My skin burns at the connection even through my jeans.

"The Lions," Ethan states, mentioning Detroit's professional football team. Though I grew up in a household where my father watched the Lions every week, I have no interest in football, never have.

I scowl, and Ollie chuckles from beside me. "Not a fan?"

I shake my head. "Nope. The NFL is not my thing. I go to Eastern's home football games, but honestly, I'm there for the tailgating. I've never seen the point of football."

"Well, the point is to get the football into the end zone and score," he teases with a hint of a smile.

"I know how it works. I just think it's boring."

"I don't know. I like it, and it's fun to play."

I raise a brow. "You weren't like your high school's star player, were you?"

He presses his lips in a line and shrugs. "Something like that."

"No way." I tap his leg. "I see you out surfing as a high school kid, not sporting pads and a jersey to run a ball around."

"Well"—he huffs out a laugh—"given the fact that I was born and raised in Michigan, surfing wasn't too prevalent. I've actually never been. I've been snowboarding, though. I feel like that's the closest a Michigan kid gets to surfing."

"Do you snowboard a lot in the winter?"

"Nah, not since I was young. I have bad knees."

"You have bad knees?" I repeat with a chuckle. "You sound like an old man when you say that."

"Compared to you." He bops my nose with his pointer finger and stands from the sofa. "I am."

My mouth falls open as I watch him make his way to the bar where Alma has the wings and sliders that were just delivered set up. I can't get over the feeling that there was weight behind his simple statement. It almost felt like a rejection.

I shake it off and follow Amos to the other side of the room where the food is. He and I make small talk, but there isn't much to catch up on since the last time I saw him.

Alma laughs at herself as she tells the guys her veggie dip saga and warns them to consume the store-bought kind. Amos and Leo take a big scoop of Alma's dip, and I can't help but smile. Leo picks up a glob of dip on a cucumber and plops it in his mouth.

"Cilantro, basil, garlic dip is my new favorite." He grins down toward Alma. She raises up on her tiptoes and kisses him.

"Yeah, it's good, Mutt." Amos uses his childhood term of endearment for Alma.

"You're both being too nice but thank you," she says

We all eat and joke around some more before finding our places at the table to try out Alma's new game. She has us number off by twos for teams, which puts me on a team with Ethan and Ollie.

"The object is to get your team to guess your word based on your clues and not to be the one holding the word finder when the buzzer goes off. Simple, but fun. Right? Any questions?" Alma looks around the table.

"Nope, seems straightforward. Go ahead and start, babe," Leo says.

I hold my hand over the buzzer. "Ready?"

Alma nods, and I press the timer. She gives one clue,

and Amos guesses it immediately, and then she passes the word finder to Ollie, who clicks it to see our team's word.

"Cold and sweet," he says.

"Ice cream!" I yell.

He nods and passes the word finder to Amos. Alma guesses Amos's word with the first clue, and he hands the word finder to me. I click it and have to hold in my laughter when the word *surfing* comes up.

"Not a sport for the Michigan kid," I say.

"Surfing," Ollie answers immediately.

I drink in the way his lips turn up into a smile, and his stare captures mine. He's sex on a fucking cracker, and I'm enamored. I wish he didn't affect me so.

The game continues. Clues are given. Words are guessed. The buzzer goes off, and points are earned. It's fun, fast, and our faces are full of smiles. I don't fail to notice that Ollie guesses my word every time after the first clue as I do when it's his turn.

I know he's eleven years older than me.

I know he's off-limits.

Yet I can't deny the connection between us. Something about him pulls me in and completely captivates me. I can guarantee that he kisses like a god, and it makes me sick that I'll never know what it feels like.

I look at Alma smiling brightly at Leo. The two of them are holding hands underneath the table, so happy and in love. There's a pit in my stomach because I know I can never venture so much as a simple kiss with Ollie.

I'd never do that to Alma or Leo, and to be honest—
myself. For a kiss from Ollie wouldn't be simple. One
taste of his lips would send me into a frenzy that'd
threaten my friendship.

It'd be magical, and I'd never want to stop.

CHAPTER 5

QUINN

I GLARE at the Starbucks cup on the table before me, angry with the wrong—albeit delicious—coffee. The hot bean water in this cup is clearly a caramel macchiato of some sort and not the skinny vanilla latte I ordered.

Nothing has gone right today, and it's put me in a total funk. I wasn't surprised when Henry, the Starbuck's manager, told me that they were out of oat milk, and I had to settle with soy. With the day I've had, of course, something would be off with my order. That's typical Murphy's law, right? So I accepted the soy even though my sister swears that GMO soy will cause me to sprout another head or something. But then I take my first sip and about choke on the sugary sweet caramel with some sort of toffee chunks. It's yummy, sure, but I don't want to chew down my coffee. *Who wants to chew their coffee?*

"Oh my gosh." Cassie plops down in the chair across from me. "Did someone run over your cat?"

I pull my glare from the paper cup. "It's just been one of those days. You know where everything goes wrong?"

Cassie lets out a chuckle. "How did Henry mess up your drink?"

A small grin finds my lips. "I ordered a skinny vanilla latte, and he gave me something with a lot of caramel and toffee." I pick a piece of the sticky coffee out of my tooth.

She rolls her eyes. "How is he even the manager? Seriously. He sucks. I'm in the back for one minute, and he screws up the simplest of drink orders. Henry!"

I place my hand on hers. "It's fine, really. I'll drink it."

"Henry!" she shrieks again, and I look around, embarrassed. Thankfully, there are only three other patrons in here besides me. The guy in the corner has headphones on and is staring intently at his laptop screen, oblivious to Cassie's high-pitched squeal. The couple on the other side of the room seems to be engrossed in an argument and are also unaware.

"Yes?" Henry appears beside the table and peers down at Cassie.

"You messed up Quinn's order. She wanted a skinny vanilla latte with..." She turns to me. "Is soy okay? We're out of oat milk."

I nod.

"With soy milk," she finishes telling Henry my order.

Henry turns to walk away, and Cassie calls out again. "Get her two Ventis. She's had a day and needs one for the road. Oh, and I'm taking my break."

Henry whips back around. "You just got off your break."

"And I need another," Cassie states. "Thanks, my cutie-patootie."

Henry sighs with a shake of his head and turns away, continuing on his path toward what might be my correct order.

"You're lucky you're dating him." I grin. "I don't think multiple breaks would fly otherwise."

She waves her hand through the air. "Whatever. We're dead anyway. There's no one in here. Plus, I practically run this place. He'd be fired without me. What *manager* messes up every drink order he does?"

I look toward Henry behind the counter and back to Cassie. I've never really understood their connection. Cassie is beautiful, and I mean absolutely gorgeous. She's funny, smart, and overall a really cool person. And Henry is...*Henry*. They don't fit, but who am I to judge?

Cassie and her best friend Tannon live in the apartment above the Starbucks, across from their guy friends Asher and Everett. All four of them are graduates of the University of Michigan. They graduated a year after I graduated from Eastern. I never met them in college even though I went to a lot of U of M parties.

I started getting my coffee from this location a few years ago when I got my job at the department store, and Cassie and I have been friends since.

"So tell me, what went wrong today?" She clasps her hands together and sets her elbows on the table, leaning toward me.

"What didn't go wrong? The manager beneath me quit without notice. One of our shipments didn't come in, and no one seems to know where it is. Then we got a huge delivery of nightwear that is on clearance this weekend for our annual Labor Day sale, and it's not what was ordered. So I have all these marketing materials out, advertising our sale, and half of the items advertised won't be available. Do you know how mean bargain shoppers can be when they can't get the items they want? This weekend is going to be the worst."

Henry comes back with my two lattes and sets them on the table in front of me.

"That sounds horrible."

I lower my chin toward Henry in thanks before he turns away. "Oh, and a sweet old lady fell down the escalator today!"

Cassie gasps. "Is she okay?"

I nod. "I think so. She's a little cut up, and she'll be sore and bruised. The paramedics came and said they think she's okay but took her into the ER just to be sure nothing was broken. I haven't heard anything since. It was a nightmare, though. It was so scary."

I take a sip of my latte.

"Better?" Cassie nods toward the cup in my grasp.

"Much. Thank you. I'm sorry. I'm being a total whiner."

"It's okay. With a day like that, it's warranted. You want to come by after work this weekend? The guys are having a Labor Day party, of course." She releases a short laugh. "You can hang out with me and Tannon, have some drinks, and relax."

The corners of my lips turn up. Everett and Asher have a party almost every weekend, and we never know who's going to be there. They invite the most random groups of people sometimes.

"Who's going to be there?" I ask.

"Well, they say, 'close friends.'" She raises her fingers in air quotes. "But what that actually means, who knows? Anyone from Everett's nerdy college buddies, to the meat heads at Asher's gym, to the whole staff of the Ann Arbor Costco could show up. It's anyone's guess."

"That could work, though. After the crazy Saturday I'm bound to have with half of our inventory MIA, I'll probably need a few drinks."

"Good!" Cassie grins. "It'll be fun. And I might have a book for you to beta read by this weekend, too. Tannon's almost done."

"Really? Already?"

Tannon is a romance writer, and I get to read her books before she publishes them to give her a heads-up on any plot holes, inconsistencies I find, or changes I would suggest. Though, I rarely have any advice for her as her books are already amazing by the time they're sent to me.

"Yep. She's been a writing machine as of late. I think this one is going to be really good, too."

"Ahh." I clap my hands together. "I can't wait. I need a spicy escape from life at the moment."

She scrunches her nose. "So no one since Beau, huh?"

"Nope. No one since Beau, and let me tell you, I miss having someone. I know I shouldn't. I should be content on my own, and I am. But it's nice being in a relationship, having that person to come home to and share your day with."

"And sleep with." Cassie quirks a brow.

"That too." I chuckle.

I grab a coffee cup in each hand, raising them toward Cassie. "Thanks for these."

"Anytime. That's what I'm here for." She stands from the table. "I'll see you Saturday night?"

"Yes, unless I'm swarmed by angry bargain shoppers and perish."

She laughs. "Always so dramatic."

"Always."

Exiting the coffee shop, I cross the street to where my vehicle is parked, unlock the driver's side door, and set my coffee cups in the holders in front of the middle console. Sliding into my seat, I close my door with a happy sigh. Good coffee makes everything better.

Dua Lipa's latest song sounds from the speakers as I push the button to start the engine.

"Yes, please." I turn up the volume and roll down the windows before pulling onto the street. There's something about singing at the top of my lungs with the wind whipping my hair around that makes everything better.

A few miles down the road, I'm belting out the lyrics to the song when my car stutters and shuts off.

"Oh my God! Oh my God!" I shriek as I guide my Jeep toward the side of the road, my heart pumping.

Once I've safely pulled off the road, I turn down the music and push the keyless start button, again and again. Nothing happens.

"You've got to be kidding me!" I hit the steering wheel with the palms of my hands as tears come to my eyes. "Just perfect," I grumble.

The stress of the day engulfs me, and my tears start flowing. Any other day, my car dying on me wouldn't be the end of the world, but it had to happen today. Resting my arms over the steering wheel, I press my forehead against my arm and cry, a physical release of the stress from this horrendous day.

"Are you okay?" A familiar voice startles me.

I whip my head up with a yelp and turn toward my open window, where Ollie stands with a front row seat to my meltdown.

"Um, what are you doing here?" I drag the top of my hand across my cheeks to wipe the tears.

"I was riding past and saw you parked here. Figured I'd check on you."

"How'd you know it was me?" I sniff.

"Pretty sure you're the only one in Ann Arbor with a sky blue Jeep with sea turtle stickers and a license plate plaque that says, 'Hit me baby one more time.'" He smirks.

I shrug with a small smile. "Well, I love turtles, and I love Britney. What can I say?"

"So what's going on?" he nods toward the front of my Jeep.

"I don't know. It just stopped working."

"Pop your hood," he tells me.

I do, and he makes his way around to the front of the vehicle and opens the hood. "Try to start it up," he calls.

I press the button, and nothing happens. He doesn't say anything else as he fiddles around beneath the hood, eventually closing it and wiping his hands on his jeans.

"Well, your timing belt broke, which is why your car probably stopped in the first place. But I think your alternator might be shot, too. I'll have to test it to be sure."

"Perfect." I sigh.

"Roll your windows up and lock it. I'll call someone to have it towed to my place where I can fix it for you."

"I thought you just did bikes."

"Well, usually, but I can do cars. Come on, I'll take you home." He pulls his cell from his pocket.

"Who are you calling?"

"Bill."

"Who's Bill?"

Ollie looks amused. "A friend."

"From NA?"

He raises a brow. "I wouldn't know since the 'A' stands for anonymous."

I drop my chin. "I'm sorry. I knew that. It's not like it matters, anyway. I was just making conversation. I'm sorry. Tell Bill thank you."

Ollie takes a few steps from my door and turns away from the road as he starts talking into his phone. I roll up my windows, collect my purse, and throw my keys and phone inside. Stepping down from the Jeep, I press the keyless lock and look behind my car. My eyes bulge when I'm reminded that Ollie rides a motorcycle.

Crap.

Dropping my chin to my chest, I take in my form-fitting pencil skirt.

Ollie walks up beside me. "Ready?"

"How am I supposed to ride on that? I'm wearing a skirt. Maybe I should get an Uber?"

He chuckles. "Don't be silly. You'll be fine. Just hike it up."

He steps toward the bike and comes back with a helmet. Placing it on my head, he adjusts the chin strap to tighten it, gently wiping a lock of hair out of my face. The caring motion causes a chill to run down my spine, and I swallow.

"Where do you live?" he asks as he continues to make sure the helmet is on just right.

I tell him my address, and I realize in all the years I've known Ollie, he's never been to my place nor have I been to his. We only see each other when we're with Alma. I feel like I know Ollie so well, and at the same time, this is the first time I've seen him outside the presence of our mutual friend. It feels strange, exuberating, and oddly...wrong.

When he's satisfied with the fit of the helmet on my head, he takes my purse and locks it into a storage compartment behind the seat of his bike and then straddles the seat.

"Hop on." He grins.

"You gave me your helmet," I say.

"Yeah."

"But what about you?"

"You're only a few miles away. I'll be fine."

"It's not safe," I offer.

I know that it's not a law that motorcyclists wear a helmet in Michigan, but I honestly hate that it's not. I get nervous when I see people riding motorcycles at fast speeds without one.

"It's fine. I promise. Plus, if it's my time to go, it's my time to go."

My mouth falls open at his statement.

"I'm kidding." He laughs. "Get on."

I shimmy my skirt up until it's barely covering my crotch and swing my bare leg over the back of the seat. My heels flounder around at my sides until I find the small footpegs. I feel, and I'm sure look, like a complete idiot.

"Hold on," Ollie calls over his shoulder as he starts up the bike.

I look around frantically for something to grasp onto and don't see anything.

Ollie reaches back for my hand and pulls my arm around his waist. My other arm circles to meet it, though hesitant as if I shouldn't be holding him this way. The entirety of my front is pressed up against his back as it vibrates in another laugh, and he pulls out onto the road.

For the first few minutes of the ride, I cling to Ollie in terror, hiding my face between his shoulder blades the best I can with this clunky helmet. He squeezes my hand as if to say that it's okay, the thoughtful movement calms me and I lift my face from his back and look around me. With a few deep breaths, and the wind in my face, the fear starts to subside, and a smile finds my lips.

The night air is warm against my bare skin, and the sun is starting to set in the distance. I bet it's beautiful out past the city where the colors of the sunset meet the grassy horizon.

He starts to slow as we approach my street.

I lean in toward his ear. "Can we drive a little longer outside of town?" I say loudly.

"Yeah, absolutely," he calls back and picks up speed, passing my street.

We drive until the neighborhoods filled with houses are replaced by fields of tall corn.

I've never been on a motorcycle, but now I understand the appeal of them. There's something about the rhythmic vibration of the engine, the wind hitting my skin and whipping around my body, and the blurred world that brings me peace after the day from hell. I'm no longer thinking about missing shipments or car problems but the simple sensations of this ride. It's so freeing.

We're the only ones on a long, straight patch of road between fields of cornstalks. I garner the courage to release my grip on Ollie and extend my arms out to the sides. Closing my eyes, I drop my head back as we speed across the pavement, and it almost feels like I'm flying as the air hits my arms and my hair flies out behind me.

With a content sigh, I wrap my arms around Ollie and allow my body to lean into him as he uses an empty four-way stop intersection to turn around so that we're heading back toward town.

Ollie's hard abdomen muscles taunt me from beneath his shirt, and his smell hits me as I press against him. His scent is a delicious combination of laundry soap, car oil, and seduction. By the time he's pulling into my neighborhood, every part of me is vibrating, and I'm a strange mixture of free, happy, and crazy turned on.

The bike slows as it pulls up my drive before Ollie turns off the engine and hits the kickstand out with his foot. He slides off the seat, standing to the side of me.

I lean to my side in an attempt to get a good view of my shoe since my heel seems to be stuck by the peg. I pull my heel free and turn back to Ollie. His face seems flushed, his cheeks carry slightly more pink than usual, which must be a result of the ride and the wind hitting his face. And yet...there's something in his eyes that I can't place as his gaze holds mine.

My mind, or perhaps ego, or maybe that small part of my heart that holds on to hope for happy endings for fruitless crushes wants to think that he's looking at me with admiration. I can't help that I want him to find me attractive. I want to be what he desires, though I know we're not meant to be. I shouldn't crave these thoughts from him. I know this. And yet I do.

He pulls his bottom lip through his teeth as his stare roams down my body. It's then I realize that my skirt has ridden up and rests bunched up above my hips, leaving my pink lacy thong in full view.

"Oh crap!" I squeal as I tug at my skirt in an attempt to cover myself, my position on the bike seat not cooperating with me.

Ollie chuckles and circles my waist in his grasp to lift me off the seat.

As soon as my feet hit the ground, I have myself appropriately covered. I press my palms against the fabric, smoothing it down. "I told you this wasn't a motorcycle-friendly outfit." I attempt a laugh.

"I don't know," Ollie says, his voice husky. "I think you looked pretty good."

"Well, yeah. I always look good." I shoot him a wink. "But still...not appropriate. Next time I ride on your bike, I'll be wearing jeans."

. . .

"So there's going to be a next time?" He quirks a brow, his gaze playful.

"Oh. Well, probably not, but if there is..." And I'm stumbling over my words yet again. I am one of the most confident people I know until I'm around Oliver Hale. His presence turns me into this thirteen-year-old girl who's yet to master the ability to talk in complete sentences to those of the opposite sex. I hate what he does to me.

I blow out a breath. "I should go but thank you so much. Do you have my number?"

He nods, his eyes assessing.

"Well, please text when you know what's going on with my Jeep. If it ends up being something you can't fix, I can have it towed somewhere else."

"I can fix it."

"I should probably give you money." I remember my purse in the back cargo area of the bike.

"Nah, I don't need anything right now." Ollie retrieves my purse and hands it to me.

"Okay." I nod, clutching my purse to my chest.

His hands reach toward my face, and I freeze. He unbuckles the helmet and pulls it off my head. The corner of his lip quirks up, and he tucks a lock of hair behind my ear.

"See ya later, Quinn."

"Bye."

My statuesque form remains planted firmly as he starts his bike and backs out of my driveway. There's a playful smile on his face as he drives away, and I get this feeling he knows something I don't. Or at least, he thinks he does.

Hell. He probably does.

My head is so fuzzy and confused with conflicting emotions that I'm not sure of much right now. And when it comes to Ollie, I'm at a complete loss.

CHAPTER 6

OLLIE

AGE THIRTY-TWO

YEAH...NO.

Stay far away, man.

Quinn's laughing at something Ethan's said, and I can feel the vibration of the sound deep within my chest. She's at the other end of the deck with Cat and Ethan, and I'm having a difficult time focusing on anything but her. Something akin to jealousy bubbles beneath the surface of my skin, and I can't quite figure that out.

I don't do jealous. I don't crush on the twenty-one-year-old friends of someone I'm sponsoring. At the same time, I can't deny that I wish I could change places with Ethan, or Cat for that matter, if only to be closer to her.

Whoa.

Once again...yeah, no.

Leo's flipping burgers on the grill and telling me about his father's recent attempt to guilt him into taking a bigger role in one of the family businesses. I've never had to concentrate on a conversation so hard in my entire life.

My brain is muddled with the vision of long blond hair, lean muscular legs on a little body, flawless skin, and brilliant green eyes. Her smile is mesmerizing, complete with the small dimple in her cheek. The contagious laughter falls from her irresistible lips, and I crave proximity if only to feel her amusement even more.

Quinn's like that. She makes everyone happy. Those near her only want to be closer. She's adored by everyone who knows her—and for good reason. She's this petite ball of light that shines brightly.

A star.

She radiates pure joy. It isn't contrived or forced in any way. It's effortless. Simply her.

And fuck me if it's not messing with my head.

She's off-limits for numerous reasons—the most important of which is Leo. I would never jeopardize my relationship with someone I'm sponsoring from NA. I'm here for him, and it's vital. His life is important, and I'd never risk it. Love or, more accurately, lust is fleeting. The fall after the high is always messy. Bringing that mess into Leo's life when he's fighting daily to stay clean, to save his life, could never be worth it.

"You agree with me, right?" Leo asks, referring to the

conversation he had with his father where he refused to take part in the future his father had envisioned for him.

"Absolutely. You'd be miserable working for your father or brother. You don't owe them anything, Leo. Not a damn thing."

"I know." He nods. "There was a small part deep within me that wanted to say yes even though I knew I'd be miserable. It doesn't make sense."

"It does. We all have this innate desire to please our parents. We all want to be loved and validated by those who gave us life. You see it all the time with kids in foster care. They come from horrible home situations, but given the choice, they'd go back to their birth parents every time. It's normal to want to do right by your family, Leo. But you'd hate working with Stephen and your dad. Not to mention the emotional triggers they'd unleash. You have to keep your boundaries and protect yourself."

Leo takes the last burger off the grill and sets it on the tray.

"You're right. I never really entertained the idea of going along with it, but at the same time, I felt a pang of guilt for not."

"Brush it off, man. Focus on yourself and what you need. Don't waste an ounce of guilt on your father. He doesn't deserve it."

"You got that right." Leo takes the platter of burgers over to the patio table, where Alma's setting down a bowl of potato salad. The table is covered with side dishes and a place setting for all of us.

"Everything looks great," I tell her.

"Thanks," she responds with a grin. Her stare, full of complete adoration, follows Leo as he takes a seat at the table.

Alma circles around the table and sits beside Leo. He leans down and kisses the top of her head. She's good for him. I think, together, they can do anything. I've grown to care for Leo like a brother over this past year and a half. He's a good guy and deserves to be loved the way in which Alma loves him.

Their friends, Amos, Ethan, Cat, and Quinn, sit at the table. I take a seat at the safe spot beside Cat where I won't have to deal with any traitorous Quinn musings. Cat is a literal supermodel, but she's no Quinn.

Alma raises her glass of lemonade. "I want to make a toast to Leo, the love of my life, who graduated today."

There're some hoots and cheers from those in attendance, and Leo shakes his head, feigning annoyance.

Alma turns to Leo, and continues, "I am so proud of you today and every day. You're going to do amazing things in this life, Leo Harding. I am so grateful to be on this journey with you. Cheers to the future."

"Cheers," we say in unison, clinking our glasses together.

"I love you," Leo whispers to Alma before kissing her lips.

"What are you going to do next?" Ethan asks Leo, taking a large handful of potato chips and setting them on his plate.

"I have no fucking idea." Leo chuckles.

The food gets passed around the table, and I take some of everything, as it all looks delicious.

"You're still volunteering at that place with the kids, right?" Cat asks Leo.

"The Boys and Girls Club," Leo says. "Yeah, it's a cool organization, and they do a lot of great things for the kids in the community, but there are definitely some aspects I'd change to make it better."

"You could start your own organization. I could help you," Alma suggests.

"Yeah, maybe. We'll see." Leo takes a bite of his burger.

We talk about what Leo would do differently to help the kids, and other volunteering opportunities in the community. Cat suggests that Leo should work with animals and maybe start a kitten sanctuary, an idea he immediately shoots down.

"Aw, but kittens," Quinn chimes in.

"Yeah, maybe someday Alma and I can rescue one from a shelter, but running a whole cat sanctuary isn't my thing." He shakes his head with a laugh.

"I got it," Ethan says dramatically. "You and me... video game developers."

"Also, not my skill set, but I can agree to several days of gaming to celebrate that fact that we don't have to sit through any more college classes."

"Cheers to that." Ethan holds up his glass, and Leo

taps it with his. "I think that new one we preordered months ago comes out next week."

"Yeah, you're right. It does."

The conversation changes from Leo's future to Cat's latest modeling campaign to Amos's prestigious summer internship to Alma and Quinn gasping in horror over the fact that I've never read a single Harry Potter book or watched any of the movies.

"Seriously? But you need to read the books," Alma urges.

"Or at least watch the movies," Quinn says, quickly turning her head toward Alma's small gasp. "Yes, Alma, I know the books are better, but the movies are good, especially for a book-to-movie adaptation, so if he's not going to read them, watching them would be the next best option. Right?"

"I suppose," Alma grumbles, and her passion for a book about wizards makes me laugh.

"I don't really have time for reading or watching TV, for that matter. I'm always busy with friends or working. If I have free time, I prefer to be outside."

Cat nods. "Yeah, I can see that. You seem like someone who enjoys being outdoors. I, myself, prefer to be inside in the air-conditioning with no bugs."

"You know what's really fun to do outside?" Alma asks me.

"What?"

"Reading. There's nothing better than reading a good book outside on a beautiful day."

"I'll think about it." I laugh.

She shrugs. "That's all I'm asking."

The rest of the meal passes with easy conversation and laughter. I'm happy that Leo has a great group of people who love and support him. As far as friends go, his circle is pretty cool. Not everyone has this quality of people in their lives. In this aspect, Leo's lucky.

I grab the last dish from the table. The others have cleared the rest of the food and taken it inside. I turn toward the house, the large bowl with remnants of what was macaroni salad in my arms, and almost knock Quinn over.

"I'm sorry. I didn't hear you come back out," I say.

"It's okay. No damage done." She shoots me a wink.

Cat comes out onto the deck. "Ah, Alma was just asking about this. I'll take it in so she can wash it." She takes the bowl from my grasp and leaves Quinn and me alone on the deck.

She places her hands in the back pockets of her jean shorts. "So you're outdoorsy, huh? What types of things do you like to do outside?"

"Ride my bike," I answer.

"Like BMX?"

"No." I chuckle. "Motorcycle."

She nods. "Duh. I should've known that. I've never ridden a motorcycle before. My parents think they're death traps." She covers her mouth. "Ugh, I'm sorry. That was rude."

"It's fine." I lean back against the deck railing. "They

definitely can be. But so can everything else. I had a cousin once who almost died choking on an onion. So by that account, I should've avoided the salad at dinner with its death-causing onions."

"I should've avoided that salad for the mere fact that it did a number on my breath." She scrunches her nose.

I can't help but laugh. "I'm sure your breath is just fine."

She bends her index finger back and forth in a *come here* motion. "I can prove it to you."

"I'll take your word for it."

"Smart. Keep your distance." The corner of her mouth tilts up. "Well, I see your point about the world being dangerous. So just do what makes you happy."

"Yeah, for the most part."

"I think I'm a live-in-the-moment type of girl. Maybe someday you can take me for a ride on that bike of yours."

The statement is innocent enough, but it carries an air of a challenge.

"Maybe." I shoot her a smile and head inside, knowing that there is no way in hell I'll ever invite Quinn on the back of my bike.

The last thing I want is her body up against mine on the back of the Harley.

At least it should be.

The fact that it's not is the problem.

CHAPTER 7

OLLIE

"So who is this girl? Something serious?" Clementine asks from where she sits atop my work bench, her legs swinging off the side.

I shake my head, tightening the bolt beside the alternator in Quinn's Jeep. "I told you. She's a friend."

Clementine starts riffling through a toolbox at her side, picking up metal pieces and dropping them back into the box with a clang. "I don't think so."

Standing upright, I set down my wrench and snatch the towel to its side and wipe my hands. "First of all, stop." I motion toward my toolbox. "You may not realize this, but those pieces were organized."

"They all look the same to me." She drops a bolt into the box and shrugs as the metal clashes with another.

"Well, they're not. And secondly." I raise a brow. "Why are you here?"

Her mouth falls open, and she grabs the empty water bottle at her side and throws it at me. "Rude," she huffs.

I catch the bottle and release a laugh. "It's a valid question." I smile.

"You're just deflecting because you don't want to tell me about your new girlfriend. I know you, and you don't fix cars, and clearly, this one belongs to a girl. You told me before that you don't date, so I'm curious."

"Clem, I told you. She's a friend. And seriously, you hang out with me too much. You should be making friends at school. What about joining a sorority?"

"Are you kidding me?" She rolls her eyes, smacking a wad of bubble gum in her mouth.

"Okay, then chess club."

She blows a bubble and sucks it back into her mouth after it pops. "I don't play chess."

"You know what I mean. You need to find some people you like, make friends. Spend time with someone other than me. Your college experience should be more than going to class and sitting in a garage watching me."

"Are you sick of me?" she asks. She forces her voice to be steady, but I hear the doubt in it.

"No, of course not. You're always welcome here...I mean, now that we've established that you carry a total lack of respect for boundaries," I tease. "I love seeing you, and you know I'm always here for you. I just want you to be happy, and I feel like you're hiding from life a little. In my experience, when someone hides, there are deeper issues at play. Are you okay?" I pin her with a serious stare. "Are you using?"

She looks down and shakes her head. "No."

"Clem." I step toward her. "What's going on?"

When she lifts her face, the unshed tears filling her eyes threaten to break my heart. The sadness radiating from her is palpable. "I haven't used," she states solemnly. "But I've wanted to. Really bad. I even asked around and found out where a dealer lived and drove to his house. I sat in my car for an hour, talking myself out of knocking on his door. I drove to his fucking house, Ollie!" A rogue tear trails down her cheek. "I hate it here. I hate the people. They're shallow and clueless. Either they're completely immature and living their life to attend the next best party or they're nerds and want to study chemistry like it's the most important thing in life. No one gets me, and I have no interest in getting to know any of them."

I pat her knee. "I get it. I do, but you have to remind yourself that these people haven't gone through the things that you have. You can't blame them for not understanding. That's what I'm here for, and the others at group. We get you. The others...they're there for your new chapter of life, the one where you get to leave all the torment behind and be happy."

"It's so hard." She sighs.

"I know, and it might always be. You have to find something to give you purpose, joy. Right now, you're going through the motions without a clear destination. Let's take your major, for example." I quirk a brow.

"General studies." Her voice is sheepish.

"Exactly." I release a laugh. "What does that degree actually mean? What does it qualify you to do with your life?"

"I don't know."

"And therein lies the problem. You know my story about fixing that first bike and finding a sense of calm and purpose while doing so?"

She nods.

"That hobby changed my life. It made me happy. You have to figure out what makes you happy, and I can help you."

"How?"

"Well, we'll start by volunteering at different places until we find something that resonates with you. Then you can choose a degree that will allow you to follow your passion."

Clementine nods, a sad smile on her face. "Okay."

Lifting my arms, I take hold of hers and squeeze gently. "Promise me that you'll stay clean. Don't drive to the dealer's house again. Stay away from people who use. Even one time, one use could kill you. You know that, right? It's not worth your life. You've come too far."

"I know," she whispers.

I pull her into my chest, and she hugs me tight. "Promise me, Clem."

"I promise."

"Someday, you're going to be happy. Maybe you'll be married and have a family. You'll be working in a career that gives you purpose. You'll have a beautiful life and be so grateful for it. And then you'll understand what this fight was for. It's hard to see it now, but trust me...it will be so worth it. Never give up on yourself and the life you deserve. Keep fighting."

"I will." She sniffs, and leans back, swiping her hands across her cheeks to wipe away her tears. "One day at a time, right?"

"One day at a time." I give her what I hope is a reassuring smile. "You know what? I have about five more minutes, and then I'll be done with the Jeep. You can hang out with Saki for a little bit and then follow me to drop off Quinn's car at her house. Then when we get back, we can go for a run."

Clem grumbles.

"Okay, star high school athlete." I shake my head. "Getting back to running every day will help. Endorphins and all that."

"I suppose." She hops off my workbench. "I'll be inside."

I watch Clem until she closes the door to the mudroom behind her and disappears into the house. The moment she's out of sight, my chest tightens as I think of a life without her. She's so young and has so much potential. This world needs her fiery spirit, and I'm going to do everything in my power to keep her here.

I cover my face with my hands and release a sigh

before forcing my fingers through my hair, so much anger pooling up within. This is what drugs do. They ruin lives. They don't discriminate but threaten to destroy everyone in their path. Some days, I hate the role in my sobriety as a sponsor. Not because I don't care for the people I help but because I love them too much, and I'm tired of the heartache. I've lost people who meant the world to me—people I've loved like family. And this shit hurts.

Some of my peers say I'm too invested, but that's who I am. When I'm in, I'm all in. There's no in-between. I would do absolutely anything to save those I love. Clementine is going to beat the odds. She's going to make it. I will do everything in my power to make sure she does.

I'm sick of the loss and the heartache. I'm done. No more. Clem is a ray of fucking sunshine, and if I have anything to do with it, she's going to be shining for decades to come.

I look toward the sky blue Jeep before me with a sense of desperate longing for something I can't have, and that's Quinn.

I'm good at my role in NA because I can read people. I usually know what someone is feeling before they do just by the look on their face. I know when people are hurt or sad or jonesing for their next high.

Therefore, I know that Quinn wants me. The truth be told, she doesn't stand alone in her attraction. I've always found her gorgeous and fun. She's a light, a free spirit—bold and beautiful and good. She's everything I could hope to obtain, yet she's not mine for the taking because I have nothing to give.

I've never had a serious romantic relationship. There have been casual flings, sure, but no one with staying power. The women I've been involved with in the past have known that, and their feelings on the matter mutual. I can't give my heart to someone when it's already occupied. Clementine and the others I sponsor come first, and I feel they always will because they need to. Their lives depend, in part, on me and my ability to see them through their darkest times.

I'm not in a position for a traditional happily ever after. Romantic love, marriage, and family aren't in my future because my life is already full. I have people who depend on me, and I won't let them down. Not ever, if I can help it. A wife and kids don't deserve to be second place.

Maybe, in part, I'm afraid. I haven't craved drugs in at least eighteen years, and I've been clean for twenty. They tell me that's rare, not to want to use again but I don't. I think my part in others' journeys toward sobriety aids me in my own. I wonder if I need them as much as they need me. Or perhaps, not, but I'm not in any hurry to find out.

My life works the way it is. I don't want more. With that realization comes the question as to why I flirt with Quinn when I'm around her though, I know she could never simply be a casual fling. It's not right, yet when I'm with her, I can't help it. She brings out the cocky side of me, the side that wants her to want me.

Last night with her arms around my waist and the breath from her laughter on my neck was almost too much. I wanted her, damn the consequences. That feeling of recklessness makes me uncomfortable.

So I'm going to finish this Jeep, drop it in her driveway, and be done with her for a while until I can get my emotions in check. And then I'm going to run until I can't run any farther with Clem because endorphins are good. They'll make me forget what it felt like to have Quinn on the back of my bike.

While Clem runs from her nightmare, I'll be running from my dream.

CHAPTER 8

QUINN

I can't pretend I didn't put more effort into my appearance than usual tonight. I'm a tad overdressed for a Labor Day apartment party, but my effort isn't intended for anyone there. It is for someone else.

Work was as I expected it would be. Once our missing shipment of clothing items for the annual Labor Day sale were found—in Tulsa, Oklahoma, no less—there wasn't time to get them back to Michigan in time. I knew there would be angry shoppers, frustrated employees, and not enough coffee to combat the day from hell—but somehow, it didn't matter.

Through it all, I knew I'd be dropping by Ollie's house before the party, and that thought alone has kept my spirit happy. I called Alma earlier to get Ollie's address. He refused to give it to me because he doesn't want payment for the work he did on my Jeep.

The day after my Jeep broke down, I got an Uber ride home from work to find my Jeep sitting in my driveway in perfect working condition. Ollie was a life-saver through that ordeal. The fact that he drove by as I broke down, set up the tow truck pick-up, drove me home, fixed my Jeep, and returned it, leaving me little time to worry, was such a huge relief. With all the fires I had to put out at work this week, it was nice not having to deal with a broken vehicle on my own.

He's adamant about not taking money from me, stating he was simply helping a friend. While that may be true, the tow truck and parts cost him money, and he shouldn't be responsible for spending his money on me. Not to mention the time it took him to fix it when he could've been working on a project that would bring in money.

Ollie's a good person, but so am I, and I owe him. There are two types of people, givers and takers. Ollie's a giver, always looking out for those around him, helping everyone he can out of the kindness of his heart, and going above and behind for his people.

I know many individuals who take advantage of others' generosity without any intention of paying it forward, and that's not me. I googled the cost of the repairs to my Jeep had I taken it to an auto shop and have that amount of money, along with take-out from the best steak house in Ann Arbor on my passenger seat.

My gaze traces Ollie's house before me. I pull into his driveway and put the Jeep in park. I'm not sure what

I was expecting, but I'm pleasantly surprised. The housing market in Ann Arbor is expensive, and his home sits on a large lot of land, as far as city lots go. He's obviously doing well for himself, and that makes me so happy for him. His home is a dark charcoal gray ranch with white trim. It's...almost sexy if houses can be considered as such. Multi-toned gray bricks create a raised flower and plant bed in front of the large picture window.

It's all very domestic, and grown-up, and I guess that's what we are. I met Ollie when I was still in college. I was young and free, dating hot frat guys and attending themed sorority parties. Most days, I still feel like that girl, but I'm not. I'm the head of my department store. I own a home and...a Jeep. *Maybe, it's time I own a pet?* I'm the woman who's admiring her friend's landscaping and paint-color choices, and no longer the girl doing keg stands in a miniskirt and crop top.

A few motorcycles sit in the drive in front of his large garage, one of which I know is his. Memories of our ride into the sunset on the country road come to mind, along with the emotions I felt that night.

These past few months have been taxing. I broke up with the *ideal* boyfriend and acquired more stress at work, and sometimes it's lonely. Being an adult without someone to share life with can be isolating. As I sit here staring at Ollie's house, his manly and sexy house, all I can think about is how it felt to have my arms wrapped around his waist while sitting on the back of his bike. I find myself wanting to tell him about my day—hell, my week, for that matter. I want to skip this apartment party tonight and go for a ride on the back of Ollie's bike instead. I'm certain that if he asked me to stay, I would.

Pulling down the visor, I glance quickly into the mirror, smacking my rose-gloss-coated lips together. I loop my hand through the handles of the take-out bag and grab the white envelope of cash before hopping down from the Jeep. I walk up to his front door, and with a hesitant sigh, I rap my knuckles against the front door.

An eternity that fits exactly into the space of two breaths passes before the front door swing opens.

My jaw falls slack when a petite girl with long red curls opens the door, holding what has to be the ugliest cat I've ever seen. My eyes go wide when I notice the cat only has one eye, but I don't have time to contemplate that fact.

"Um, hey. Is Ollie here?" My voice raises an octave, and I momentarily question whether I have the correct address before remembering that his bike is literally sitting in the driveway, indicating that I'm at the right place.

The girl looks young, twenty at the oldest. She's wearing short, tight running shorts and a sports bra.

"He's in the shower. Do you want to come in?" She sounds nice enough but something about this whole situation makes me feel uncomfortable.

I shake my head. "I don't think so." I drop my attention toward the bag in my hand and toss the envelope with cash inside it. "He fixed my car, so I was just dropping off the money for that and a dinner to say thank you."

"So you're the Jeep." The corner of her lip quirks up.

"Yeah, um..." I extend my arm. "Would you mind giving this to him when he gets out?"

"Sure." The redhead takes the bag from me.

"And tell him I said thanks again."

"You got it." She nods, and takes a step back, and I swear the cat in her arms glares at me with its one eye. "Bye." She waves.

I raise my hand to wave back, and she closes the door between us.

Is that his girlfriend? I stand, stunned. It takes me a few seconds to come to my senses and turn from his front door.

She's cute, sure, but I didn't picture Ollie with someone so young and peppy. *I was peppy once,* I think as I climb into the Jeep. When Ollie first met me, I was just like that girl but with blond hair and sans ugly cat. Now, I'm a twenty-seven-year-old, going on fifty-three.

Maybe a loud apartment party is just what I need tonight. I've had enough adulting this week to last me a while. It's time to drink and forget about those fleeting moments on the back of a certain someone's motorcycle.

———

"You came!" Cassie cheers when I find her out on the balcony of Asher and Everett's apartment.

"I came." I smile.

She grabs my hand and spins me around. "You look hot!"

"Thank you. You, too."

Cassie's roommate, Tannon, pulls me into a hug, followed by Asher and Everett.

"What do you want to drink?" Everett asks.

I press my lips together. "Hmm, surprise me. Anything but beer, though," I say over the Fleetwood Mac song that blasts from the speakers. The music and people at their parties are always a surprise.

"You got it." Everett grins, and disappears into the apartment.

"Who are all the people, Ash?" I ask, noticing that many of them are dressed up quite a bit.

"Well, Benny, over there in the tux"—Asher points at a tall, dark, and handsome guy across the room—"is a client of mine. He got married today, and these are the guests from his wedding. They only had money to reserve the hall until eight, so I told him to head on over here."

"Your party consists of an entire wedding reception?" I let out a laugh.

"So random, right?" Tannon chuckles beside me.

"As always," Cassie adds before taking a sip of her drink.

"Well, they didn't all come. His grandparents, great-aunts, and stuff went back to the hotel," Asher says.

I nod slowly. "Right...I guess that makes it totally normal then."

"Normal is overrated, Quinn," Everett says. Stepping onto the porch, he places a glass of clear liquid into my hand. "It's a vodka and soda with lime." He motions toward the glass.

"Thank you," I say and take a sip.

"You're looking hot as hell. Where are you coming from?" Asher asks me.

"Nowhere, really. This is all for you," I tease.

Asher clutches his heart. "Babe, you shouldn't have. I already kind of promised a bridesmaid she could stay over."

I shrug. "Bummer. I guess it's not meant to be. I really thought we could be something, Ash."

Before Asher can respond, a woman dressed in a tangerine dress wraps her arms around Asher's waist. "I need another drink, Asher," she whines.

"I got ya, babe." He spins around to face her and leads her off the porch and into the living room of dancing bodies.

I raise my brows. "Unfortunate wedding color."

"I know, right? Orange bridesmaid dresses." Cassie makes a gagging face.

Everett excuses himself and heads into the apartment to make rounds with their guests.

"Cassie told me about your day from hell earlier this week. How was the rest of your week?" Tannon asks.

I tell them about the past few days, including the part about breaking down after leaving Starbucks on Wednesday. I leave out foolishly wanting someone who I can't have nor need.

"Do you miss Beau?" Tannon inquires.

"Sometimes," I tell her honestly.

"You know, one of the groomsmen, actually he's the groom's brother, is gorgeous. We should introduce you," Tannon suggests with a mischievous grin.

"Then why don't you want him?" I ask with a chuckle. Tannon is beautiful, single, and writes gut-wrenching stories about love. She's a total catch.

Cassie stands to Tannon's side and wraps her arm around her back. "I already tried," Cassie says, looking from me to Tannon. "You know our girl is too shy to hook up with a guy from a party."

"I am not. I'm just not interested," Tannon corrects her roommate. "Plus, I'm busy. I don't have time for that right now."

"There's always time for that." Cassie nods toward the guy, and I follow her stare to the tall guy standing at the bar in the kitchen talking to Everett. He's wearing the pants from his tux and a white button-down shirt that's rolled up his very muscled forearms.

"I'd definitely make time," I blurt out, causing the girls to laugh.

"Go talk to him," Tannon urges.

"Yes, ask Everett for a drink refill and get to know the best man. I'll find Asher and make him play better music. I mean, Cat Stevens is classic and all, but you need some swoonier music. It's not 1970. Seriously."

Cat Stevens's "Wild World" plays through the speakers. "No, leave the music. It's sexy. I can make it work." I grin and turn toward the open threshold between the deck and living room. "Wish me luck, girls."

Moments later, I have a fresh drink in hand, and I'm chatting with the best man from the wedding, whose name is Mason.

Besides his startling good looks, Mason is smart and charming. He owns a business in Novi, a city about forty minutes from here. He checks all the boxes, and even if he didn't, I wouldn't care. This week has been too much seriousness and not enough fun. I'm channeling my inner college girl tonight. When he kisses me as we dance to Jim Croce's "Time in a Bottle" because apparently, Asher has a seventies playlist on, it makes me weak in the knees, and I know tonight's going to be fun.

CHAPTER 9

QUINN

I'M HALF-NAKED, sprawled across my king-sized bed under a sheet with an equally half-naked and snoring Mason beside me. My entire body is exhausted from our late night of drinks, dancing, and heavy make-out session.

College Quinn is back! But man, is she tired. I don't remember feeling like this back at Eastern. My sorority sisters and I would stay out dancing the night away at Theo's, our favorite bar, on Thursday for Greek night until two in the morning and then hang out at one of the guys' houses for an after-party until at least four. I always arrived at my nine o'clock Friday morning class with a pep in my step. Half the time, I was still drunk and wearing my wristband from the bar.

I miss those days.

I reach for my cell phone on the end table, and the

time reads eleven. It's almost midday, and my body aches like it's five in the morning. *Crap, I'm getting old.*

I toss on a T-shirt and shorts, and close my bedroom door, leaving a slumbering Mason behind me. First things first, I need water. My mouth is dry, and I'm beyond parched.

Once in the kitchen, I chug two glasses of water and think about last night. Despite the fact that I currently feel as if I were hit by a train, it was fun. *Wasn't it?*

Yes. It was.

Mason is a great guy and, not to mention, gorgeous. He's a good dancer, a good kisser, and well...pretty much aced all areas of foreplay. And yet...I don't know. I didn't let it go as far as sex last night, and I'm wondering why. Truth be told, college Quinn, probably would have. A small part of me, buried deep beneath the intoxicated lust-filled moments with Mason, that just wasn't all-in.

Perhaps, I was right to hold off with Mason. Something's missing. I should want to climb back into bed with him and finish what we started, but I don't. There are no butterflies. No nervous excitement and underlying jitters of new possibilities. I just feel...blah.

It's just because I'm tired and hungover. The excitement will come.

An incessant buzzing sounds from the living room, and I go to check it out. Our attire from last night is thrown about the room, evidence of our frenzied actions to remove all articles of clothing on the way to the bedroom. *Ah, yes...college Quinn is definitely back or at least visiting.*

After a year of playing house with Beau, the sight before me makes me laugh under my breath simply because it's been so long since alcohol and poor decisions have led to such a night.

Searching for the sound of the buzzing, I locate Mason's phone lodged beneath the couch. A woman named Sarah is calling. I let it go to voicemail, and after her name leaves the screen I notice several more missed calls from her and at least a dozen texts. Clicking on the text icon, I read the first few, and it's clear that Sarah and Mason are together. She can't be his wife, or I think she would've been at his brother's wedding with him. I'm not sure why she wasn't there last night, but they are definitely in some sort of a relationship.

And I'm an idiot.

Well, the butterflies refused to surface for a reason. My gut had him pegged, even if my brain was a little slow on the uptake.

With a sigh, I make my way toward my room and toss the phone toward him.

"Mason!" I yell, startling him from slumber. His confused stare catches mine. "I'm going to take a shower. I want you gone by the time I get out. Call Sarah back. She's blowing up your phone," I say, heading across the room to my bathroom. Once inside, I close the door behind me without so much as a backward glance and lock the door.

I take a long, hot shower, and when I emerge from the bathroom, a blanket of steam following me, Mason is gone. He retrieved all of his items of clothing and left. I double-check the rest of the house and lock the back door, suddenly feeling creeped out that he was here in the first place. *What a douche.*

The week from Hell—Eighty-Five.

College Quinn—Zero.

I get dressed, throwing on a pair of jean shorts and a faded tank top. I have no plans today except to wallow in my shame as a human. Well, that and to get rid of this headache.

An Excedrin and two espressos later, I finally feel like I could be a viable member of society again.

Friends plays on the TV, and I laugh at a scene I've seen a hundred times. I grew up with this show, and it will never not be funny. I love it so much.

My phone catches my eye, from the arm of the couch where the notification light flashes. Sure enough, the text icon is present on my notification screen. Clicking on my message icon, I find a text from Cassie making sure I got home okay and another from Ollie.

I quickly mute the TV, needing to concentrate. Before reading Ollie's text, I shoot a quick reply to Cassie so she doesn't worry. Then I open Ollie's and stare at the words before me.

. . .

Hey! Thanks for the money and the dinner. Completely unnecessary as I told you, I was just helping out a friend. But since I know I can't convince you to take it back, I'll just say thank you.

A smile comes to my face. His words are friendly and completely platonic, yet I'm giddy as I write him back.

You're welcome, but seriously, I'm so grateful for your help. I had a shitty week, and you made it a little easier. I appreciate you. Thank you so much. And I met your girlfriend. She seems nice. ;-)

I just can't help myself with those last two sentences. I'm fully aware that I'm fishing for information, but clearly, I have no shame.

My heart beats wildly as his response comes through mere seconds later.

I don't have a girlfriend.

I roll my eyes, thinking of last night and wondering what Mason classifies Sarah as since he stated he didn't have a girlfriend either. Shame consumes me when I realize I'm

comparing Ollie to Mason because there's no comparison. On Ollie's worst day, he wouldn't even come close
to be Mason's creep status.

Well, whoever answered your door.

His answer is immediate.

She's just a friend.

Okay. I respond, not knowing what else to say but
knowing that Ollie wouldn't lie to me.

I have something for you. Can I stop by today?

The butterflies have shown up full force and are now
flipping wildly in my stomach.

Sure. I play it cool.

Great. Be there in five.

. . .

"What!" I scream, jumping from the couch.

I turn and start frantically fluffing my couch pillows. "What am I doing?" I shake my head and sprint toward the bathroom, where I proceed to brush my teeth for several minutes. I drag the toothbrush across my tongue and then rinse with mouthwash. Nothing says gross like coffee breath.

I hurry back to the living room and snatch the dress, bra, and panties I wore last night from the floor and jog back to my room, where I toss them into the hamper. I take in my appearance before the full-length mirror on my bathroom door. My hair is still wet. I have zero makeup on, and my clothes aren't the least bit cute.

As I'm trying to prioritize which is most important— hair, makeup, or attire—the rumble of Ollie's motorcycle can be heard from my driveway.

Crap.

Well, I told myself that I can't be interested in him. A relationship with him is too dangerous. So this is for the best.

I give myself another once-over in the mirror, and with a sigh, I turn to leave my room as a light knock comes from the front door.

I pull the door open.

"Hey," I greet him.

"Hey." He smiles back, and my chest literally hurts

because as cute as I thought Mason was last night, he's nothing compared to Ollie. No one is.

Ollie's wearing a pair of perfectly fitted, faded jeans, and they aren't the type of jeans made to look faded by the manufacturer. They're faded from use, worn countless times by Ollie over the years, and there's something about that, something that makes his jeans look even sexier on him. He's wearing a plain white T-shirt, which clings to the lean muscles of his chest and arms. There's something very James Dean about his appearance today, classic and hot, and I'm here for it.

"Do you want to come in?" I stand back, allowing him entrance.

"Um, sure." He takes a step inside, and I close the door behind him. "So I have something for you."

"So you've said." I grin.

He reaches into his back pocket and pulls out...my driver's license.

"It was in the envelope with the money." He extends the small piece of plastic toward me.

I frown, remembering that the bank teller always puts my ID in the envelope with the cash and a receipt each time I get out cash from my account at the drive-through bank window.

I'm not sure what I thought Ollie was bringing me, but I'm definitely bummed.

"Thanks." I force a smile and take my driver's license from him.

"You're welcome. Just thought you might need it."

I hold it up, pressing my lips in a grin. "Yep. I definitely will."

He wipes his palms against his jeans. "Alright, well, I should get going. I just wanted to make sure you had that."

"Well, thanks again," I say as he turns to leave.

He twists the doorknob, opens the door, and takes a step, then he stops with his back turned to me. I watch him, curious. He seems to be thinking with one foot out the door and the other still in.

Finally, he turns back toward me. "Do you want to go for a ride?"

I'm so happy, I could cry. I nod my head. "Yes. Let me get ready."

His ocean-blue gaze travels down my body. "You're perfect the way you are."

I swallow. "Well, I need a hair tie at a minimum."

"Okay. Grab your hair tie, and let's go." His lips turn into a smile, and the sheer sexiness of it threatens to end me right here. To be on the receiving end of one of Ollie's smiles, I'd happily sink into oblivion. And that realization terrifies me but not enough to stay away.

CHAPTER 10

OLLIE

AGE THIRTY-FOUR

I STUDY Leo closely as he sings along with the rest of the crowd. A dozen people circle around Alma singing happy birthday. Their core group of friends, along with some others from The Lair, are in attendance for Alma's twenty-third birthday.

Everyone, especially Alma and Leo, seem happy. His entire face smiles when he looks at her, so much love and pride in his eyes.

Yet I can't shake this feeling in my gut that something's off. Leo has opened up to me a few times over the past couple of months about him going through a rough time. We always talk it out. He says all the right things, indicating he's on the right path, and we continue with life.

One day at a time. Because that's all we can do.

More so than the few conversations that we've had is the fact we haven't had more. Usually, when people go through rough patches, it lasts longer than a single conversation. It feels as if Leo is pulling away from me. When my friends are struggling, they tend to rely on me even more, not less, as in Leo's case. Perhaps, he is doing great, and I'm being paranoid, and it wouldn't be the first time. It's an unfortunate side effect of my job, worry. It's constant.

I try to start conversations, and he ends them quickly, reassuring me that he's good. I can only go by his word. He's the only one who truly knows what's going on inside his head.

I have no other choice but to believe him, yet...that feeling remains.

Alma blows out the candles and turns to Leo. He presses his mouth to hers. She wraps her arms around his neck, deepening the kiss, and their friends cheer.

He's happy.

"Let's eat cake!" Quinn cheers.

Quinn is petite, maybe five feet two inches with a killer body, yet she can knock out desserts more than anyone else I know, and I love it. I love women who can eat.

Alma breaks the kiss, and Leo's gaze lingers on her face before he kisses her forehead.

"What flavor of cake is it?" Quinn asks.

Amos carries over a pile of plates, forks, and a cake knife. "It's a white cake with raspberry and custard filling," he answers her.

Quinn's current boyfriend whispers something into her ear, and she nods. He grabs a beer from the ice bucket and walks into the living room to where I'm assuming he's continuing to watch the Detroit Tigers play baseball on the TV.

Amos starts cutting the cake when the lights go out. A collective gasp sounds as the room goes dark.

"We lost power?" Someone from The Lair asks the obvious.

"I'll get the candles!" Alma feels her way out of the kitchen and returns with a basket of candles.

After the interior of the home is lit with warm light from the flickering candles, Leo scrolls through his phone.

"Apparently, the whole grid is out, so all of Ann Arbor and surrounding areas. Some computer glitch," Leo says.

"Oh my gosh. That's crazy. Does it say how long it'll take to fix it?" Cat asks.

Leo shakes his head. "Doesn't say."

"How exciting. This will be a birthday party to remember. We could play a board game or something by candlelight?" Quinn suggests.

"Oh, that would be fun," Alma says.

"I could start a bonfire in the firepit for those who wanted to hang outside," Leo chimes in.

Ethan nods. "Yeah, man. I can help you."

The rest of the evening is fun, maybe even more so because of the lack of power. There's something about a power outage that's nostalgic. I'm not sure why, but it makes me feel like a kid. Like we're on this adventure living by candlelight and our imaginations. Some of the partygoers left after the lights went out. A few stayed indoors and played Scrabble, and the rest joined Ethan, Leo, and myself at the bonfire.

After a few hours around the fire, I step away from the firepit to head inside for a bottle of water. Making my way up the steps to the deck, I spot Quinn leaning against the wooden railing and looking toward the sky. Her long blond hair hangs over her shoulders. Her features are accented in the distant flickering light of the bonfire and the glow from the moon. She looks like a goddess, pure and beautiful.

"Scrabble finished?" I swallow the lump in my throat.

"Yeah, they've moved on to Monopoly."

"Who won?"

"Amos, of course." She chuckles. "Guy's a genius."

"Not a Monopoly fan?" I inquire. Stepping up to her side, I rest my arms beside hers on the deck railing. I drop my head back and follow her gaze toward the sky.

"No, it's fine. I just wanted to see the stars. You can

never see them in the city. There are always too many lights. My family lives up by Mt. Pleasant, out in the country where the night skies are just brilliant. Growing up, I never wanted to live in the country, and I definitely don't miss it except for the night skies. I miss those." She sighs contently, her stare never wavering. "My dad loves astrology. He told us all the stories of the constellations growing up. I used to find it so magical. Do you know any of them?"

"No, I can find the big dipper, though. It's the only constellation I can recognize." I point toward the big dipper in the dark sky above us. "And I think one of the stars in it is the North Star? But that's my entire knowledge base right there."

Quinn smiles and points upward. "Yeah, the top right star in the bucket portion of the big dipper actually points at Polaris, which is the North Star and the top star in the handle of the little dipper."

"So the North Star is actually in the Little Dipper? Well, I've apparently been wrong my whole life." I huff out a laugh.

"You weren't completely wrong. You had the gist of it. Do you want to hear more?" she asks.

"Sure."

"Well, the big dipper is actually part of a larger constellation called Ursa Major, and she's a bear." Quinn scoots right up next to me until the sides of our bodies connect. She take hold of my arm and points it upward. "Find the handle of the big dipper."

"It's right there." I point.

"Right, so that's actually the tail of the bear and then you follow it down." She positions my hand so I'm pointing toward the stars as she's explaining them. "Then there's the body and the legs, and those three make the face of the bear. See how it's like a triangle?"

I nod but in truth she lost me after the tail of the big dipper. I'm not sure what she's pointing to but it looks nothing like a bear. It's irrelevant because honestly, I just love hearing her talk.

"Several legends surround Ursa Major depending on what version you follow but the one that my dad told me was that Ursa Major was once a beautiful woman named Callisto who had an affair with the god Zeus. From that affair she had a son, Arcas. Zeus's wife, Hera, found out and was so jealous that she turned Callisto into a bear so she would no longer be beautiful. One day when Arcas was older he came upon his mother in her bear form in the woods. She was so happy to see him that she started to approach him but he was frightened so he shot an arrow at her. Zeus stopped the arrow from hitting her and felt bad for Callisto because she longed to be with her son but couldn't. So Zeus turned Arcas into a bear as well and then he picked both bears up by their tails and tossed them into the sky where they could be together and live in peace forever in the heavens. Ursa Minor is the little bear, Callisto's son, he's right there and his tail is the handle of the little dipper. See?"

She moves my arm over, presumably pointing it

toward the other constellation. No, I'm not sure exactly which stars I'm looking at but I agree regardless. "Yeah."

"You don't see, do you?"

"No."

She throws her head back and laughs. "It's okay. It takes a while until you can really start noticing the shapes of the constellations." She releases a happy sigh, and lets go of my arm. "I love this though. Gosh, I should get home more often, if only to lie outside at night."

Once again, I lean against the deck railing beside Quinn, our faces toward the sky. The world around us is dark save for the flickering light of the dwindling fire behind us. It's peaceful. The sides of our bodies are still connected, neither of us have stepped away. It doesn't mean anything, though. Just two friends watching the night sky.

We stare, content in our silence.

"Oh my gosh!" she grabs my arm. "Look! A shooting star. Make a wish!"

Sure enough a little ball of light is soaring across the sky. I can't remember the last time I've seen a shooting star, if ever. Standing here with Quinn as one passes across the sky causes goose bumps to form against my skin, an awareness of something greater than this moment present.

She takes my hand in hers and squeezes it. "Make a wish, Ollie." Her demand is urgent.

"I am," I say through a smile.

A moment later the star has disappeared into the horizon.

"How lucky are we?" she whispers, her voice in awe. "What'd you wish for?"

"I can't tell you or it won't come true."

She purses her lips. "I don't think it works like that."

"Just in case we should keep it hush. It's not every day that one gets a shooting star wish."

"True. Well, I hope you made a good one." She peers down at our hands, still connected between us, and releases her grasp.

"Don't worry. I did." I clear my throat. "I should get back to the guys."

"Yeah." She takes her bottom lip into her mouth. "Well, thanks for stargazing with me."

"Anytime."

I leave Quinn on the deck and head back toward the guys, completely forgetting the water, my initial reason for going toward the house in the first place.

I'm lost in thought, thinking about the past few minutes. I made a wish at that moment, one that just came to me. The star was there and the thought immediately popped in my head. It happened so quickly that I didn't have time to question it. It was just there taking up residence in my mind.

A single wish.

Her.

CHAPTER 11

OLLIE

WHAT WAS I THINKING? Oh, that's right. I wasn't. What do I expect to come from this outing? Nothing because that's what I can give to a relationship. Absolutely nothing. My plate is full.

I get that I shouldn't be dating, and at the same time that's exactly what I'm doing. I know the way in which I affect Quinn because the feeling is mutual. We can't be friends that actively hang out because whether we admit it or not, we both want more.

There is no *more*.

There can't be.

That's why this is stupid, and I'm a complete dumbass. But...the way in which her arms wrap around my waist, clinging to me, and how her giggle can be heard over the wind whipping past us is captivating. I can't be in her presence and not be completely drawn in, enamored.

It's always been that way with Quinn. We've flirted at Alma's gatherings for years. It was innocent because it never went further. But this...hanging out, beyond the presence of Alma and our mutual friends, just the two of us, is very different. It's dangerous.

I drive us outside of the city of Ann Arbor and continue down the long country road passing a couple of small rural towns without a destination in mind. That's the thing I love about being on my bike, the ride is a destination in itself. As we enter Chelsea, a quaint town, I pull over in front of the small market on Main Street.

"I'll be right back," I tell Quinn as I step off the bike and make my way into the shop.

I grab a couple of prepared sandwiches, bottles of water, and a bag of chips. Next to the checkout counter is a display of beach towels. Pulling a towel from the wooden crate, I place it on the counter.

"Going on a picnic? It's a lovely day for it," the little old lady behind the counter asks as she slowly rings up my items and places them in a paper bag.

"It's a beautiful day," I agree.

When I've paid, I head back outside where Quinn remains, leaning back on the leather seat of the bike, looking like a vision in her ripped jean shorts.

She must've just gotten out of the shower when I arrived at her house. Her hair was wet, and she didn't wear an ounce of makeup and she looked more beautiful than I've ever seen. Quinn is drop dead gorgeous, always. But today, she's even more-so, somehow. It's why I couldn't leave her even though I tried.

"What'd you get?" she asks as I approach.

"Lunch," I tell her, opening the back cargo hold and pushing the bag inside. The towel makes it a tight fit, but I'm able to close and latch it.

"Where are we going?" she smiles and I swing my leg over the seat and start the bike.

"You'll see," I say as she wraps her arms around me once more.

We continue out of town which takes us down the tree-lined, winding road leading to the lake. Michigan has tons of lakes, this area especially. We're surrounded by state park land, and there has to be at least a dozen lakes in this area alone. There's one in particular that's smaller, and a ways out from the others. My parents took me there when I was young, and I remember thinking it was so cool because we were the only people there.

I drive slowly down the winding dirt road until the small patch of gravel, intended as a parking lot, shows through the clearing of trees. I pull my bike to a stop and kill the engine.

Giving Quinn my hand, I help her off the bike and retrieve the bag of food.

There's a path through the trees, wide enough for two people to walk side by side.

"So mysterious," Quinn whispers as we make our way down the trail.

"My parents brought me here once as a kid, and I remember thinking it was so cool. It's a lake on state land but not many come here. Either they don't know about it or prefer one of the larger lakes," the lake comes into view. The sunshine reflects off its shiny blue surface. Behind the lake is a backdrop of nothing but trees, and along the edges, hundreds of bright green lily pads.

"Oh my, so pretty," Quinn says in earnest.

"Right? It's just as I remembered it." I lay that beach towel along the grassy patch near the waters' edge, and pull the food from the bag. "You hungry?"

Quinn looks to the sandwich in my extended hand and takes it from me. "Yes. I haven't eaten yet today." She sits cross-legged on the big towel.

I sit across from her. "Really? It's like two in the afternoon." I chuckle.

She pulls back the sandwich wrapping. "I know, but I slept in. Some friends had a party last night, and I was out quite late."

"Ahh." I nod in understanding before taking a bite of my sandwich.

"I don't party all the time," she clarifies. "It had just been an awful week."

"Dude. I'm not judging you. I'm not like that," I say.

"Dude?" She chuckles.

I shrug. "I'm old-school, remember? That's what we said back in my day."

"Well, *dude*...do you ever wish you could go to

party? Drink a lot, and resent your choices?" she asks before taking another bite of her sandwich.

"Definitely not." I laugh. "I'm high on life, Quinn, and that's all I need."

"I believe that." She nods. "You're like the chillest person I know."

I unscrew the cap of my water bottle, and take a swig. "I really don't judge or care if others drink. It's just not something I want to do. You know? And most people don't have a history like mine either. That changes things."

"Yeah. I guess it would," she says before squinting. "Why are we here, Ollie?"

The carefree air around us is suctioned away. My chest tightens with her question.

"What do you mean?" I play dumb.

She shakes her head. "You know exactly what I mean. We don't do this, you and I. It's different, and I want to know what you're thinking about it all."

I tighten the cap of my water bottle, drop it to the towel and stand. I pull off my T-shirt, and unbuckle my jeans.

Quinn jumps from the towel. "What are you doing?" Her voice is shrieky, and it causes me to laugh.

"Swimming." I kick off my boots and remove my jeans, leaving my boxer briefs on. "You should try it. It's fun." I wink before turning and running into the water because avoidance is my friend.

"I don't have a suit," she calls out.

CAPTIVATED SOULS / 113

"You're wearing panties and a bra, yeah? Basically, the same thing." I lie back into the water, floating on my back and staring at the clouds. The water covering my ears mutes the world around me.

I hear when she enters the water and I look up. She's wearing white cotton panties and a simple white bra, and it's the sexiest thing I've ever seen.

Fuck. I'm in trouble.

I feign calmness and retreat to my back floating position. Quinn lies atop the water beside me, and extends her hand toward my own. She entwines her fingers through mine and for some reason, I let her. The two of us float silently, save for the light movement of the water, and weighted breaths as our hands connect making it all so real when I don't think either of us want it to be.

There are some things in life that are inevitable, for instance, the sun will always rise in the east and set in the west. Birds will always chirp in the newness of spring. Ice will always be cold to the touch, and water will always be wet. The earth will always circle the sun, and fire will always burn.

Quinn is my inevitable. For me, she's always shone brightly, and, like a star, she's a ball of fire that could possibly burn me, ruining everything I've worked so hard to build. But like any shooting star, she's impossible to ignore. I find myself putting my faith in her, wishing and hoping, that we'll work. For, I don't know how long I can be in her presence, in her light, before I'm forced to look —at her, us, and everything we can be.

Just as one isn't supposed to look into the sun, I'm not meant to hold my stare on Quinn for too long. Her light will blind me.

I'm not sure exactly when it happened but there's been a shift. For years, I was content with our light-hearted flirtation knowing that it'd never be more than that. Now that I think about it, something changed between Quinn and I at Alma's birthday party. Our words became needier, our shared breaths heavier. The air between us was charged with more than friendship. Quinn was emitting desire, I felt it. From how she looked at me, to the way her body leaned in toward mine, needing to be close—it was there.

Everything's different, and at the same time, nothing has changed. My reasons for avoiding relationships still stand. Commitment scares me because I'm already committed to so many others. A relationship with Quinn would put nothing more than her feelings on the line whereas the relationships I have in NA, the one's that depend on me like Clementine could mean her life if I fail.

I can't fail.

I'm torn between what my heart wants, and maybe even needs, which is Quinn and what's right, which is my commitment to others. Some people could do both but I'm so terrified of failing that it doesn't seem worth the risk. But is it even a choice anymore?

Look at me. I'm out here holding hands with Quinn.

It's already gone too far.

Quinn releases my hand and swims out deeper, and I follow. She stops, and stands to face me. The water is up to her chin.

"What are we doing, Ollie?" her plea, a mere whisper.

I tread water, circling her. "I don't know."

"You want to know a secret?" she asks.

I nod, pulling my lip between my teeth.

"I'm scared," she admits.

"Me, too, Quinn."

"Really? Of me?"

"Definitely." I scoff. "You have the power to ruin everything."

She furrows her brows. "I wouldn't, though."

"You don't know that."

"Well, you could destroy me like Leo did to Alma." She gives voice to her fear and I get her hesitation. Alma's grief over Leo's loss was devastating. Of course that affected her.

I can't picture myself relapsing, ever. But I don't tell her that because maybe it's best if whatever we've started ends here. "Maybe."

"Seriously?" Her voice quakes with emotion and I realize I can't do that to her.

I release a sigh. "No, Quinn. I'd never do that to you. There are many ways in which someone becomes an addict. Mine was circumstance. I was a kid who was prescribed too many pain pills. I had a happy childhood. I've never experienced abuse or trauma. And quite honestly, I have no desire to ever use again. I don't crave it or miss it in any way. It's been twenty years, and I'll never go back. But you're right to be concerned. My history will always be a part of me, and I can't change that. Truthfully, I wouldn't want to because it's led to others that need me."

She presses her lips into a line and nods, seemingly satisfied with my response.

"What do we do now?" she licks her lips and I swim toward her until our faces are mere inches apart.

"Now." I lean toward her slowly, and plant a peck on the tip of her nose. "I take you home."

"What?" she protests as I start swimming to shore. "That's it?"

"That's it." I release a chuckle.

CHAPTER 12

QUINN

I'm one of those people who don't dread Mondays because I love my job, usually, and I love working. It feels good to be productive and work hard in a field I love.

And yet...when my alarm went off this morning, I grumbled, literally almost full blown yelled in protest.

Crazy thing is it's not even Monday. Yesterday was a holiday, Labor Day, and I had the entire day to contemplate my choices. And still...the weekend needed to be longer because I need more time to process what happened.

Ollie kissed me.

Okay, so it was on the nose, and very wet because we were in water. But it was something. I know now that the feelings between us are mutual, all the feelings, both the desire and apprehension.

That peck on the nose turned me on more than my entire evening with Mason or a year with Beau. Ollie exudes ridiculous hotness. Everything that I find attractive in a man, was put into Ollie. He's all that I've ever wanted, and deep within my gut tells me to give in to him, and the idea of us.

After the infamous nose kiss, Ollie and I dried off, put our clothes back on, and rode back to my house where he dropped me off. He told me that neither of us can think clearly around the other, and that we need time apart from each other to think about what it is that we want.

He had a solid point. My head is always cloudy when I'm with him. I put it off to lust but the fact is, I don't think straight when I'm near him. He surrounds me in his Ollie bubble of perfection where I'd do anything if he asked me. I would've given him anything he wanted, right there in the lake without any thought to the consequences because that's what he does to me.

I called my sister Holland last night to seek advice, and my other sister Willow happened to be over. The two of them are very close and both live within a few minutes or our parents, and are often together. Holland put me on speaker and I explained the situation with Ollie to both of them. I was honest, telling them everything I know because I wanted honest feedback. Or at least I thought I did, until they unanimously told me to stay away from Ollie. Even when I tried to expand on his good qualities, they didn't want to hear it. They heard addict, and it was cut and dry for them after that.

They don't know him, and how amazing he is, though. As outsiders with only a few minutes of explanation to go on, of course they would warn me not to get involved with him.

I need to talk to someone who understands.

Alma.

It so happens that today is Love's first day of preschool, and I don't have to be in to the office until noon. So I'm heading toward Love's school to see that cutie on her first day, and then I hope to snag some time with my bestie because I need it.

———

Love was so cute as she made her way into the school with her teacher but I knew she would be. I have a handful of nieces and nephews that I adore. But if I'm being honest, I have to admit that Love's more adorable than all of them. She's just a beautiful little girl. She got the best traits from her parents, the very best parts.

I took Alma to this trendy new restaurant in Ann Arbor. We sit out on the patio on faux leather chairs. Sleek black table umbrellas block us from the sun. It's a hot day for September. Fall may be around the corner but today is still screaming summer.

We order veggie and feta omelets and talk about everything. She and Amos are doing well, and I'm so happy for them. She deserves someone like Amos, someone who loves her with everything he has, and will never hurt her. She's been through so much pain. The universe owes her the perfect happily ever after, and it appears to be delivering.

I'm trying to decide how to bring up Ollie without bringing up Ollie. I need advice but I'm not ready to tell her that it's Ollie simply for the fact that if it doesn't work out or I opt not to go through with it, I don't want anyone to feel awkward about inviting us both to events as they always have. I refuse to make this weird.

I stare at my plate, flicking around a piece of onion that's fallen from the omelet.

"Is everything okay with you?" Alma raises a brow. "Sounded like you wanted to talk about something earlier?"

I lower my fork to the plate and drop my hands to my lap. I chew on the corner of my lip and level a gaze toward Alma. It's now or never. "There's someone."

She sets her fork on the table and gives me her full attention. With a reassuring smile, she asks, "A guy, someone?"

"Yeah." I pull in a breath. "I think I like him a lot."

"Okay," she draws out, squinting toward me. "I'm sensing a but?"

She knows me too well.

"I think I like him a lot, but I don't want to." I pull my bottom lip into my mouth, raking my teeth over the skin beneath my lip. "He's an addict. Or was, though I think they still use present tense, so technically is. I don't know."

I take a few deep breaths and continue. "He's clean and has been for almost twenty years. He's a little older than me. I've been attracted to him for a while but haven't acted on it. You know?" Alma's eyes widen ever so slightly, perhaps wondering how old this mystery guy is or maybe realizing that she, too, knows someone who's been clean for twenty years. If she knows I'm speaking of Ollie, she doesn't let on, so I continue. "I mean, after what you went through...I don't ever want to love an addict. It's too hard. I admire you so much, Alma. I think it's incredible—what you went through and how you came out of it stronger than before—but I don't think that's me. It would destroy me. I know it. I can't take that risk."

"Yeah." She sighs quietly.

"He could stay clean, of course, and we could be happy. Yet there would always be that fear in the back of my mind that he'll relapse. Leo was clean for four years, and he relapsed. It could happen." I look at her for answers.

"It could," she admits. "That's the thing. You never know. Twenty years is a long time to be clean to falter, but it happens. Though, it may not. You really like him?"

"I do. God, I mean, we've had this flirtation thing going for a few years. Every time I give in to it just a little, I'm drawn toward him like a magnet. Seriously, everything about me craves everything about him. I've been fighting it because I'm so scared. I talked to a couple of my sisters, and they told me to run far away from him and fast. But they don't understand."

"It sounds to me like you're wanting me to tell you to go for it," she says.

I shrug. "Maybe I am but at the same time, I'm hoping you don't."

Perhaps Ollie was right, it might be easier to call it quits now before anything has happened. Is that what I want Alma to say? Do I want her to tell me that it's not worth the risk? I find myself praying that she tells me the opposite.

"I can't tell you what the right answer is, Quinn. You just have to follow your gut and your heart. Is this guy worth it? Is the possibility of something great worth the possibility of something horrible? Only you know that answer."

"Would you change anything? If you knew then what you know now, would it have mattered?" I ask.

She shakes her head. "No. I wouldn't have changed a thing. He was worth it."

And just like that, I got the answer I needed to hear.

Because Ollie's worth it, too. Deep within the most sacred part of my heart, where no man has held residence, the answer pounds loudly...*he is*.

CHAPTER 13

QUINN

AGE TWENTY-THREE

TEARS FALL SO hard and fast I can't see. My hand shakes as I try to push the key into the lock. *Where is the stupid keyhole?* I want to scream.

I'm so furious at the world that I'm having a hard time focusing on anything. As far as funerals go, this was the worst. I would gladly walk around with days of the week panties in full view every day of my life than sit through another second of anything as awful as what I just experienced.

I can't stop thinking about Alma and her tearful—yet incredibly brave—speech. My heart literally aches for her. I don't know how she's doing it, managing to go on amid so much grief.

None of this makes sense. It seems like a mere month ago we were all laughing together at Alma's birthday. And now...

I'm so insanely furious. At the world. At Leo. Not at Leo. At Leo's father. At the Universe. *At this fucking key that refuses to go in the hole!*

"Hey," a gentle voice comes from behind me. "Hey," Ollie says again, taking the keys from my trembling hand.

I blink away the tears, and his fuzzy face comes into view. I pull hot August air into my lungs, trying to calm my panic, but I can't stop—the tears, the shaking, any of it. I'm a mess.

"Let me drive you home." He slides his arm through mine and leads me around the car. He opens the passenger side door, and I get in.

Ollie slides into the driver's seat and starts the car. I lean my head against the window. The Hardings' blurred estate passes as Ollie drives us away from this horrible place.

No words are spoken as he drives me home. The only sounds that surround us are those of my sadness.

He pulls my car to a stop in my apartment parking lot, and an arm around my shoulder leads me inside the building and to my apartment.

"Well, I'm going to get going." His voice is sad, and I know that this day must be killing him, too. He loved Leo.

"Stay. Just for a while. Please. I don't want to be alone." My plea is a broken whisper.

He nods and toes off his black leather dress shoes by the door. Removing his suit jacket, he leaves it on the entryway table and follows me into my room.

I take off my heels and climb into bed, exhausted. "Will you lay with me? I'm exhausted."

Silently, he climbs in and scoots in behind me, his front to my back. He wraps his arm around my waist and pulls me into him.

It's comforting.

"I'm so mad and sad," I cry.

"Me too."

"I'm heartbroken for Alma."

"Yeah," he whispers.

"And for Leo."

"Yeah."

"I'm so sorry, Ollie." I squeeze his hand that's around my waist.

"Me too." The sorrow in his voice is palpable. "Me too."

No more words are spoken, and my breaths even out until my dreams pull me under away from the nightmare of this reality.

When I wake, hours later, Ollie's gone.

CHAPTER 14

OLLIE

Cruising down the main street of my hometown brings back a wide range of emotions, and not all of them bad. This town and these people are good—a little too obsessed with sports—but decent nonetheless. Nothing that happened here was intended to send me down the path toward addiction. I wasn't the only one who learned valuable lessons from my time as an addict.

The ride is almost an hour from Ann Arbor, not too far away that I can't go home whenever I want, but far enough to give me some distance which, when I moved away from home initially, is what I needed.

My mother rushes out of the house the second I pull into the driveway, her arms extended out ready for her hug.

I step off the bike, and she collides with me, wrapping her arms tightly around my middle. "It's been too long," she says into my chest.

"Mom, it's been a month."

"A month too long! Now, come inside. I made all your favorites!"

All my mother ever wanted to be is a wife and mother, and that's what she did. She was the type of mother who always had fresh baked cookies ready for my friends when we got home from school. She went to every class party I ever had, every banquet, every PTA meeting, and every game. She was, and still is, my biggest fan.

She had complications after my delivery and had to have a hysterectomy, leaving me as a permanent only child, and while I'm sure there was a time she mourned that fact, it never showed. My mother, Christine Hale, is adored in this town. She still volunteers at the school even though I moved out almost two decades ago. She uses her giving spirit and loving nature to help others in the community.

"Bill! Look who's home." She pulls me into the house where my father sits in his recliner watching college football.

He turns his face from the big screen. "Hey, son. Good to see you."

I open my mouth to reply, and he's already turned back toward the television. My father is a good man, but our relationship isn't very deep. There have never been any long conversations between us as he's a man of few words.

My mom waves her hands through the air, dismissing my father's actions. "Oh, you know him and football. Anyway, for starters we have cream cheese, dill pickle, and ham roll-ups."

She grabs a tray of the appetizers from the refrigerator and places them on the table. "Sit. Sit." She motions. "These were your absolute favorite when you were young. There was a time you could've lived off nothing but these when you were about nine. Remember?"

"I do. You packed these every day in my lunch for a year in fourth grade." I chuckle.

"Well, I had to. You would've thrown a fit had I not."

"Remember what I else I was obsessed with?"

"Cheesecake!" She laughs. "Don't worry. I made one of those for you, too."

I shake my head and toss a ham roll-up into my mouth. "You're too good to me, Mom. So what's got you taking a walk down memory lane of my fourth-grade year?"

She fills up two glasses with iced tea and takes a seat at the table across from me. "Well, the other day, the movie *Beethoven* was playing on one of the cable channels. Remember, I took you and all your friends to see it in the theater for your tenth birthday over spring break of your fourth grade year. You loved that movie, and begged us for a Saint Bernard for a solid year after that."

"I do." I bob my head. "Dad said he was allergic but now that I think about it, I think that was lie." I grin.

"Maybe a little white lie." She presses her lips in a line. "Anyway, watching that movie again after all these years brought back so many memories of you at that age. I love that age. Still a kid but wanting to be a teen," she smiles, joy and nostalgia line her features. "You know, you have a home with a yard. You could get yourself one of those big, hairy, slobbery dogs now if you wanted." She chuckles.

I shake my head. "I don't think Saki would appreciate that. She's the queen of the house."

"I can't believe that cat's still alive."

"She is and doing well."

My mom places a hand on mine. "Honey, that cat has never been doing well. She is the most homely looking thing."

"Mother, so much judgment," I chastise in jest. "She is perfect exactly the way she is."

"Well, I suppose that's true, as we all are. So tell me. How's everything? Your motorcycle business and druggie counseling."

"Mom," I say on a laugh. "It's sponsoring not druggie counseling."

"You know I didn't mean anything by it," she says in a sweet voice, and it's true. My mother would never say a mean word about anyone, but her choice of words could use an adjustment sometimes.

"I know and it's going well. We're all doing well."

"That's good to hear, Sweetie."

"And I actually just finished up a huge bike rebuild, so I decided to come visit you before starting my next project."

She raises her hands in praise. "Hallelujah for that. I've missed you, and I'm so proud of you."

We make easy conversation over one plate of food after the next. I'm bursting at the seams and we haven't eaten dinner yet. Mom updates me on all her committees and community projects. I pull out my phone and show her pictures of my latest Harley rebuild which turned out incredible.

"Somethings different about you today," she says suddenly, her brows furrowed. "There's a girl, isn't there?"

My eyes widen. "Mom, there's no girl."

She squints her eyes, accessing. "Don't tell me I don't know my own son. There's a girl and I want to hear about her."

"She's just a friend, Mom."

"Okay, well tell me about this friend," she urges.

"Well, we've known each other through a mutual acquaintance for almost eight years. She works in fashion, in Ann Arbor. She's kind, fun, and beautiful. But it's just not a good time for me. I have other responsibilities and it wouldn't be fair to them or to her to explore anything beyond friendship."

"I'm not buying it. What else?"

"Well, she's eleven years younger than me."

Mom flips her wrist. "So what? That doesn't matter. You know your father was three years older than me and we worked out just fine.

"Three years is much different than eleven, Mom." I laugh.

"Not when I was sixteen, and he was nineteen. It was a very big deal. We were in love and couldn't be together. My father would've killed your father if he'd known. So we waited, in love but apart until I was eighteen and then we eloped. And look at us now, all these years later. Love is love, my boy. Don't let a little age difference ruin it."

"Honestly, it's not really the age at all. It's more the responsibility I feel toward others. I'm so afraid to let them down."

"Honey." She puts her hand on mine. "I get that it makes you feel good to help others. I understand that you feel obligated to do so. But you've spent twenty years putting the happiness of others above your own, and that's just not right. You have paid enough for your past. When are you going to start living? You have the kindest heart of anyone I know and you deserve happiness. We all do. It's time, Oliver. It's time."

"It's just not that easy, Mom. I can't just walk away."

"Then you find a balance, a new way of doing things. One that puts your happiness on the list, and more than that—makes it a priority. It's all about time management. Readjust. You're capable of having a life, and helping others. Don't tell me you're not."

"Maybe."

"Definitely." She scoffs. "There is no maybe about it. Definitely because you, my boy, are worth it."

I wish everyone had a mother like mine—fierce in her love, and unwavering in her support. If they did, I think the world would be a better place. I'm in no way close to perfect but the good I do possess within, can be accredited to her.

CHAPTER 15

QUINN

Amos chases Love around the backyard with a squirt gun as she giggles. Alma and I sit beneath the large umbrella canopy on the patio, lemonades in hand watching the sight before us. It's one of those hot September days that feel like full blown summer, hiding the fact that autumn is right around the corner. This is my type of weather—hot.

I've often thought about moving away from Michigan. The seasons are beautiful, sure, but I would love to live somewhere with an eternal summer, as long as there's air conditioning. I don't think I could leave all those I love, my friends and family. Well, maybe I could if I got offered an incredible fashion job in New York City, not that it's any warmer, but because it's *New York City*. I grew up watching reruns of *Sex and the City* and dreaming of living in the epicenter of high fashion one day. But I put roots down here, and as much as I love clothes...I love my people more.

"Quinny! Save me," Love runs toward me, giving me just enough time to place my glass of lemonade on the table before she springs into my lap.

"Safe zone!" I yell out, and Amos stops his pursuit with a wide grin.

"Phew, you're lucky Love Dove." He bops her on the nose. "Well, it's probably a good thing you found the safe zone because I have to get the grill going for dinner." He turns toward Alma. "Can I get you anything?"

"Nope, we're good. Thanks," she says.

"Okay." He leans down and gives her a quick kiss. "I'm going to get dinner started then."

"Sounds good." She smiles up to him.

I'm still wrapping my mind around Alma and Amos as a couple. I met them both when Alma moved into our dorm freshman year. They've always been close, the best of friends since childhood. Admittedly, when I first met them, I thought they were together. They just had this natural chemistry and ease with one another. Then Alma fell in love with Leo, and it was once-in-a-lifetime love. Anyone who saw them together would agree. But I'm glad that Alma's found love with her lifelong best friend. If anyone could've worked his way into her broken heart, it would be Amos. He's loved her since they were children, and he's good—such a great person. I know he would do anything for Alma and Love and they both deserve someone who loves them that way.

Amos walks away and Alma looks to me with a shy grin. I nod, and smile back. Reaching out, I squeeze her hand. I'm so happy that she's happy.

I wipe Love's wet locks away from her face, and kiss the top of her head. "You know what I think?"

"What?" she asks, eyes wide.

"I think that we should work together to get Amos back when he's not expecting it," I say dramatically. "We need to make a plan."

Love shoots up from my lap. "I have water bayoons!"

"Ooh, balloons! Yes, good call. Go get 'em and we'll fill them up with a hose. Don't tell Amos, though."

"Okay!" Love jumps off my lap and runs indoors giggling.

I can't help but laugh. "God, she's adorable."

"She's perfect," Alma agrees.

"Where's Lee-Anne?" I ask of Alma's mother who is normally here.

"You know...I'm not sure. She's been busy a lot lately ever since she, Cat, Love, and I went to lunch at Leo's favorite Coney Island on the anniversary of his death. I think she and Luca are hanging out but she won't admit it."

Luca is the owner of the Coney Island and a widow like Alma's mother. "Oh, that might be nice."

"Yeah," Alma furrows her brow. "I mean I want her to be happy and find love again. She's still so young but she also has quite the history and I don't want her to hurt Luca. He's been through so much."

"As you've said, she's different since your father's passing. She's better. So hopefully she'll stay that way."

Alma nods, "I really hope so and speaking of love and dating...what'd you decide to do about Ollie?"

I gasp. "I...I never said anything about Ollie."

"Come on, Quinn," Alma laughs. "I've been your best friend for nine years. I *know* you."

"But I didn't mention Ollie."

"You didn't have to. First, there's the fact that you've been crushing on him forever. Secondly, how many former addicts that have been clean for twenty years do you know? It's not rocket science." She reaches over and taps my knee. "I think it could be really good for you both."

"You do?"

"Absolutely. Ollie is the best there is, and so are you. Honestly, I don't think you have anything to worry about with him. I mean, I know—never say never—but if there were ever an addict that you could trust not to relapse, I think it'd be him. He was a kid when he was using, and he's spent his entire adult life helping others. I just can't see him ever using again."

She goes quiet and I know she's thinking what I'm thinking. *No one ever thought Leo would either.* Yet, Ollie isn't Leo, and it's not fair to constantly compare them.

"Yeah, I think that's true."

"What does Ollie say about all of this?"

I shrug. "He's hesitant, too. For other reasons, and I'm not completely sure why."

"Well, he's never been in a serious relationship. His life is dedicated to his people at NA. Maybe he's scared of what a real relationship would do to his life. He's had the same routine his entire adult life, bikes and NA. It'd be a change for him. But he likes you?"

I nod. "I think so."

"I think so, too. In fact, I think you've both always liked each other but out of respect for Leo never acted on it. You know what you should do?"

"What?"

"Talk to him."

"You make it sound so simple."

"Maybe not simple but straightforward. The only way you're going to figure it out is by talking to him."

I smile at my best friend. "You're so wise."

"I try." She shrugs.

Love comes back onto the porch with a bag of balloons in her hand. They're the kind that I saw on an infomercial once where you connect the hose to a spout that has lines to each balloon and it fills them up all at once. Apparently, they plop off and seal themselves shut when they're full.

"I got 'em!" she holds up the bag.

"Oh, I've always wanted to try these. I've seen them on TV. Do they really work the way they're shown?" I ask Alma.

"Yeah." She huffs out a laugh. "It's really cool."

"Wow. How fun, Lovie! Let's go fill them up and do a sneak attack on Cookie." I use Amos's nickname which is what Love normally calls him.

"Come on, Momma!" Love extends her hand to Alma.

"I'm coming! I'm coming!" Alma jumps from her chair and follows Love and I.

The three of us sneak off to the side of the house to fill the balloons that actually do work the way the infomercial said they would, and prepare for our ambush.

Everything about today is just what I needed. The hard stuff will have to wait. For now, I have a water balloon fight to plan.

CHAPTER 16

OLLIE

Taking my ratchet, I break the axle nut loose. The rear axle has had the washer welded to it, so I thread it out part way, and push with my thumb to get the axle to slide out of the wheel. Stepping behind the Yamaha, I put my foot under the tire, and my hand under the rim. Sliding the axle all the way out, I move the chain off the sprocket so it's out of the way allowing me to pull the tire assembly out.

The owner of this Yamaha R6 wants a new look, a spiced up paint job. He told me to make it look kick-ass, and unique. I've had some designs working in the back of my mind, and I'm excited to use one on this bike. Jobs that give me total creative freedom are my favorite.

First things first, I gotta remove the tires so they're out of the way when I spray the base layer of paint.

I set the back wheel on the shelf, and grab the ratchet to tackle the front when I hear a car pull into the drive. A moment later, Quinn is standing at the entrance of my garage looking drop dead gorgeous as always. It's been a week since our ride to the lake. A week of back and forth scenarios juggling in my mind. A week of questions and uncertainty. A whole week without *her*.

God, how I've missed her. My entire body hums at her mere presence.

I drop the ratchet on the table. "Hey. What's up?" I play it cool, and immediately hate myself. I see her and my walls immediately go up, and this unaffected version of myself shows up when I am anything but.

Her face wears a look of determination and without a word she walks toward me until her body is pressed against mine. Reaching up she grasps my face between her hands and pulls me toward her. Before I can rationalize her actions, her lips are on mine.

The kiss is firm and unwavering. Quinn is taking what she wants. Though, caught off guard, it takes my body less than a second to act on instinct and take what it wants in return. I thread my hands through her hair and pull her in, needing her closer. Kissing Quinn is everything I imagined it'd be. Her lips are soft but determined. The kiss, sensual and needy, sends electricity though my entire body. On a sigh, her tongue enters my mouth and entwines with mine. All I see and feel is hot, red desire.

I push Quinn back until her body is pressed against

the wall. I cradle her face as my tongue explores her mouth. My body presses against hers and she wiggles beneath my touch. She releases a soft moan that vibrates through my mouth and it's almost too much.

This moment is all-encompassing.

This kiss is everything.

I'm submerged in all that is Quinn. The smell of her hair, the taste of her lips, and the quaking of her breaths causes my heart to race to an explosive speed.

This is years of desire exploding in a single moment. Hot and needed. More than that, it's overwhelming because I've wanted to know what it felt like to kiss Quinn Kirkpatrick since the first moment I laid eyes on her years ago.

I've been inexplicably pulled toward her from the start. She's all I've ever wanted but was too afraid to hope for. My body craves every inch of hers. My heart beats adoration for only her. She's the only woman I've ever wanted to risk it all for.

Simply put—she's everything.

My life has existed to put others back together. Focusing on their terrors has allowed me to forget my own. I knew that one instant, one kiss would change everything, and it has. For a single kiss, a solitary stolen moment will never be enough. Now that I've tasted her, I can never stop. That loss of control terrifies me to my core but for Quinn I will slay all the demons. For her, I will risk it all.

I pull my mouth away, just a fraction, and touch my

forehead to hers. Her chest heaves against mine, mirroring my own struggle for breath.

I squeeze my hands closed, pulling at her silky locks between my fingers. "Quinn," I say on an exhale, all rational thoughts and words a jumbled mess in my head.

"I've waited eight years to do that, and I wasn't about to wait a second longer," she whispers against my lips.

I smile, feeling her plump lips grinning against mine.

"It was incredible," I say.

"It was everything." She puckers her lips, giving me a peck that sends another round of heat down to my toes. "Now that I finally have your attention, I'm never giving it up."

"Promise," my voice is husky with emotion.

At this moment I want Quinn more than anything in this world. Nothing is standing in our way, yet—my history as my own worst enemy terrifies me. I have the power to screw this up. I know I could, easily.

This is a first for me, kissing a woman with true emotion, and wanting her beyond the physical. It's new terrain, and I can't deny that it's frightening. I could've lived without knowing what Quinn's lips felt like on mine. But now that I know, I can't live without her.

Quinn presses her palms to my face. Her bright greens are inches away, the soft gold specks visible. "I know this is new for you. In the past, maybe we weren't possible, but we are now. You want me and I want you. It's that simple. Sure, there could be more to it, baggage that could ruin us. Let's not let it in. We'll keep it easy—we like each other. That's all that matters. I've tried to be happy with others. I lived my life but the fact that you were out here and not with me was always in the back of my mind. I'm going to fight for us, Ollie. I don't want any more excuses. I just want you."

I nod, the gravity of her words setting in. I suppose, I'm now dating Quinn after almost a decade of fighting it. She won just as I knew she always would.

She rubs her thumb across my cheek. "Are we good?"

"Yeah." I kiss her softly. "So good. You're an amazing kisser."

"I know." She pulls my bottom lip into her mouth. "You should see what else I can do." She kisses over my jaw, onto my neck and below my ear. The kisses are soft and her breath is hot. I'm covered in goose bumps and hard as a rock. My head is so muddled with lust, I can't think straight.

Quinn's lips work back across my face until they're on mine. Pressing my body against hers, she moans as I deepen the kiss. Our tongues entwine with one other—slow, hard, and seductive—in a dance that was always meant for just the two of us.

Hands roam.

Bodies squirm.

Sounds of desire surround us.

Our tongues dance.

I never want to stop, maybe ever.

"Sorry if I'm interrupting," a voice states from behind me, and it's like a bucket of cold water falling over my libido.

I jolt away from Quinn, taking a step back and turning toward Clem. I wipe the back of my hand over my mouth. "Clem, I..."

"Oh, calm down," Clementine scoffs. "I'm nineteen. I've seen people kiss before. Not a big deal."

"Right. Well, this is Quinn." I motion behind me. "And Quinn this is Clem."

"Yeah, we've met," Clem states.

Quinn takes a step so she's beside me. "Yeah, when I brought you dinner and money for fixing my Jeep."

"Oh, that's right," I say.

Clementine narrows her eyes, accessing me. "We're still on for tonight. Right?"

It takes me a second to remember what she's talking about. *A&W. Root beer floats and chili dogs.* "Yes, of course. Quinn just stopped by."

"It was an unannounced visit," Quinn adds.

Clementine purses her lips, "Well, it was obviously well-received." She shoots me a knowing look.

"I should probably go then," Quinn's gaze darts from me to Clementine and back.

There's a moment of silence before Clementine pipes up. "It's fine. You can come with us if you want—at least to the first part. We're going to A&W for dinner before the meeting. It's kind of our thing."

"Are you sure?" I ask Clementine.

"Yeah, it's fine," Clem says again. "We should hang out. I mean, if you guys are going to be a thing, we should get to know each other." She turns toward Quinn, her expression darkens. "Because I'm here to stay."

Quinn's eyes go wide, and she looks at me. I give her a smile because I don't know what else to do. This new development was sudden, and we clearly have some dynamics to work out.

"Thank you for the invitation," Quinn addresses Clem. "But I think I'm going to pass this time. Ollie didn't know I was coming over, and you already had plans. But let's get together another time because I'd like to get to know you, too."

"Okay, that's fair." Clem nods. "Well, I'll see you around, Quinn. I'm going to go visit with Saki before we leave."

Clementine walks past us and opens the door to the house before closing it behind her.

Once Clem is inside, I turn toward Quinn and take her hand. "I'm sorry."

She shakes her head. "No, it's fine. You had plans. I get it." She squeezes my hand. "We'll get it all figured out. Don't worry."

Biting my lip, I nod.

Quinn pops up onto the tips of her toes and throws her arms around my neck. "I made you a promise, Ollie.

I want you, and you want me...and that's all that matters."

Our lips meet.

The kiss isn't as heated as our last, but it's somehow even better because it holds the promise of more. And with Quinn, I'll always crave just that.

QUINN

HEELS KICKED off to the side of my office, I sit on the carpet amidst a pile of purchase orders that need sorting. The manager who quit a few weeks ago sure left things in a mess. This week has been one late night after another. With many of our part-time summer help leaving to go back to college, I've been helping out on the floor during the day and up in my office at night sorting out everything else.

We're trying to hire additional staff, but it takes time, and until then, it falls onto me to sort it out. Truth be told, I usually wouldn't mind. I love being busy and feeling productive. It's the simple fact that my mind has been elsewhere this week while my body's wanted to be there for real.

Thoughts and daydreams of Ollie aren't life-sustaining. I need the real deal.

Patience.

He had this whole complete life before me, as did I. One kiss isn't going to automatically change everything, allowing our lives together to fall magically into place. It's new and will take time.

We've been in touch through texts, both of the sweet and sexy nature, and I suppose it's better than nothing. I place my fingers to my lips, where I swear they still burn from that kiss.

That incredible first kiss.

"Hey."

His voice startles me, and I yelp, clutching my hand to my chest. Ollie leans against the doorframe of my office.

"Oh my gosh." I hop off the floor. "What are you doing here? How did you get in?" The store closed an hour ago.

Ollie steps toward me, careful not to step on any of the messy piles on the floor. He sets a white plastic bag on my desk.

"First," he says before taking my face in his hands and kissing me senseless. I'm a pile of mush when he pulls his lips from mine. "I needed that." He grins, carefree and beautiful. "I met Franky in the back on the forklift, moving boxes from a truck into the back warehouse. I told him I was your boyfriend and wanted to surprise you with dinner. So he let me in."

"Oh my gosh." I look up toward him, smitten with everything Oliver Hale. The fact he's here, and I'm in his arms as he looks at me with so much adoration is hard to wrap my mind around. "Well, first of all, you could've been a murderer for all Franky knew. *Thanks a lot Franky.*" I laugh. "And more importantly, *boyfriend?*"

"Here's the thing, little one, the second you traipsed, all sexy and confident, into my garage and kissed me, you were mine. I'm too old to play games. You wanted me? You have me."

"Okay." My reply is breathy.

Ollie's lips find mine once more, and I can hardly believe this is happening. I've wanted Ollie for so long, and he just told me that he's mine.

Mine.

It's surreal really.

He kisses me until my lips ache and my legs threaten to give way. When he pulls away, I remember something he said from moments ago.

"Did you say dinner?" I quirk a brow.

I haven't eaten since breakfast, and I'm famished.

A low chuckle rumbles free. "Well, that's a bit of an exaggeration. I actually only brought dessert. I stopped at the cheesecake place in the mall and got you a variety."

I squeal, smiling wide. "Even better! You know my love for all things sweet and yummy."

"I do." He grins.

"Take the bag," I tell Ollie and grab his free hand, pulling him out of my office. "It's a mess in there, and honestly, I need a break from that space." I lead him over to housewares. The store is dark save for the ambient lighting coming from the *Exit* signs above the doors throughout the store.

I grab a blanket from a display and place it on the ground, and we take a seat.

"Let's see what you brought me," I say, wide-eyed.

Ollie chuckles and starts pulling out containers. He hands me a plastic fork. "There's plain, caramel swirl, strawberry topping, chocolate chip, and one with a bunch of different berries. Take your pick."

"I'm thinking a little bit of each of them, and when I say a little bit—I mean, a lot."

Ollie grins as I dig into the cheesecake. He takes a fork and tries a bite of the plain cheesecake. "This is good."

"Amazing."

"So what was that mess on your office floor?"

"Purchase orders and receipts...crap I need to organize. Not my favorite part of this job, that's for sure."

Ollie scoops up a large bite of the caramel cheesecake and holds it out to me. I take a bite. "I missed you."

I lick the caramel off my lips. "I missed you, too."

"I know you texted that everything went fine Sunday night with Clem at *A&W* and the meeting but is everything really okay with that situation? She seems quite attached."

Ollie sets down his fork and leans on his propped knee. "She is. She is one of the reasons I was hesitant about us or a relationship in general. She needs me, and honestly, she isn't in the best place right now. She's having a hard time. We spend a lot of time together. I've been told that I get too close to those I sponsor, but the truth is, I don't know another way. It's who I am. I'm an all-in type of person. If I commit to someone, that's it. I'm in 100%. Honestly, that's why I've never done relationships because they'd interfere."

"I would never want you to stop helping her or seeing her. I completely understand how important your role is."

"I know. I just worry."

Reaching out, I grab his knee. "Try not to. I want you exactly the way you are. I know that you have this big important role that was a part of your life well before I came along. I think what you do is amazing. You're an incredible man. I'm prepared for dates being canceled, and plans changed because you're needed elsewhere. I'm not coming into this blind. I've thought long and hard about us, and I want this even if it comes with obstacles. We both had reservations coming into this. Heck, it's taken years to get past them just to get here. But now that we're here, I don't want to be anyplace else. You can do both, you know? You can help others and have a relationship of your own."

"Yeah, that's what I've been told."

"By who?"

"My mother."

"Well, she sounds like a brilliant woman, and I agree with her wholeheartedly. You can have both. You deserve happiness, too." I lower my eyes for a second before raising my gaze to his. I swallow. "I know I can make you happy."

He leans forward, and I automatically move toward him until our lips meet in a short and sweet kiss. "I know you can," he says. "That's not even a remote worry. You're perfect, Quinn. The girl of my dreams."

"Okay," I whisper against his lips.

We bag up the cheesecake containers and lie on the blanket, propped on our elbows we face each other.

"You know how you became a part of Leo's life, and became friends with his friends? I was thinking, can't we do that with Clem? Like all hang out together so she has you, but I have you, too."

"Yeah, we could try that."

"And you sponsor others?"

"Yeah but they're all at different stages of recovery, and require different levels of support from me. I have some that have been clean for a long time and only need to check in with me every once in a while. Clementine is newly clean and she's not close with her family, and lost all her friends. So she's kind of fragile in that way, and needs me more."

"You know when I first saw her, when I dropped off your money, I thought she was a girl you were seeing or hooking up with." I cringe just saying the words out loud.

"Yeah, I remember your text," he says amused.

"Well, you didn't know, I guess. Though, she's a little young for me, don't you think?"

I scrunch up my nose. "I thought so but who was I to judge."

"Well, rest assured. There has never been anything romantic between Clem and I. She's like a little sister to me."

"I know you said you don't date, or *didn't* date but you have been with women before?" I've always been curious about his past with women but have never felt the time was appropriate to ask. I guess it's now or never.

He throws his head back and laughs. "Yes, Quinn. You think I'm a thirty-eight-year-old virgin?"

"I don't know. You've always been so mysterious about your love life."

"Well, that's the thing, I haven't had a *love* life. Love and sex are not mutually exclusive. You've never slept with someone you didn't love? Had a one-night stand or a hookup?"

"Yeah, but I've been in love, too."

"Well, I haven't. Just sex."

"That's kind of sad," I say.

He tucks a strand of hair behind my ear. "It's not. It worked for me."

"I really like you, Ollie. I don't want to be just sex."

"Quinn." He sighs. "You could never be *just* anything because you're quickly becoming everything."

"Say more words like that." I grin before leaning in for a kiss.

"Let me take you home where I can *show* you everything I want to say."

My entire body tingles. "I'd like that."

We clean up our impromptu dessert picnic on the sales floor and I grab my purse from my office.

"I can take you back to your place on my bike and bring you back to work tomorrow. Leave your Jeep here?"

"That sounds perfect."

We walk hand in hand out the back of the store, passing Franky.

"You know he could've been a murder?" I tease Franky as we pass.

"Nah, I could tell he was good. It's in the eyes," Franky responds.

I smile wide. "Yeah, you're right. He's good. Have a good night." I wave toward Franky, practically running beside Ollie as he leads us to his motorcycle.

I don't know who's more excited to get back to my place, him or me. We've both been waiting eight long years, so I guess we'll call it a tie.

CHAPTER 18

OLLIE

AGE THIRTY

It's the first time I'm meeting Alma though I feel like I know her already. For the past six months, she's been a constant part of conversation between Leo and me. He worked so hard to get better, for her, and I can see why. The two of them have a special connection, a chemistry that's undeniable.

Leo and I have become friends over this past half year, and he wants to start introducing me to his friends. He wants me to be a part of his life, and I think it's awesome. Despite our obvious connection through NA, he's a great guy to hang with, and I'm sure his friends are just as cool.

Tonight, it's going to be me, Leo, Alma, and Alma's best friend...Quinn. Leo told me that Alma invited Quinn because she didn't want me to feel like the odd man out and something about even numbers being better.

Leo just bought a grill and he and Alma are outside trying to figure it out. I offered to help but they said they had it taken care of.

"I'm sorry I'm late!" A female calls from the foyer. "You will never believe what Kingston did to Abby last night. So I was talking to her. It's kind of a mess. I'll tell you all about it, but I am here now and ready to defuse all tension!"

She steps into the living room, and her mouth falls open when she sees me.

"Tension?" I question with a smirk.

"Oh my gosh, you must be Ollie...and you're early! Ahh, I'm sorry. I'm Quinn." She closes the distance between us and takes my hand in a firm shake.

I'm momentarily stunned by her proximity, confused at my reaction. My heart thumps within my chest at the feel of her hand in mine. She is the most beautiful woman I've ever seen. Short, rocking body, mesmerizing green eyes, long blond hair, and a smile that leaves me breathless. *What the fuck? Breathless? Who am I right now?*

I pull my hand from hers. "It's cool."

"Alma didn't think it'd be weird or anything. She only wanted to make sure that you didn't feel singled out or anything. Plus, maybe we'll play Euchre or something, and the teams will be even."

"Euchre?"

"It's a card game. Do you know how to play?"

"Of course. It's kind of a requirement of growing up in Michigan."

"You know, I would've thought so, too. Yet, I've met many people here at college that've never played."

"Odd."

"Indeed." She waves her hand before her. "Well, anyway, Alma loves games and all candy. It's two things we have in common."

"Games and candy. Got it."

"You are really gorgeous," she blurts out. "You're thirty? You don't seem that old."

"Well, it's not really old, and do you always say whatever comes to your mind?" I chuckle, quirking a brow.

She scrunches her nose. "Usually. It's a problem. But also a blessing because who doesn't like to hear that they're attractive? Right? I can keep my mouth shut. Like, if you looked like a troll, I wouldn't have said anything. I'm not mean." She extends her palm in a circling motion in front of my face. "But clearly, you are like the opposite of a troll. Total opposite."

"Well, thanks, little one." I chuckle.

She beams at the pet name and shoots me a wink. "You're welcome, gorgeous."

You're fucking beautiful. I want to tell her, but I

don't because while random honesty works for her, it'd just be weird coming from me. Not to mention, I'm here for Leo, not to screw his girlfriend's nineteen-year-old best friend.

CHAPTER 19

QUINN

THE SHORT RIDE from the mall to my house is one giant turn-on. My work attire really doesn't lend itself to being the *girlfriend* of a guy who's always on a motorcycle. I can't believe after years of lusting after Ollie, I'm finally —*finally*—dating him. I honestly didn't think this day would come.

My skirt is hiked up to my thighs, enough to allow my legs to straddle the seat. My arms are wrapped around Ollie's waist, as I lean against his back. I can imagine what it'll be like to touch the skin beneath his clothes, and it's almost too much. He smells of perfection, leather and a rugged scent—maybe his body wash or shampoo. Ollie doesn't seem like the type of guy to wear cologne but he always smells like heaven.

The night air is cool as it hits my exposed skin, and I can feel Ollie's forthcoming touches. The wind whips across my skin in a seductive rhythm teasing my body with what's to come. I have wanted this man, more than I've ever wanted anyone, since I was nineteen years old. There's been this innate pull toward him from the very first second I laid eyes on him. Maybe it's chemistry or destiny, the label is irrelevant, but the feeling is real.

Ollie pulls into my drive and turns off his bike. He steps off, and then circles his hands around my waist lifting me off the seat. My heels hit the ground as Ollie's lips meet mine. The kiss is needy and urgent as if the ride was a total aphrodisiac for him, too.

The kiss slows, and he leans his forehead against mine, his breaths heavy. "You know what's going to happen when we get inside, yeah?"

I nod.

"You're ready for that?"

I slide my hand over his abs until it rubs against the rock hard evidence of his desire. "I've been ready for eight very long years."

"Me too." He groans. Grabbing my ass, he lifts me from the ground and I wrap my legs around his middle.

Our tongues collide as he walks up to my front door. I awkwardly riffle through my purse for my keys without breaking the kiss. Keys found, I hold them behind me, as Ollie pushes my body into the door, expecting the key to magically open the door like one big epic movie seen. But atlas, it doesn't work that way.

"Dammit," I hiss as I pull my mouth from Ollie's and turn from him to unlock my door. My hands shake with adrenaline for what's to come that it takes a few seconds to open the door.

The door clicks open and I sigh with relief. I'm crazed with need and hating anything standing between me and Ollie.

"We good?" Ollie smirks.

"Yes!" I wrap my arms back around his neck and attack his mouth with mine needing to feel his tongue entangled with mine.

He walks us inside and kicks the front door closed with his foot. He leads us to my room, and sets me down beside the bed. The moment my feet hit the ground, he pulls off his shirt. My heart races at the sight of his bare chest, and my gaze roams down his abs to the perfect V, and my breath hitches as he unbuttons his jeans and pulls them off, along with his boxers, in one swift movement.

This man has been the star of my dreams for years, and even the best dream can't hold a candle to Ollie in real life. He's perfect.

"Quinn," my name is a husky whisper.

"Yeah." I lift my stare to meet his.

"Do you need help?" he nods at my fully dressed form.

I make quick work of ripping off all articles of clothing separating my skin from his. When I'm naked before him, his gaze darkens as he takes me in. His blues burn my skin as they assess me from head to toe. He runs the back of his finger along my collarbone, down my peeked nipple, over my abs, and stops at my hips.

"You're perfect, Quinn," he says, his voice low with desire. "I knew you would be." His other hand cradles my chin and pulls my face toward him.

His kisses are soft and reverent as he pushes me back onto the bed. His mouth worships mine as our hands roam, exploring each other's bodies. His finger enters me and stars explode beneath my closed eyelids just knowing that it's Ollie who's touching me. Ollie's single touch replaces everything. I never want to be loved by anyone, other than him, again.

He kisses down my neck, and across my chest. Stopping at my breasts, his mouth plays homage to my nipples as he adds another finger he continues to work me into a frenzy below.

"Ollie," I plead, wanting to feel him inside me.

"Patience." He kisses down my belly. "There's something I've wanted to do for a very long time."

He spreads my legs wide as his tongue explores my most sensitive area. My body immediately starts to shake and I moan loudly, the sensations—too good. His fingers pump in and out of me hard as his tongue circles the ball of nerves between my legs. I feel the rush building, and my cries become louder. The journey toward release is more intense than I've ever felt. I'm chasing what will be the most powerful orgasm of my life, and every inch of me trembles.

Ollie's fingers curl toward the front wall, rubbing my

G-spot. His free hand reaches up and pulls on my nipple, eliciting pleasure from so many areas. He sucks my clit into his mouth, and I fall. Hard. Every cell in my body erupts with a sensation more incredible than I've ever felt. Electricity rushes from my toes, up to my scalp, and I cry out as wave after wave pulls me toward a utopia that I know I'll only ever feel with this man.

He continues to lick me as my body quivers with release. I'm spent, and sated. My limbs are heavy as I reach for him. "Ollie," I plead.

He kisses up my body until he hovers above me, and takes my mouth in a kiss.

"I need to feel you inside me," I beg.

He rolls off me and I miss his proximity.

"Where are you going?"

"Condom," he answers.

I tug at his arm. "No. I'm on the pill, and I've been tested. Have you?"

"Yeah, I'm clean and always use a condom."

"Then no." I pull him toward me. "I don't want anything between us. I've waited too long for you, Oliver Hale." I press my palm to his cheek.

"You sure? I don't mind." He covers my hand with his.

"Please," I beg.

He straddles my body and stares at me below him, his eyes full of adoration and need. He lines his hard length up with my opening and I close my eyes.

"Look at me," he orders and I comply. "Keep your eyes open. I want to see you."

He slides into me and I gasp. His mouth falls open. "Fuck Quinn," he hisses.

His brilliant blues hold my stare as he starts moving inside me. We're frantic as he picks up the pace, a mess of moans, and heat as his body slaps against mine filling me up so completely. I close my eyes, pressing my head back into the pillow, needing to focus on the sensations as my release starts to build.

Ollie drops his head, his arms caging me in. His pants sound almost pained as he continues to work inside me. I claw at his back urging him to move harder and faster. Feeling my orgasm building I grab his face and kiss him hard, moaning into his mouth as pleasure takes me. He plunges his tongue in deep, the intensity mirroring his movements below. He growls, loud and wild, as he spills his release inside me.

Exhausted and sated, he falls atop me and I trace circles on his back, slick with sweat, with the tip of my finger.

"I knew you'd be perfect," he says, supplying my shoulder with a peck.

"That was amazing."

"Amazing," Ollie sighs.

"We're going to be doing that a lot." I thread my fingers through his hair.

"Fuck yeah we are."

CHAPTER 20

OLLIE

QUINN's hot little mouth moves up and down my shaft as the warm water of the shower hits my back, and I'm trying to remember why it took me so long to take what I wanted.

All the reasons, all the worry—literal years of it—left the moment I touched her. She was made to be mine. Designed to fit me perfectly. The thing is, I knew it. From the moment I met her, I knew she'd be perfect for me. I fought it for so long, and for what?

People still die, or they don't. They use, or they don't. I can be there for everyone, lend an ear or advice, but ultimately I can't choose for them. The decision to use is solely their own.

But Quinn...I could've lost her. She could've married Beau or any of the other perfectly acceptable boyfriends she's had over the years. I allowed irrational fear to keep me from the one woman who was put on this earth for me. I've spent eight years wanting someone I thought I couldn't have. Eight years of not feeling...this.

I thread my fingers through her wet hair. She moans as if sucking me off is the best thing she's going to do today, and to be honest, it's insanely hot. Everything about her is, always has been.

At thirty-eight, last night was the best sex of my life. Bar none. That fact is tripping me out. Is Quinn just a little sex goddess, or is it merely because feelings are involved, which is a first for me. I've never wanted more from anyone I've slept with. It's always been just sex.

With Quinn, it's different. It's so much more. The want, desire, and fondness I've felt for her over the years were there last night and now—making everything feel so much...better. Indescribable.

"I'm coming," I groan, giving Quinn a chance to pull away as I steady myself against the tiled wall of the shower. She doesn't move, though, and the sight of her on her knees below me makes my orgasm hit hard.

She takes every last drop of my release, and I'm so turned on, I'm almost ready to go again. I pull her up from her knees and kiss her. "That was incredible," I say against her mouth.

"I'm glad you liked it." She grins, running her palms over my wet skin.

I twist her around and pull her back to my front. Leaning down, I suck on her neck and bring my hand around her waist, my fingers finding the spot I crave. Her legs widen on instinct, allowing me deep access, and I work my fingers in and out of her, rubbing her clit with my thumb.

She leans her head back into my chest, "Ollie," she whines, pushing her pelvis toward my hand.

"I know, baby. You and me. We fit so good together," I whisper into her ear, pulling her lobe into my mouth before I start licking and kissing down her neck.

My hand pumps harder, and Quinn's thrusts grow in intensity as she fucks my hand. Suddenly, very jealous of my fingers, I pull them away. Turning Quinn around, I hold her against the wall and lift her leg up to the side so she's wide open for me.

Her mouth is slack, and her heady eyes beg for more. Bending my knees, I position myself at her opening and thrust inside. She cries out, a mix between a whimper and a scream, and it makes me throb with insane need. She's so vocal, letting me feel how I affect her with each touch.

"Does that feel good?" I groan as I take her against the wall.

Her eyes are squeezed shut, her face turned to the side, her mouth open as she cries out in pleasure with each thrust.

"So good," she manages to get out between breaths.

I lick my thumb and start rubbing it against her little mound of nerves as I thrust harder into her. She starts to shake, and I lean against her, holding her to the wall as I chase my own release and fall over the edge with her.

We kiss gently under the spray of the water as we come down from our high.

"I don't want to go to work," Quinn says. "I want to stay here and make love to you all day."

I kiss her forehead. "Me too, believe me."

I feel like a teen who's discovered the true power of his dick for the first time, and I never want to leave this shower. I want to stay in here all day and come with Quinn over and over again.

"Tonight," I promise with a soft kiss to her lips.

I squirt some soap into my hand and start to wash Quinn's body. It doesn't take long to realize we are too new into our relationship for this, as I'm already hard and ready to go again.

"Maybe we should wash ourselves, or you may never get to work." I grin.

She bites her lip and looks down at my growing desire. "I don't know. Work is overrated."

"Quinn." I chuckle and take a step back.

"Fine." She pouts in mock protest and grabs the shampoo.

We wash up and get out of the shower. I put on the same clothes as yesterday, and Quinn puts on a new outfit for work. I notice that she's wearing a black pair of dress pants today, which, although not really bike wear, are definitely more suitable than the tight skirt she had on yesterday.

I watch, fascinated as she puts on her makeup and brushes out her hair. It would suck to be a girl, so much shit to do just to leave the house.

"What?" She notices me staring at her through her mirror.

"Just enjoying the view." I grin.

"Well, I'm not even going to bother to do my hair." She twists her hair into a bun. "Motorcycles are sexy but not conducive to good hair days."

"See, making your life better already. You don't need to spend tons of time on your hair. You're gorgeous without all the fuss."

"I like the fuss. It makes me feel pretty." She puts a silver hoop earring in each ear.

"You're beautiful, Quinn, regardless. Even with wet hair and no makeup, you're the most beautiful woman I've ever seen."

She walks over to me wearing a sexy smile. "Are you saying nice things to get into my pants, Ollie Hale?"

I grab her hand and pull her down to me, so she's sitting on my lap. I circle my arms around her waist. "You know I have no trouble getting in your pants."

"That's true." She grins. "You're welcome anytime. So what are you doing today?"

"Working on a Yamaha, meeting up with a couple of people. How about you?"

"Dealing with customers and filing paperwork."

"Sounds fun."

"Oh, yeah." She raises her brows. "Can I see you tonight?"

"Yeah. Do you want to come over to my house after work? I don't want to leave Saki alone all night."

She nods. "Sure. I'll try to get out of work at a normal time today. I won't work until after the mall closes." She grins. "I can drive back here, and grab some things and then head over to your place. Maybe we can do dinner together?"

"Sounds like a plan."

It feels right making plans with Quinn, like the two grown-ass adults we are. It only took years of desire, months of flirting, a hot garage kiss, a week of suggestive texts, and cheesecake to get to this point. I'm just glad we're finally here because *here* feels good.

"I can make you breakfast before we go." Quinn swipes her thumb over my cheek.

"I'd like that."

She hops off my lap. Extending her hand, I take it, and she helps to pull me up. Hand in hand, she leads me toward her kitchen.

"Would you like Golden Grahams, Apple Jacks, or Cocoa Krispies?"

"Oh, wow. So many choices. I guess, Cocoa Krispies."

She opens the cupboard and reaches for the bowls. "I agree. It is a Cocoa Krispies kind of morning."

I open the refrigerator to find a half gallon of milk and some condiments.

Quinn reaches behind me and grabs the milk. "Hey,

I'm making breakfast. You take a seat." She motions toward the table.

I do as instructed, and she serves us each a bowl of cereal.

"Now, just to be clear, I'm actually a really good cook. I haven't been grocery shopping in a while, and I hate buying a lot of groceries because I'm never here, and they always go bad before I can use them."

"I get that." I nod. "You know, I think you work too much."

"Yeah, probably." She shrugs and takes a bite of her cereal. "I like my job, and besides hanging out with friends, I don't do a lot. So I figure...why not work?"

"Well, I've never had a girlfriend before. But I'm thinking that I might be a little high maintenance as a boyfriend." I smirk.

"Oh, really?" Quinn giggles.

"Yeah, and I'm thinking that I'm going to want to see you a lot," I tease.

"See me or do me?" She quirks a brow.

"Both, obviously."

She shakes her head with a smile. "Well, I'll try my best to keep normal work hours because I, too, see myself being a little needy when it comes to time with you."

"Good."

I clear our dishes, rinse them out, and place them in the dishwasher while Quinn brushes her teeth and finishes getting ready for work.

Minutes later, she's straddling the back of my bike, and we're on the way to the mall.

I pull up in front of the entrance doors to her store, and she slides off the bike, handing me my helmet back.

"I'll see you tonight." She gives me a chaste kiss and heads into work.

I feel like I'm going a little insane because I miss her already.

CHAPTER 21

QUINN

THANKFULLY WORK FLEW BY, aided by the fact that I had very little time to miss Ollie because I was putting out fires everywhere. I'm glad it was hectic because a slow day where I had nothing better to do than count down until I'd get to see Ollie again would've been torture.

I'm afraid to get too confident in this new relationship. A part of me wants to believe that because it's something that we've both craved for so long we're simply going to ride off into the sunset and live happily ever after. And yet—there's the other part, the more rational part, that fears that something lies just around the corner waiting to derail us and our happiness. After all, a thirty-eight-year-old man doesn't go his whole adult life without a serious relationship for nothing. *Something* will threaten what we have going. I just don't know what. Yet I want to be with Ollie enough to risk it.

I pull into Ollie's drive at seven, a respectable time. Plus, I'm taking the rest of the weekend off. I can't wait to wake up next to Ollie tomorrow and not have anywhere pressing to go.

"Hey, Little One," he greets me at his door and pulls me into a kiss.

"Hey, Gorgeous." I step into his house.

Ollie's house is nice. It's clean and modern. The interior is a color palette of whites, creams, and blues. It's quite stunning, really.

I'm not sure what I expected his design taste would be. I suppose, given the fact he's a free-spirited lifelong bachelor who works on motorcycles, I imagined something a little more eclectic. Perhaps mismatched, hand-me-down furniture, and a random futon that he's held on to since high school. At the bare minimum, I thought he'd have a couple of posters on the wall.

"What are you thinking?" Ollie asks as I stare at a framed piece of art hanging over his white leather sectional sofa. It's an abstract painting of a motorcycle, but it's more than that. The colors and textures that the artist used are mesmerizing.

"I love this painting. I've never seen anything like it."

"Yeah, I got that from a local artist a few summers ago at the Ann Arbor art fair. He's such a talented guy. Right?"

"Definitely. It's amazing."

"How was your day?" he asks.

"Good. It was..." I'm startled when something with fur vibrates against my leg. "Ahh!" I say, pulling up my leg before looking to see what is buzzing against it.

Ollie laughs. "It's Saki." He bends and picks up his cat.

"Oh, right." I scrunch up my face and take in the unfortunate creature in his arms.

"Why are you giving her that look?" He raises a brow. "Don't even tell me you hate cats or something because she's a deal breaker."

"No, I love all animals. She's just a lot to take in at first." Seriously, is he blind? The cat is scary-looking.

"Because she's so stunning?" His crystal blues peer down at me.

"Uh, yeah. Totally."

He chuckles and kisses the cat's head. "Don't worry. In an hour, you'll be in love with her. She has that effect on people."

I follow Ollie onto his back deck. He gives Saki another squeeze and then sets her down. She purrs and rubs herself against his leg.

"I thought I'd grill since it's such a nice night. You like shrimp and veggie kabobs?"

"Yeah, sounds good." I take a seat on the porch swing as Ollie starts the grill. Saki stretches out in an area of sunlight coming through a patch in the treed canopy above. "What happened to her leg and eye? And why does she look like two cats sewn together?"

"Well, it was the summer after my senior year of high school. I had finished rehab and was struggling a bit. I saw this old Kawasaki bike in a junkyard, so I decided to buy it and fix it up. When I was at the dump, I found Saki as a kitten. She was hiding under a heap of metal and was missing an eye and a leg. I don't know what happened to her, but I took her home with me and named her after the bike that brought me to her. She's been my constant companion for twenty years. I rescued her from that junkyard, but I think we saved each other. It was her, fixing that bike, and eventually riding it that kept me clean that first year. It was a rough part of my life."

"That's sweet." I look at the skinny little thing and try to see her the way in which Ollie does...but, gosh, she looks rough. "That makes sense. I thought you named her sake after the Japanese wine, which I thought was a little odd given your sobriety."

Ollie chuckles. "No, at eighteen years old, I don't think I knew what Sake was. Alcohol wasn't my vice. And as far as her fur, I have no idea. Her coloring is unlike anything I've seen. She really does look like part one cat, part another. Adds to her charm, I guess."

"Yeah." I nod, trying to hide my thoughts from my face.

Ollie laughs. "I promise. Give her a day. She's literally the sweetest."

As if on cue, Saki hops up into the swing and bumps

her head under my hand, an invitation for me to pet her. "She's skinny."

"She's old. I feed her all the time, and the good high-fattening canned stuff, but she can't keep on weight the same as she used to."

She purrs loudly as I pet her head, and every now and then, she sneaks a lick against my hand, making me giggle.

I rock in the swing, pet Saki, and watch Ollie grill, and it's perfect.

"What do you think about Alma and Amos?" I ask him of our mutual friends.

He turns a row of kabobs with his metal tongs.

"I think it's great. Amos is a good guy, and he loves Alma and Love. That's all the matters. Leo would be happy. You know he'd want his girls to be happy and cherished."

"Yeah, I think it's a good match, too." I pause. "Do you think about Leo a lot?"

A wistful smile crosses his face, and he looks past me as if lost in thought. "Every single day. I miss him."

"Do you think he's happy wherever he is?"

Ollie's gaze finds me. "Absolutely," he says with conviction.

I shake my head. "I don't know how you do what you do. I mean, I couldn't deal with loss like losing people that are so close to you. I just couldn't."

"Yeah, that part sucks, but I don't lose them all. In

fact, most make it, and it makes me feel good knowing that I was a little part of someone's happiness."

"That's true. It would be a good feeling."

"Every happily ever after makes the hard stuff worth it. And I get these people. I've been there. I don't judge them. They connect with me, and sometimes—only me. I truly think most people are capable of fighting the worst demons if they have at least one person in their corner, one person fighting along with them. Everyone needs to know they're not alone."

"That's what Alma used to say when I asked her how she turned out so good despite her horrible childhood. She said she had Amos, and he believed in her and supported her, so she felt she could do anything."

Ollie nods. "I believe that. One person really can change someone's life."

We chat more about our day while we eat dinner outside in the warm breeze. In all the years I've known Ollie, I've dreamed about this exact scenario—coming home from work to good food and good conversation with the most beautiful man I've ever known. It really doesn't get better than this.

I could get used to this life. It feels right.

After dinner, I help Ollie take in the dishes. All the while, Saki stays at my feet, purring and rubbing against me. I think I've realized that she's so skinny because all of her daily calorie intake goes into fueling her robust purring habit.

"If you want a break from her at your feet, give her a

can of her food. They're right there in the pantry." He nods toward a white door on the other end of the kitchen. "She'll love you forever, and she likes to nap after eating." He grins.

I take his advice and grab a can of food for her. "It's not that I mind. I just feel like I'm going to step on her, and I don't want to hurt her," I say, scooping the food out into her dish before throwing the can in the recycle bin.

"Well, eventually, you'll realize that it's just easier to pick her up and carry her everywhere, which is what she likes."

"Ah, so that's her motive."

"Pretty much."

We've finished loading the dishwasher and cleaning up. I dry my hands off on a towel and turn to find Ollie staring at me.

"It's crazy how much I missed you today." He shakes his head with a laugh. Taking a step forward, he takes hold of my hips. "It's like I've been trying to stay away from you for so long, and now that I can touch you whenever I want, it's all I want to do."

I wrap my arms around his neck. "I know."

"Everything about you captivates me. Your body draws me in to the point of heady intoxication. The only thing I can relate it to is chasing a high, and it scares me. I don't ever want to be reliant on anything again."

My chest swells, and I cup Ollie's face. "You don't have to be afraid of me. I'm not a drug, Ollie, because I would never hurt you, and what you feel with me is real, not chemically induced. This type of high, the kind we're both feeling, is good and natural. Does it feel like you're falling, and even though you have no idea what you'll reach at the bottom, the fall is so thrilling that you want to fall faster, harder, and longer?"

He nods, kissing my lips. "Something like that."

"That's called falling in love, and it's the best high there is."

CHAPTER 22

OLLIE

QUINN PULLS her Jeep into a spot in front of Lion's Lair, an organization that my late friend Leo and his wife, Alma, set up years ago. It's now run by Alma and her best friend, Amos. Well, they're more than best friends now, I suppose. Alma and Amos have been dating for several months. The Lair has so many programs that help children to young adults with issues ranging from school to drug programs to financial supports. If there's a need in the community, Alma makes sure the Lair provides a solution. This place is a gem, a true gift for the people they serve.

Alma lends out the gym to programs that need space to hold meetings or events. In tonight's case, the gym is reserved for a self-defense class run by a local police officer, which is why Clementine has opened her door and is jumping out of the back seat before the vehicle's engine is shut off. This is her second self-defense class here, and she's been looking forward to it all week. I'm sure it has nothing to do with the, and I quote, *"hot god,"* who runs the class, Jude.

"Jude better be careful with that one coming his way." I chuckle, watching Clementine's fire-red hair bounce against her back as she disappears into the building.

Quinn shakes her head. "He's used to it. He can handle himself."

"Yeah, he's a good guy."

"He is. He's actually dating, or at least trying to date, a friend of mine." Quinn swings the driver's side door open and hops out.

"Trying to date?" I step around the front of the car, extending my hand out toward her.

She slips her hand into mine. "Yeah. She's hesitant about it. I don't know why."

I furrow my brow, causing Quinn to laugh. "Not because I want him or anything, but he is a catch. So I don't get the hesitancy." She halts her step and twists her body to face me. "Jude's hot and all, but you, Ollie Hale, are perfection. There's no one else for me."

Her words, so sincere, cause a pang of *something* to shoot through my chest—panic comes to mind, but that doesn't seem right. It's a combination of fear and lust and adoration all at once. Quinn's the only woman to ever elicit such a plethora of emotions within me, most of which I can't accurately decipher.

I smile down at the beauty before me. The tiny golden specks in her bright greens are sparkling in the light of the descending sun. Her full lips—one of my favorite features—constantly call out to me, begging to be kissed.

I press my lips to her, and she sighs.

I'm falling for her.

I should've known she'd win in the end. Fighting this attraction for so many years was futile. Quinn Kirkpatrick is someone who gets what she wants.

I'm hers.

As much as that thought freaks me the fuck out, it's true, and it's about time I accept it.

I lean back, breaking our connection. "Are you going to the class?"

"No. I've taken it several times. I can kick your ass if I need to," she kids.

"Is that so?"

"Oh, definitely. I can take you down."

I laugh. Quinn's tiny. I have a hard time imagining her *taking down* anyone. But I know Jude teaches the women ways to stop a potential attacker that doesn't require brute strength.

Fingers threaded together, we continue toward the building. "Well, for my sake, I hope you never have to."

"Me too. That would be counterproductive to all the things I'd rather do instead." She shoots me a grin.

"Oh my goodness!" Alma cheers the second we open

the glass entryway doors. "You two are so cute together. I love it so much."

Alma hugs us both.

Amos is right behind her. He extends his hand toward me after giving Quinn a hug. "How're you doing, man?"

"Good," I answer. "No complaints."

"Clementine barely had time to say hi as she raced toward the gym," Alma says with a chuckle.

"Oh yeah. She's *super* into self-defense." Quinn grins.

"Hope you came with your appetites because Alma had enough tacos to feed an army delivered," Amos says.

Quinn raises her arms in cheer. "Tacos!"

"Of course. Only the best for my favorites," Alma answers her before addressing me. "And Love is setting up a tea party for her Uncle Ollie as we speak."

"I bet she is." I chuckle.

"You know you're her favorite tea party guest," Alma says.

We follow Alma and Amos toward her office.

"Why is that? What is it about me that screams tea party?"

Alma looks back toward me before opening her office door. "I think she just knows how much you love them." She shoots me a wink.

"Right," I draw out.

I'm not a huge kid person, in all honesty. Most little kids annoy me, but Love never has. She's the most adorable three-year-old I've ever seen. She looks a lot like her dad with dark hair and bright blue eyes. Leo was one of the best, and I miss him. I feel close to my friend when I'm around his daughter. It's almost as if she carries his spirit somehow. It's probably just wishful thinking, but nonetheless, I see him in her.

"Quinny! Owwie!" Love calls out when we walk through the door. She hasn't mastered her 'L' sounds, and my name coming from her lips makes me smile every time. She runs over to us, and Quinn pulls her into a hug.

She hugs me after Quinn, and says, "I made us a tea pawdy."

Sure enough, her pink plastic princess cups are set up on the small table by the window.

"That's awesome, Lovie. I can't wait. Are we going to eat Tacos with our tea?" The room carries the aroma of a Mexican restaurant, and it smells good.

She nods excitedly.

"Perfect. I can't wait."

We chat—Quinn and Alma more so than the rest of us—eat our tacos, and drink our "tea," aka lemonade.

I've been in the same room with this group of people countless times over the past eight years. It's comforting and feels like home. I love Alma like a sister and would do anything for her and her family. As I clink my teacup against Love's in a "cheers," I think about how my role as a sponsor comes with some heartache, it's outshined by the love that comes with it. And just maybe, I can let go of this underlying worry and trust that it's all going to be just fine.

———

We drop Clementine off at her apartment and head back to my place.

"Let's go for a ride," Quinn says, pulling into my driveway.

"It's dark."

"I know, but I'm in the mood for a ride." She shrugs.

"Are you turning into a biker chick right before my eyes?" I quirk a brow.

"No," she protests, flipping her long blond hair away from her face. "But I like it. It's a rare warm October night. Maybe one of the last ones. I don't think we should waste it."

"Okay. Let's go."

Helmets on, we straddle the bike seat, and I pull out of the driveway. Quinn's right. It's abnormally warm for this time of year and an ideal night for a ride. I love feeling Quinn's body behind me. She's so close, her arms wrapped so tight I can feel the heat of her body amidst the night air that whooshes around us.

I take us out of town toward the rural area that lies outside of Ann Arbor. We pass empty fields, already cut and harvested and acres of woods.

As always, when I'm on my bike, I feel free and with Quinn behind me—happy.

Her hands move up under my shirt, and she splays her palms across my chest. I pull in a sharp breath when her fingers circle my taut nipples. She lowers her touch as her fingers slide into the front of my jeans before pulling them out and unbuttoning my jeans.

Releasing a hand from the bike handle, I clasp her hands beneath mine. "I don't think that's a good idea," I yell back toward her.

"I think it is," she says, barely audible through my helmet and the rushing wind.

She wiggles her hand beneath my grasp and manages to pull down my zipper. I inhale a sharp breath as she finds her way beneath my boxer briefs. I return my hand to the bike handle feeling the need to steady us.

She starts to move her hands up and down along my shaft as her body moves against my back.

Fuck.

I slow down. Spotting a small clearing between two large oaks, I steer us off the road and into the woods just far enough to hide us from a passing vehicle. Coming to a stop, I turn off the bike and hit the kickstand with my boot. I remove Quinn's hands from my boxers and slide off the bike.

"That's a dangerous game, babe. You know I can't concentrate when you're doing that."

She takes my hand and swings her leg over, stepping down from the bike. She splays her hands over my chest once more. "I know, but I couldn't help it."

"No?" My voice is low as she works her magic touch

down my torso. This time, she pulls my jeans and boxers down until they're mid-thigh.

The moon is full tonight, and it shines through the treetops, making everything about Quinn even more beautiful.

"No," she says as her hand circles me and starts moving faster.

I step back until the bark of the wide tree behind me scratches my skin through my shirt.

Quinn straightens up on her tiptoes and kisses my neck. "Sometimes, just being near you makes me so horny I can't resist you," she says in a whisper as she peppers kisses against my skin. "I feel like I need to touch you, or I'll die."

"Well, that's...a little...dramatic," I say through shallow breaths as her hand moves faster.

"I've never claimed to be anything but." She grins and drops to her knees, taking me into her mouth.

I let out a moan into the night air. "Fuck, Quinn."

Eyes closed, the back of my head leaning against the tree, I finger her hair as her head moves below. My muscles begin to tighten, and stars appear beneath my eyelids. I grasp her shoulders and push her back.

"Not. Yet," I pant.

She takes my hand, and I pull her up from the ground, twisting her around to change places. She leans against the tree as I pull off her shoes and remove her jeans and panties. Wanting to see her bare in the moonlight, I take off her bra and shirt.

"Ollie," she whines, pulling my head down toward hers and connecting her lips with mine.

After a while, I step back from the kiss. Slowly, I scan her body.

"You are the hottest thing I've ever seen. Fucking beautiful."

Falling to my knees, I lift one of her legs and place it over my shoulder.

"Ollie." Her voice shakes with need.

"I got you, babe."

Spreading her open with two fingers, I find the spot needing attention from my tongue and start working. I slide my other hand up her legs until two fingers enter her. She cries out, and I start to pump my fingers as my tongue licks her greedily, loving every second.

Everything about Quinn is a turn-on—the sounds she makes when she's chasing her release, the way her body moves beneath my touch, and how she pushes into my face needing more. It's all so perfect.

Her breaths come faster, mixing with wanton cries as she approaches the edge. She grips my shoulders and moans as her body starts to tremble, and she falls into orgasm. I groan, tasting her release.

Her trembling body slowly abates. I leisurely kiss up her body until my mouth finds hers.

"I want you," she says against my lips.

"I want you," I breathe out.

She wraps her arms around my neck, and I lift her off the ground. Her legs circle my waist. I carry her to the Harley. Positioning myself at the back of the bike, I lay her down across the seat.

"Hold the handlebars."

She reaches back and grasps the handles on either side. I press her knees out to the sides and take her in, bare against the leather seat of my bike. She's my fucking dream.

"Hold on, baby," I warn before I enter her with a collective groan. She feels so good. We both cry out as I start the delicious assault.

In. Out.

Perfection.

Her tits bounce up and down as I move inside her. Nothing has ever made me feel as good as this.

Nothing.

We come together. Hard. Crying into the night air.

I pull her off the bike, kissing her as I hold her in my arms.

"I love you, Ollie," she says between kisses.

I can't respond, so I simply kiss her harder.

CHAPTER 23

QUINN

I CAN'T KEEP the visions of the moonlit motorcycle lovemaking session out of my mind. I've been on a high all week from it. After Ollie licked me to heaven against the tree, he took me lying on the bike before making me orgasm a third time as he entered me from behind as I stood leaning over the leather seat.

It was straight from the sexiest porn movie ever created except it was so much more than incredible, mind-blowing sex. It was raw and emotional, romantic and hot. It was love.

Ollie may not be ready to say it back, but I know he feels it. Honestly, I think he's felt it for a very long time because if I'm honest with myself, so have I.

"He's the one," I answer when my sisters Holland and Willow ask how Ollie and I are doing.

I drove an hour north to my parents' home today to go apple picking with my mom and sisters. Apple picking is one of my mother's favorite family activities. We've gone every year since...well, since forever. There isn't an autumn that we didn't go.

We almost missed this year, though. It was near impossible to get the five of us girls home on the same day with our schedules but we managed. Barely.

It's late in the season, so my favorite apple—honey crisp, was picked out. Today was mainly Rome and Braeburn apples which aren't the best for eating plain. They're great for pies and applesauce. We did manage to pick a big bag of Fuji and some yellow delicious, which are good eating apples.

As per tradition, we're back at my parents' home now, where we'll bake apple treats, make applesauce, and eat apples until our bellies hurt, as we do every year.

"Really," I say. "I love him. I think I always have."

"Does he love you?" my youngest sister Willow asks.

I nod. "I know he does."

"But has he said it?" Holland chimes in.

"Not in words, but everything he does says it."

Willow shakes her head and throws the pieces of apple she just cut for the pie into the bowl. "I don't know. If he can't say it, Quinn."

"Men are different. Maybe his love language is acts of service or something else. Your sister knows his heart," my mom adds from across the kitchen, where she stands washing a sink full of apples.

"That's true," Willow says. "I'm just worried for you, Quinn. You really seem to like him a lot and his history..."

"It's bad," Holland finishes her thought.

The two of them are as good as twins. Born less than a year apart from one another, they've always been close. Whereas my older two sisters, Iris and Harper, are twins and have been at each other's sides since birth. There are a few years between both my older and younger sisters and me. It's like mom had Iris and Harper and took a break for a few years before having me before taking another break prior to having Willow and Holland.

I've always been close with my sisters, and they would do anything for me, as I would for them. Yet the two sets have a deeper bond with each other than they do me, and that's totally fine. Alma's my soul sister. Despite the fact that she was engaged, living with a guy, and then married, almost our entire relationship—we've been close from the start. Relationships are funny that way. When they're meant to be, they just are.

Like Ollie and me.

"It's different," I disagree.

Now that I know Ollie so much more than I used to, I can't see his past as bad. He's one of the greatest people I know. His journey made him who he is, and he's pretty spectacular.

"He's an addict, Quinn. How can you trust that?" Holland says.

"We're just worried about you," Willow adds.

"He was a kid," I say. "The meds that got him hooked were doctor prescribed. He's been clean for twenty years and is seriously the best person I know. I promise you, I'm good."

"And it doesn't bother you that he's old?" Willow scrunches her nose.

I can't help but laugh. Willow isn't much more than a kid herself. "Wait until you meet him. He isn't *old*. He's gorgeous."

"Girls, stop giving your sister the third degree. You haven't seen each other in months. Surely, there are other things to catch up on," my mother comes to my defense, but the truth is I don't need her to. I know my heart, and I'm not ashamed of it.

"It's fine, Mom. I don't mind the questions. You'll all see when you meet him. He's pretty great, and I'm happier than I've ever been."

"I'm glad, sweetie." My mother shoots me a smile that lets me know she's on my side no matter what.

"I'm going to go outside and hang with the kiddos for a bit," I say before taking off my apron and hanging it over the back of one of the kitchen chairs.

The kitchen door is closing behind me when I hear Willow say quietly to Holland. "I thought Beau was the one."

"Me too," Holland agrees.

I smile as I step outside so grateful that I didn't settle for Beau.

"Hey, Quinn-a-lynn." Iris uses my childhood nickname that she and Harper came up with, though I have no idea why. I've never thought it made sense.

"Hey, what are you doing?" I ask.

"Finding the cutest pics from today to post," Harper says, scrolling through her phone.

My nieces' and nephews' giggles can be heard across the yard as my dad pushes them on the swings. Harper and Iris got married within a year of each other, and each have two toddler-aged kids, a boy and girl each. Even for twins, they're ridiculously in sync.

"Oh, I bet there are a lot of them," I say.

"So many," Iris says.

I take a seat on the porch swing beside my sisters, and watch my dad and the kids. I loved growing up here. It's so peaceful. My parents' home is a hundred-year-old farmhouse that they've renovated. There are two large red barns out in the distance that stand empty. When I was young, they housed our sheep we showed at the county fair every year in 4-H and sold their wool.

I had a great childhood full of love and adventure. I have great parents and family. I feel nothing but happiness when I think of my life growing up. I hope to give that to my own kids one day. They probably won't be raised on a farm as I'm pretty much a city girl at this point. But I want to give them the same amount of happiness and security as I had. And I want to do it with Ollie by my side.

We've only been together a couple of months, but I simply know he's it for me. He's the eight-year crush that's finally mine.

And I'll never let him go.

CHAPTER 24

OLLIE

QUINN IS SO beautiful lying in my bed with nothing but a white sheet covering her body. Truth is, she's gorgeous —always. Yet, there's something about her in the morning. Hair in disarray, no makeup, and eyes still puffy from sleep is when I find her the most stunning.

I carry the wooden tray in my hands.

"Babe."

"It's too early," she grumbles into her pillow.

The two of us were up late, entwined in all sorts of positions. My entire body was sore when I woke up this morning so I know hers must be hurting as well. The two of us are insatiable. It's crazy, really. I've never been with someone who fits with me the way that Quinn does. It's a whole new experience, one that I will never tire of.

"I brought you breakfast," I say.

She bolts up in bed, her bed head looks like a lion's mane, and it's fucking adorable.

"Food?" she sits back against the padded headboard. "I will never tire of waking up to a feast, Ollie. Oh my goodness. It smells so good." Quinn yawns from my bed, stretching her arms out over her head.

The sheet from the bed falls below her breast, and I internally groan and look away. We have plans today, and I can't risk becoming distracted, which is easy to do when Quinn, especially a naked Quinn, is around.

"Do you mind covering yourself up?" I instruct.

"Seriously?" She chuckles.

"Quinn," I warn.

"Fine. All covered." She pulls the sheet up over her chest and tucks it beneath her arms. "But seriously, that looks amazing." She eyes the tray.

"You know it's my favorite meal of the day." I set the tray over her lap.

"This is incredible." She looks at the spread. "I still can't believe you make such elaborate breakfasts, and here I was serving you stale *Cocoa Krispies* the first night you stayed over."

"I liked your *Cocoa Krispies*," I say.

"Lies." She shakes her head.

Bending down, I give her a chaste kiss. "I will eat anything you serve, and it wasn't that stale. There was a slight crunch left to it. Give me a second. I'm going to go grab my tray and join you."

Moments later, I'm returning to my room with

another tray of food. I sit beside Quinn and place the tray over my lap.

Our trays contain French toast, bacon, scrambled eggs, strawberries, orange juice, and coffee. It's a typical breakfast. If I don't have anywhere to be in the morning, I usually make a big meal. My mom always made big breakfasts for me, even on school days. I must've inherited my love for this meal from her.

Quinn pops a strawberry into her mouth. "I love your breakfast obsession."

"Good. I'm glad."

Saki hops onto the bed and starts purring loudly.

"Hey, lady. I gave you canned food," I tell her as she walks over to my tray. "She wants the eggs," I tell Quinn. "She's been obsessed with eggs since she was a kitten. It's weird."

"Can cats have eggs?" Quinn asks.

"Well, she's been eating them for twenty years so I'm thinking so." I laugh.

"I've never known a cat to eat eggs before. Maybe they're the secret to her longevity."

"Perhaps they are." I dump the strawberries from the little bowl onto my plate and scoop some eggs into the bowl before placing it on the bed for Saki. "Spoiled girl."

"She really is," Quinn agrees.

"It's true. No use in denying it. She's a princess and she knows it."

"She has to be approaching the world record for her age."

I shake my head. "No, the oldest cat was thirty-eight years old when she died. Her name was Crème Puff. So Saki has a good eighteen more years left in her."

"Thirty-eight years old? And you know her name?" Quinn laughs.

"Only because Clem looked it up a couple of months ago and told me." I grin

She stuffs a large piece of French Toast into her mouth and groans, "This is amazing. Do you seriously make food like this all the time or are you just showing off?" she puckers her lips.

"This is a pretty typical Sunday morning breakfast. I told you, it's my favorite meal."

"Well, then, it's official...I'm marrying you."

I jerk my face toward hers.

She starts to laugh. "It's an expression, Gorgeous. Calm down. We're not getting married."

"Just eat your food." I scoff. "We have a full day."

"So you really want to go clean out cages and pick up animal feces instead of staying here with me all day?" she lets the sheet drop from her chest.

"You better pick that sheet right up," I warn. "And I told you that you didn't have to go with us."

She blows out a breath and covers back up. "I know but I want to spend the day with you, and it's important that I get to know Clementine better. But tell me again, why is cleaning cat litter boxes going to help her with her sobriety?"

I fork a strawberry and hold it out to her. She takes it

in her mouth. "You're so focused on the shit aspect of the day. You know there will be puppies, cats, and maybe bunnies to snuggle. And I told you, Clementine needs a purpose. She needs to find something in this world that she enjoys, that she looks forward to, that makes her happy. So we're volunteering at several places to find what it is she loves."

"Like your first bike that you found in the junk yard did for you?"

"Exactly. That bike changed my life. Clementine is flailing through her days without a purpose right now, and she needs one desperately. She's going to college but doesn't know what for. She doesn't have any friends besides me. So I'm hoping if we can find a place that resonates with her she could find both, you know? A future job prospect, and maybe some cool co-workers with similar interests that she could become friends with. She loves Saki so much, I thought somewhere with animals would be a good place to start."

Quinn takes another bite of her French toast and leans her head against my shoulder. "You're so sweet, Ollie. Like, seriously, you're one of the best people I know in this world. I love the way you care for others so much."

I brush off her compliment. "You're sweet, too."

She sits up and shakes her head. "No, I'm different. I care about those close to me. You care about everyone."

I kiss the top of her head. "Your heart is one of the things I love about you, Quinn. You're a good person."

"Maybe." She shrugs. "But Clementine is lucky to have you. You're incredible. I want you to know that I see that in you, and I'm in awe."

I take a piece of bacon between my thumb and forefinger, and flick it toward her. "Eat up. You're going to need the energy for all the cat shit you'll be picking up."

"Hey! I thought we just agreed that I'll be in charge of puppy snuggles."

"We'll see." I slide off the bed, leaving my tray behind, and shoot her a smirk. "I'm going to shower."

"Oh!" Quinn's voice is filled with excitement.

"Don't join me," I warn. "I'll be quick and then you can go. We need to meet Clem soon."

The reality is that I want nothing more than for Quinn to join me. I'd love to stay naked with her all day —in the shower, my bed, the kitchen counter—wherever lust leads us. She's addicting, and it scares me how much I want her, all the time.

Once the water of the shower is hot, I step in. Seconds later, the shower curtain is being pulled to open to reveal a naked Quinn with a wickedly sexy smile.

Well, shit.

"Quinn." Her name is meant as a warning but sounds more like a plea.

"I can be quick, too. You know?" she drops her gaze to my evident arousal and slowly takes me in until her eyes meet mine. Her green stare holds me, as she bites her bottom lip.

"Fine," I relent in a heated whisper, gripping her waist and pulling her toward me. "Quick."

"Quick," she says against my lips as she wraps her arms around me. The second her tongue enters my mouth, I lose all concept of time.

———

"I want this one," Clementine holds an old gray cat against her chest, as he purrs loudly.

The three of us spent the past few hours making sure all the animals in the shelter were fed and watered. We cleaned out cages, and mopped the concrete floors. Now, we're in a large cat patio, or catio as the cool kids say, playing with the cats and kittens.

A little black kitten swats at my hand, and falls over, his legs shoot in the air causing me to laugh. The black fur ball's siblings climb up my shirt with their sharp claws and bounce on my shoulders like a jungle gym.

I'm going to reek of cat when I leave here. Saki is going to be jealous, and probably angry with me when I come home smelling like cats. I'll have to give her extra attention tonight so she doesn't pee on my laundry which she's done before when she was mad at me. Cats are weird like that. They don't put up with shit.

"You said the same thing about the orange tabby kitten a minute ago," I remind Clem.

She looks to the orange tabby now in Quinn's lap and smiles. "Yeah, he's cute but he's a kitten, so he'll get adopted. This guy's old and will be looked over. He probably has some tragic story. Like, maybe his owner died and he had to come here to this scary place after losing his whole world or even worse, what if he's never been loved? What if he was a stray and got caught and spent years here? It's so sad. I don't want him to die in a cage in the shelter."

"That is so sad," Quinn agrees. "He seems to really like you. I've never heard a cat purr so loud."

"Clem, you're going to want to take all the animals home. Every week there will be one or more that will break your heart but you need to be content with the fact that you're making their lives better just by coming in here and playing with them, and showing them love," I say.

"That's true but I want to adopt him. He needs me."

"And you need to focus on yourself for a while, and keep getting better before you take on the responsibility of another life." I hate the words as they leave my mouth but I just worry that a pet will be too much for Clementine.

"Um, you said Saki saved your life. Gave you a purpose." She pins me with a stare, ready for a fight.

Quinn presses her lips together holding in a laugh.

"What?" I look toward Quinn and she shakes her head. "No, tell me."

"I mean, you do say that. So it's kind of like the same situation," she says with a chuckle.

Clem gives Quinn a nod of approval, and then turns to me. "Exactly."

"Maybe that's true but you can't have pets in the dorm anyway." I pull out my next reason.

Clem sighs, pouting out her lips. "That's true. I could sneak him."

"You'd get caught."

"You could keep him until I leave the dorm and get an apartment next year," she says to me.

I shake my head. "I can't do that to Saki. I'm sorry. I can't stress her out when she's so old. That's not fair to her."

"No, that's true. She'd hate it," Clem lets out a resigned exhale. "I have to figure out a way."

"You could volunteer here a few times a week to visit him," Quinn suggests.

"Yeah, I should," Clem wears a content smile as she rubs the elderly cat's neck. "I just want him to know he's loved. You know?"

"He definitely knows," Quinn says with a grin.

Clem smiles down at the cat with such genuine affection and I can breathe a little easier. She's always so tormented, everyday a constant battle. At this moment, she's happy.

CHAPTER 25

QUINN

OLLIE PACES across the back deck. His free hand cradles the back of his neck as he speaks into his phone. I'm not sure who he's speaking to, but it's obviously someone from NA, and it's clearly stressing him out.

I hold Saki to my chest and pet her head as she nuzzles into my neck. "I shouldn't be spying on him, huh?" I whisper to the cat. Releasing the curtain, I let it fall and cover the window before retreating to the living room.

"I just worry about him, you know? I mean, I always thought he was so carefree. He never seemed to worry about anything, and now that I really know him, I realize he worries about everything and everyone."

Saki purrs louder and licks the top of my hand. I smile down at the odd looking thing. "Ollie's right. You are a good listener. You want some scrambled eggs?"

I set the cat down and open the refrigerator to retrieve an egg. I laugh at myself as I whip the egg in a bowl. Ollie told me that Saki would have me wrapped around her paw in no time, and he was right. I remember thinking she was the ugliest creature I'd ever seen, but I can't picture her that way now. She's just so...adorable and sweet.

I stir the eggs in the skillet, and they cook up in no time. Once finished, I blow on them for several minutes before scraping them into Saki's bowl. She presses her body against my leg in a purr of thanks before she eagerly consumes her favorite treat.

"Such a little queen," I say with a grin.

Inside Ollie's living room, I notice a set of the *Harry Potter* novels on his bookshelf. I think back to all the times that Alma begged him to read them over the years.

"You made her scrambled eggs?" Ollie asks, a smile in his voice.

I turn toward him. "She wanted them." I shrug.

"Oh, I bet she did." He grins.

"Is everything okay?" I nod toward the phone in his hand.

"Yeah, it's fine...or it will be. I don't know."

"Do you want to talk about it?" I ask.

He shakes his head, forcing a smile. "Nah. Nothing you need to be worried about."

"Okay, so..." I change the subject. "I totally just saw your *Harry Potter* collection. Did you read them?"

"I tried." He laughs dryly, taking a seat on the sofa.

I climb up on him, straddling his legs with my arms on his shoulders. "You tried?"

He nods. "I got through a few of them. I wanted to be able to talk about them with Alma. You know how much she loves them."

"I do." I grin.

"To be honest. They're such downers. The writing's good, and the wizard stuff is interesting, but it's so goddamned depressing. I mean, Harry has a shit life. Everyone is mean to him—that Malfoy douche, his family, and Professor Snape. It's annoying. Everyone he loves dies. No one seems to stand up for him. Like you think Dumbledore is an okay dude, but he doesn't stop Snape from bullying this kid. No one really stands up for him. It's infuriating." His hands hold my waist.

I can't help but smile. "You seem to have distinct opinions about this."

"Well, yeah, the kid has a shit life. I have enough real-life stress and shit to worry about with real-life people. I can't waste my energy worrying about a fictional kid."

"Good things happen, too. Ron and Hermione are there for him. And Dumbledore is amazing, and Snape is actually kind of good in the end, though still a bully. I mean, yes, a lot of people die, but he's not alone."

He shakes his head. "I'm sure the series has a satisfying ending. I just don't think it's my type of read. As I said, I deal with too much unfairness in my real life."

"So what do you like to read?" I ask.

He presses his lips together. "Um, like magazines."

I laugh. "What kind of magazines?"

"Motorcycle magazines, I guess."

"Really? There are motorcycle magazines?"

"Of course. There's *Cycle World*, and *Motorcyclist*, and...*Rider Magazine*, to name a few."

"Well, okay then." I chuckle. "I had no idea."

"Yep. There's no drama. Just reviews and information on bikes. What do you like to read?"

"Anything with drama." I grin. "Romance novels with lots of angst are my favorites. The more drama, the better."

"That doesn't surprise me."

I lean down and press my lips to Ollie's. "Well, at some point, you're going to have to at least do a *Harry Potter* movie marathon with me."

"Okay, fine, but right now, we have to go."

———

I move the straw in a circle, swishing the root beer around the ice cream of my float. Clementine and Ollie are laughing together between bites of their chili dogs. We're at Clem's favorite restaurant, A&W. It's not so much a restaurant as a mix between a diner and a fast food place.

Servers in striped uniforms bring the food out, and everyone eats outside in their vehicles. Or, in our case, sitting on the hood of Clementine's VW bug.

"I have one," I say. "If it were possible, would you rather know the day you're going to die or not?"

"Definitely not," Clem says.

"Not," Ollie agrees.

I bob my head. "Yeah, I'd say not know too. Oh, I have another one. Would you rather kill twenty puppies or one human?"

"Dark, Quinn," Clem states.

"Do we get to pick the person?" Ollie asks. "I mean, it's a no-brainer if it's a pedophile or murderer."

I shake my head. "Nope. A random person."

"The person," Clem says.

"The puppies," Ollie scrunches his nose, and Clem smacks him in the arm.

"You'd kill puppies?" she shrieks.

"Yeah. I wouldn't want to, but I wouldn't kill an innocent person who could be someone's child or parent, someone who might cure cancer someday. You never know. Every life is valuable."

"Well, puppies are innocent," Clem argues.

"So are most people," Ollie says.

Clem scoffs. "Hardly. What about you, Quinn?"

I bite the side of my cheek. "I can't answer."

"Not cool. That's not the way the game is played. You have to answer, especially if you're going to ask such barbaric questions," Clem protests, tossing the card-board container from her chili dog into the paper bag of trash.

"Well, I'm surely not going to kill someone's child or

sweet little grandma, and I couldn't kill adorable puppies. So I can't answer." I shrug.

"Cheater," Clem grumbles and turns to Ollie. "You're dating a cheater," she states before plopping a chili cheese fry in her mouth.

I feign remorse. "I'm sorry. I won't ask questions I can't answer anymore. How about would you rather eat nothing but super sour food or super spicy food for the rest of your life?"

"Now you're just lame." Clementine hops off the hood of her car.

"Hey! That's a legit question," I argue.

"A legit lame question." She picks up our discarded food containers and walks it toward the trash can.

"You still have to answer!" I call out.

"Sour!" she shouts over her shoulder.

I turn toward Ollie, who's wearing a satisfied grin. "Spicy."

"What's so funny?" I ask.

"You two. You argue like sisters. It's cute."

"Cute?" I lift a brow.

Ollie leans over and places a kiss on my lips. "Adorable. Thank you for being so cool and hanging out with Clem and me. I like having you here."

"Well, I like being with you, and she's part of the package. Right?"

"Right." He nods.

Clementine returns, and Ollie slides off the car hood. Turning back toward me, he lifts me from the hood and sets my feet onto the concrete parking lot of the restaurant.

"We should get going, Clem. Do you want to ride together on my bike, and Quinn can drive your car back to my place?"

Clem shakes her head. "You know. I think I'm going to skip the meeting tonight."

Ollie's expression darkens. "What do you mean? You always go to the Sunday night meeting."

"I know, but I have a paper due for psych class tomorrow that I haven't even started yet. I'll just go to tomorrow's meeting."

"Are you sure?" The concern in Ollie's voice causes my heart to beat faster as worry settles in.

Clem playfully hits Ollie's arm. "Totally sure. Calm down, Papa Bear. I'm completely fine. I really have to finish my paper. I'm already precariously close to failing this class as it is. The professor is an absolute bore. Delaying the meeting one day isn't a biggie."

"You're good?" Ollie questions.

"Yes. I promise."

Ollie releases a breath. "Okay, but you know that Sharon and Marty attend Sunday night meetings. There's likely to be less complaining and judging at tomorrow's meeting." Ollie's face of concern morphs into one of amusement.

"I know. How will I ever survive a week without Marty's judgmental eyes and Sharon's constant pity party?"

I'm not sure who Marty and Sharon are, but I'm grateful for their tension relief.

Ollie pulls Clementine into a hug. "Tomorrow then."

"Yep." She pats his back and pulls away to look toward his face. "And you can use this night to brainstorm how I'm going to adopt Oliver."

"Oliver?" Ollie questions.

"Yeah, he seems like an old worrywart, doesn't he? The name seems fitting," she says, unable to hold in her chuckle.

"Funny," Ollie deadpans.

"Fine. I haven't decided on his name, but you really should be thinking about how to make him a reality for me."

"I'll do my best." Ollie grins.

"Bye, Clem. See you later." I wave as she opens the driver's side door.

"See ya, Quinn," she says before the door closes beside her.

Ollie takes my hand and leads us toward his bike.

"You okay?" I ask.

"Yeah," he says. "Just had a weird feeling there for a minute. I guess paranoia is a side effect of this gig."

"I see that."

He hands me a helmet. "You want to sleep over?"

"Of course." I tighten the strap of the helmet under my chin. "Can we stop at my place for a few things first?"

"Sure."

———

Ollie sits on the other end of the couch. Saki purrs in his lap as he watches a Lion's game on the large flat screen. My laptop rests on my thighs as I put the final touches on a PowerPoint presentation I need for work tomorrow. Just being here makes me so happy. It all feels...right.

We haven't been officially dating that long, yet it feels like we've been together forever—though, not in the *bored married couple* kind of way. Our forever feels exciting, and sexy, and comfortable all at once. I can be completely myself with Ollie. Every second with him is precious. Even the simple act of sitting on the sofa, each doing our own thing, feels amazing, like this is where I'm supposed to be.

I don't regret the past eight years of knowing him but not being with him. It wasn't our time. Had we hooked up back then, it wouldn't have worked out. We were meant to be together now.

"What?" Ollie's asks, breaking my stare, his tone is one of amusement.

"Nothing." I shake my head and turn back to my computer screen.

Ollie chuckles. "It wasn't nothing. What were you thinking just now?"

I close my laptop and set it on the table beside me. I

turn to face Ollie. "I was just thinking that I'm happy, here with you."

"Yeah?" His voice is deeper and sexy. Lifting Saki, he kisses her on the head, sets her down on the floor, and then pats his lap. "Come here."

I make my way toward him and straddle his lap. He tucks my hair behind my ears and looks at my face so reverently as if I'm the most beautiful person he's ever seen.

"What else?" His question is a husky whisper.

"I was thinking how easy it is with you like this life has been waiting for me. Being with you is comfortable and exhilarating all at once."

"Yeah?"

I nod. He runs his palms down my arms, causing a torrent of goose bumps in their wake.

"I feel the same way." His fingers dig into my hips. "I wish it wouldn't have taken so long."

I shake my head. "It had to. That was our journey. It wouldn't have worked any earlier. We both had to be in the place we are now. I had to experience my life up until now to be ready for what we have. Same with you."

His desire grows beneath me, and I rock into him. "I've wanted you since the moment I saw you. You were nineteen and way too young for me. Yet you had this fearless energy. It was enthralling, and I felt this pull toward you that shouldn't have been there. It wasn't right, yet I couldn't stop myself from wanting you. I've wanted you since."

"I remember, and I felt it, too. I called you gorgeous within seconds of meeting you."

"You did." He smiles. "My desire for you these past eight years has bordered on addiction, Quinn. Every time I hang out with Alma, I hope you're there."

"Same." I thread my fingers through his short hair. "You don't have to want me anymore because I'm yours."

"I'll always want you, even if you're only a room away."

I press my mouth to his in a gentle kiss. "You can always have me," I whisper against his lips.

He deepens the kiss, his fingers sliding against my scalp as he pulls me closer. There are no more words to be said but so much more to say, and it's our bodies that do the talking now.

I break the kiss, only to stand and remove my clothes as Ollie does the same. I straddle him once more and slide down onto him with a heated groan.

"God, Quinn," Ollie huffs out a broken whisper as he digs his fingers into my waist, guiding me.

Every time I make love to Ollie is different. Sometimes, we're so frenzied that we're straight-up fucking hard and rough and fast. Other times we make slow, purposeful love. I've worshipped every inch of his body with my mouth and tongue as he's done mine. This connection with him is perfect every time. His body was made for mine. I've had some great sex in my life, but nothing compares to this. Nothing.

Our tongues twirl together amidst moans of pleasure

as I continue to ride him, moving my body so he hits all the right spots.

His breathing increases as he pumps his hips harder against me, and I know he's close. I move my hips faster, chasing the orgasm that threatens to explode. I drop my forehead to his shoulder, unable to concentrate on anything other than the sensations invading my entire body.

Ollie releases a hand from my waist and settles it between my legs, where his thumb rubs against my bundle of nerves, and I throw my head back with a scream as I fall over the edge. Two more thrusts and Ollie's groaning as he falls with me.

Like every time, it's perfect.

CHAPTER 26

OLLIE

QUINN'S BODY lies against me, her soft skin warm against mine. I've never been a snuggling type of person. My body has always craved distance after being intimate with a woman. I've always wanted her on the other side of the bed or preferably out of my house. But not Quinn.

I love the feeling of her against me. I crave her silky skin beneath my touch. I want to touch her every moment of the day. My need for her is insatiable. She's different than any woman who's come before her. I've never needed anyone the way I do her.

The room covers us in darkness and is silent save for Quinn's breaths as she sleeps. I woke up a few minutes ago, unable to fall back to sleep. Extending an arm, I reach for my phone on the bedside table to check the time.

It's three o'clock in the morning, but it's not the time

that causes my veins to run cold. It's the missed call and voicemail from an unknown local number.

Shit.

I slowly remove my other arm from beneath Quinn and quietly roll out of bed. Taking my phone, I exit the bedroom and play the voicemail as I put my phone to my ear.

This message is for Oliver Hale. This is Diane from St. Joe's hospital. You are listed as Clementine Allen's emergency contact. Please call me back at...

As Diane lists off a phone number and extension, I fall to my knees.

No.

No.

No.

I knew something was off, and I ignored it. There were signs tonight. She didn't want to go to the meeting and then the story about the paper she had due. I didn't buy it. I believed an addict, so I could come home and fuck my girlfriend. *What is wrong with me?*

It was all too good to be true...because it is.

I pull in two fortifying breaths before I have the strength to rise from the floor. Diane's message didn't give me any details. I have no idea why a nurse from the hospital called me, but I can bet it's not because Clementine needs her appendix out.

I don't know if she's dead or alive, and I'm terrified to find out.

Racing back into my room, I switch on the lights. Grabbing my jeans from the floor, I pull them on before reaching into my dresser drawer for a clean shirt.

Please be okay.

Please be okay.

I chant over and over in my head. I can't lose Clementine. *Fuck, I can't lose anyone else.*

"Ollie?" Quinn's tired voice startles me. "What's going on?"

In my panic, I'd momentarily forgotten she was here.

I turn to face her, and I feel sick. I don't blame her. It's my own damned fault. I went against everything I believed to have her. I knew I'd become distracted. I knew I shouldn't be with her. Hell, I've been single my whole adult life for a reason. I can't be everything for everyone.

Thankfully, she insisted on driving her Jeep over after picking up some things from her house. Getting her home is one less thing I have to worry about.

"It's Clementine. I don't know," I say truthfully, grabbing the back of my neck.

"What happened?"

"I don't know, but I have to go, and I'm sorry, Quinn, but I need you to go, too." I shake my head. "I can't do this. It's just...too much," I say before turning to leave.

"Wait!" Quinn calls out from my bedroom, but I can't focus on her right now. I have to get to the hospital.

I don't remember a second of the trip from my house to the hospital. One minute, I'm starting my bike, and the next, I'm running into the hospital lobby.

My face is numb from the cold wind on the ride here. The night air is chilly, and I probably should've driven my truck, but the bite of the frigid air was a needed sensation. Any feeling that rivals this hollow dread in my chest is welcome.

Fear guides my steps as I enter the hospital lobby.

I've been here before—not knowing what I'm going to find when I enter—and I hate it. Even if she's alive, she may already be lost. Sometimes people never recover from their first relapse, unable to muster the strength within them to get clean. They're forever lost until it's over.

I despise this place. For me, hospitals mean tragedy, heartbreak, and loss. Everything about my surroundings causes bile to turn in the pit of my stomach. The smell, harsh and pungent, assaults my senses, causing an instantaneous headache to surface. The tiled floor, cleaned with chemicals, feels sticky beneath my feet.

The lobby is quiet. The only person in sight is an elderly security guard.

"I need to check on someone who's here," I tell him.

"You're going to have to wait a few hours, sir. It's not visiting hours."

222 / ELLIE WADE

"I know, but I need to see her," the desperation in my voice a warning.

"What floor is she on?" he asks.

"I don't know," I say. "A Diane called me. She said"—I think back to the voicemail—"extension 865."

"Extension 865 is the eighth floor, the mental health unit." I say a quick thanks and break into a jog toward the elevators. "Sir, you can't go up there right now. Visiting hours start at nine."

He's still calling after me as the elevator doors close with a ding. Eight floors up, I step out into a dimly lit hallway. The hospital is asleep, but I can't wait until it wakes. I need to know if Clementine is okay. I'm petrified to find the truth, but not knowing would be even worse.

A middle-aged woman sits at the front desk behind a glass window. Her brows furrow as she concentrates on the computer screen before her. Her fingers, complete with a bright red manicure type furiously against the keyboard.

I clear my throat and tap on the clear partition. She looks up with a small gasp, startled.

I shift back and forth nervously on my feet as she reaches up, opening the window a few inches. "Sorry. I'm looking for a Diane."

"I'm Diane," she says slow and hesitant.

"Hi. I'm Oliver Hale. You called me about a Clementine Allen. You left a message."

She pauses a moment, uncertainty lines her features.

I'm sure she's not used to a crazed man showing up at four in the morning.

She drops her hands to her lap with a small exhale and nods. "She's here. She checked herself in a few hours ago."

"Checked herself in?"

"Yeah, said she was in danger of self-harm, so she's here for a week as we assess her."

"Self-harm? As in suicide?"

Diane nods again.

"Was she on anything, or had she done anything to hurt herself?"

"She didn't act as if she was on anything. She says she wasn't. I ran a panel on her to know for sure. The results aren't back yet. She hadn't hurt herself prior to coming in."

"So she's okay?" The stupidity of my question isn't lost on me. Of course she's not okay. She's a patient in a mental ward on suicide watch. She's far from okay, but she's alive, and that's what matters.

Diane presses her lips in line and raises her shoulders. "For now, yes."

The way she answers causes my chest to hurt, and I can't imagine having this job working with individuals that aren't stable and are a danger to themselves. Nothing is guaranteed when the mind isn't right. She's probably seen an unfortunate amount of loss.

"Can I please go sit with her?" I see the answer on Diane's face before she says it. "Look, I know it's not the time. I get it, but I'm begging you. Please. Please let me see her."

Diane hesitates a moment longer and finally dips her chin.

"Thank you so much."

She steps to the side of her desk and opens the locked door separating us. I follow her down the hall, wiping my palms against my jeans.

Clementine is sleeping in the hospital bed. There are cloth-lined leather cuffs around her hands strapped to the bed rail. She's always looked so young and small. But lying here in this bed, she looks like a kid. Innocent and fragile. Too small to be dealing with the horrors of mental health and addiction.

I pull the chair beside her bed and sit. As much as I hate seeing her like this, I'm so grateful she's breathing. People can come back from scary situations as long as they stay alive. With air in her lungs, there's another chance to make it all better.

Head dipped, I pick at some paint that's stubbornly stuck to my fingers from the paint job I was working on this morning.

Her small voice startles me. "I'm sorry."

My head jolts up. "Clem. Are you okay?"

"Yeah."

"What happened?" I reach out and take her hand. "Did you want to kill yourself?" I can hardly get the words out.

"No." Her voice cracks. "Not really. I wanted to use

so much that I felt like I couldn't stop myself. So I called 911 and told them that I was going to kill myself. An ambulance showed up ten minutes later and brought me here. It's stupid, maybe. I just knew that I had to save me from myself. You know? I needed to make sure I was somewhere where I couldn't hurt myself. It's not a total lie because every time I use, there's a chance it will kill me anyway."

Tears escape my eyes and roll down my cheeks as I pull in a breath. "I don't think it's stupid at all. I think you're incredibly strong and brave."

"I feel weak," she chokes out.

"That's how drugs make you feel, but it's not true. Resisting makes you so strong, Clem. But you shouldn't be here strapped to a bed. You should be in a good rehab facility where they understand what you're going through. I can make some calls tomorrow and get you in."

"Okay." She squeezes my hand. "I've been clean for a long time. It feels wrong to go back to rehab."

"It's not," I assure her. "You only have to stay as long as you feel you need to. It can be a reset to help you keep going with your sobriety. The demons you faced when you were first getting clean, and the ones you're facing now are different. The counselors there can help you navigate these new struggles so you don't relapse."

"That sounds good," she says weakly.

"Do you want me to call your parents?"

She shakes her head. "Not right now. I mean, they'll

find out because my health insurance is still under them, but I don't want to deal with them right now."

"Okay, well, get some sleep."

"You're staying?"

"I'll be right here when you wake."

"Okay. Thank you, Ollie. Thank you for being here for me. I don't know what I'd do without you." She sniffles as tears roll down her cheeks.

"You'll never have to find out because I'm not going anywhere."

CHAPTER 27

QUINN

TODAY SUCKS. This whole week has sucked. Ollie isn't answering my calls or texts. He's completely ghosting me except for the one text he answered, letting me know that Clementine will be okay. I hate that I feel bitterness toward her because I know it isn't her fault. At the same time, it feels like he's choosing her over me.

I mean, are we broken up? I don't even know. I've been trying to replay the conversation, and I use that word loosely, that we had at three in the morning. I specifically remember him saying that he can't do this. Do what? Us? Middle of the night visits to the hospital? Sleeping naked? A lot of things were going on that night that perhaps he *can't do,* but I'm having a hard time believing he was referring to our relationship.

We are deliriously happy...*were* deliriously happy. *Weren't we?*

I knew there'd be bumps in the road when I pursued him. It's the reason I didn't for so long. A man doesn't stay single his entire life and be issue-free. I mean, that's a no-brainer. I'm willing to work through everything with him because he's so worth it. There are many things that I *can't do*, and giving up on him is one of them.

But what if he's already given up on me?

I lie in bed another minute, contemplating my actions. A part of me wants to go see Alma, or call my sisters, or visit Cassie at Starbucks and tell my sad tale of a broken heart. Misery loves company, and I want to tell them all about this shitty hand I've been dealt. Then what? They'll give me advice, or they won't. It will be good advice, or it won't. None of it will change what I know I have to do.

I have to get Ollie back.

Now that I know what it's like to be on the receiving end of Oliver Hale's love, there's no way I'm going to be satisfied with a life without him.

———

His bike is in the driveway when I pull in.

He's home.

My heart pumps faster within my chest, and my stomach twists as anticipation rises. I'm nervous to see him, but at the same time, I can hardly wait. I miss him. A week is far too long.

As I approach the garage, I hear the tinkering of metal.

Flutters erupt in the pit of my stomach when I see him. He's bent over a motorcycle wheel, some metal tool in his hand. He looks gorgeous in jeans and a plain gray T-shirt that clings to his biceps just right. I want to run to him. Hug him. Kiss him. Do all the things. But I can't because I have no idea where we stand. Given the week of silence, I'm guessing—nowhere good.

"Hey." My greeting is hesitant.

He looks up from the bike and releases a sigh. His shoulders fall, and his chest deflates on a long breath.

"Hey."

He doesn't give me much. His voice is monotone, almost resigned.

"Can we talk?"

He nods and sets the metal tool down on his work-bench. "Yeah. Come on." He motions for me to follow him into the house.

"Do you want anything to drink?" he asks when we enter the kitchen.

I don't, but I reply anyway. "Water's fine."

He grabs a glass from the cupboard and fills it with the filtered water from the refrigerator. It feels awkward. The room is filled with tension as my apprehension swells.

I came here thinking that I'd smooth over whatever it is that's going on. Reassure him. Talk things out. This palpable unease has me losing confidence by the second.

He passes me, hands me the glass of water, and continues into the living room. I follow. The glass in my hand is so heavy. I set it down on a coaster on the side table and take a seat on the sofa. Ollie sits in the over-sized chair facing me.

I'm not sure how to start or what to say. I'm not used to feeling like this around him, and I hate it. The past couple of months have been the best of my life. He's become my home, my sanctuary. Now, he's so far away. It's impossible to find him. The man before me isn't my Ollie. He's someone completely different.

"Ollie." I pause. "What's going on? Why haven't you called all week?"

He leans forward, elbows on his knees, and threads his fingers through his hair, clutching the back of his neck before raising his tormented gaze to me. Confusion lines his face, and if I'm not mistaken—sorrow.

"Quinn..." My name is a sigh, a sound of resignation. "I don't think I can do the relationship thing. It's not you. It's me and my life. There's only so much I can handle, and I have to do the right thing."

The words leaving his lips are so foreign that I can barely register their meaning. At the same time, I knew they were coming. I didn't want to believe it, but deep down, I already knew.

"The right thing? What does that mean? What changed? I thought everything was going great."

"It was, but with my life, there's always the inevitable fall after a high. The good doesn't last, and it's always followed by heartbreak. I can't live like that."

"You're not making any sense. You have to give me more. Explain," I urge.

He presses his lips in a line and pulls in a breath. "You know my role as sponsor and what that means for people like Clementine, Leo, and the others. I am literally the person standing between them and death. Here's the thing. If addicts use, they die. Sometimes it takes years of abusing one's body. Sometimes, it's one moment of weakness or a bad batch of a drug that ends everything. I'm closer with these people than I am with anyone. I know everything about them—their fears, their passions, their deepest and darkest moments. I know it all, and it creates this bond between us that can't be explained. I love them. I would do anything for them, and it's my job to be that person in their lives—the one who fights to save them."

Ollie's bottom lip shakes, fighting off the emotion that's building inside. He takes a moment, pulling his lip between his teeth. He's visibly shaken up, and it hurts me. It kills me to see him like this.

His hauntingly beautiful blue stare finds mine again. "It's not fair to you, Quinn. I know it's not. Maybe, it's not even fair to me. But I signed up to be this person. It's my job, my purpose. I was so lost in you that I didn't see the signs in Clementine. A part of me felt them, and deep down, I think I knew they were there, but I ignored them because I was caught up in you and us. I could've lost her. Had she made a different choice than the one she did, I could've lost her." The emotion is thick in his voice.

"You didn't lose her," I say.

He shakes his head. "I could've. I have before. I lost Leo. I knew he was struggling, and I didn't get through to him. I wasn't able to save him, and that's on me." His eyes fill with tears, and it breaks my heart.

I swipe away the tears that roll down my cheeks. "No, it's not." My words are loud and firm. "That is not on you."

"It's my fault. I failed him. You don't know what that's like...to have someone's life or death on your conscience. It's fucking hell, Quinn. The weight is too much. I can't go through that again. My happiness isn't worth someone's life. It's just not."

"No," I state, firm. "You listen to me. Leo's death isn't your fault. Whatever happened to Clementine isn't your fault. They are responsible for their choices. You can't live their lives for them. You're only human, Ollie. You have limitations. You can't be everything to every-one." I shake my head and take a breath to compose myself. "You were so important to Leo." My voice breaks as tears fall freely. "You did everything you could. You were always there for him. He loved you and would hate that you're carrying this guilt. It wasn't you. Maybe it wasn't even Leo. It was the addiction, the abuse, and the demons. You can give everything, and in the end, some people aren't meant for this world. I don't have all the answers, but I'd like to think that Leo is happy now. He's free from pain and torment. He's watching his family from heaven with a smile on his face. Some demons are too strong to live with forever, and I think he lived with his as long as he could."

We sit in silence save for the sounds of our broken hearts, the wounds from the loss of Leo freshly open.

"That isn't on you." My broken words come out barely a whisper.

"It feels like it is."

I shake my head, and my lips turn up into a sad smile. "It's not. I promise you, it's not. You are the kindest, most caring and selfless man I know. You give your all for everyone you love, and that's enough. Whether they make it or not, it's enough. It has to be. Ultimately, it comes down to them and their choices, and you have to be content knowing you did your best. They have to choose to beat addiction. They have to choose to fight. You can't do it for them. And if they give in and you lose them, you have to make peace with their decision and let it go. The alternative is a life of loneliness. You deserve to be happy, Ollie. You do. You've given twenty years of your life to service, to what? Make up for your wrongs? Yes, to help others, but at what cost?"

"Life is priceless, Quinn."

"It is, and that includes your life, too."

I stand and take a deep breath. I feel like I can't get enough air into my lungs. This space is so saturated with heartbreak that it's suffocating.

Ollie rises from the chair and faces me.

"I love you, Oliver Hale. Real love. I want to spend an eternity with you love. I know you feel the same about me. Here's the thing, you haven't dated, but I have. And I'm telling you that the connection we share is special, and it won't come around again. You're mine, and I'm yours. You can deny it all you want, but it won't change the fact we belong together." I reach up, cupping his cheek, damp from fresh tears, in my hand. "But I won't be what you throw to the side when life is hard because parts of life will always be hard. Instead of discarding us, you should be leaning on our bond to get you through the difficult times. You have to choose *us* above all else because I love you too much to be thrown out and ignored. You deserve a life of happiness with real love, and so do I."

Lifting my other hand, I take Ollie's face in my grasp and pull his mouth toward mine. Our lips meet in a soft kiss. It's short, not nearly long enough, but more than I can bear with the uncertainty of our future weighing down on us. Knowing it could be our last kiss makes my heart twist in exquisite torture, but I hold on to hope. Ollie's never let me down before, and I'm praying he'll come through like he always does.

"You're my happily ever after, and I'm yours...if you choose...but only you can make that choice," I whisper against his lips before stepping back.

Ollie is silent as I turn and walk out of his house with barely enough vigor to do so. Holding on to what I know to be true gives me a semblance of strength, just enough to make it to my car without succumbing to the sadness that threatens to drown me.

I won't let it because my heart knows the truth.

He's the one.

When Ollie comes to terms with that fact, I can only hope he chooses to fight.

For me.

For him.

For us.

CHAPTER 28

QUINN

I'VE THROWN myself into work this week, as I often do when I'm stressed or sad. Lying around in a self-imposed pity party has never been my style. I guess avoidance is more my speed. Perhaps it isn't the healthiest of coping strategies, but it's not as painful as the alternatives.

I haven't given up on Ollie. I refuse to believe we're over. Maybe my stubborn heart is holding on by means of self-preservation, but I'd like to believe it's because I have faith that he'll come around. He has to.

"So that's a no to the party tonight?" Cassie asks as she hands my coffee across the counter.

"No." I shake my head. "I'm not in a partying mood."

Yep, Ollie broke me because I'm quite sure those words have never left my lips. Quinn Kirkpatrick has never met a party that she didn't like. Maybe I'm getting old. I am almost twenty-eight. It could be the fact that I was in a relationship with someone who hasn't partied in twenty years and my best friend, Alma, hasn't partied her whole life. They're all finally wearing off on me because the last thing I want to do is drink and dance tonight.

"But don't you want to see who comes? It could be the Detroit Tigers for all we know. It's part of the adventure." She shoots me a wink.

"You think a professional baseball team is going to show up at an apartment party in Ann Arbor?" I chuckle.

Cassie shrugs. "You never know. Asher does work with one of them at the gym, and it's off-season."

"Still, I'll pass but have fun. Tell Everett, Ash, and Tannon I said hi."

"I will. Tomorrow is *Survivor* and taco night if you want to come over and hang out," she offers.

I nod. "Yeah, that sounds more my speed. I'll text you if I can make it."

"Sounds good. See you later."

"Bye," I say with a wave before taking a sip of my latte and exiting Starbucks.

Alma lives a few minutes from Starbucks. I make it to her house before I'm even halfway through with the latte. We're having a girls' night in—just me, Alma, and Cat. It's just what I need.

"Hey, babe!" Alma pulls me into a hug.

"Hi."

"Quinny!" Love jumps into my arms.

"Hey, Love Dove. How's my favorite girl?"

"Good! Gigi made bawk bwead like fwom a twee. It's not very good, but it's weal healfy for you."

I look at Alma for translation.

"Bread that tastes like bark. Very healthy," she says with a laugh.

My eyes widen. "Oh, yeah...I'll have to try that," I lie. "Your gigi loves you so much, doesn't she? She's always making you good food to keep you healthy. Isn't she?"

Love nods, and I set her down. "She does yuv me."

"How could she not? You're easy to love."

Love runs off to the kitchen.

"What's in this bread?" I ask Alma.

"Not sure. Some kind of root, I think. Lee-Anne tells me, but sometimes it goes in one ear and out the other," she says with a grin.

"Is Cat here yet?" I ask.

"Yeah, she's talking with Amos. Come on." She motions me toward the living room. "Can I get you something to drink?"

"Wine?"

"You got it." She nods and disappears into the kitchen.

After I greet Cat and Amos, I take a seat beside them on the sofa. They're engrossed in a conversation about the value of the dollar on the world market. Cat's parents live and run a business in Russia. She's so smart when it comes to the world, and Amos is smart when it comes to almost anything. I'm all in if they want to have a conversation about autumn trends of collage fabrics and pleated skirts or the return of high-waisted baggy jeans. World economics isn't my forte.

Alma comes back with a glass of wine and hands it to me.

"Thank you," I say as she takes a seat beside me.

Love runs by us, waving a fairy wand and giggling.

"It's almost bedtime, right?" I say to Alma.

"Yeah." She chuckles. "Can't you tell? She's winding right down." She shakes her head.

Alma's mother, Lee-Anne, comes into the living room. "I think I'm going to go unless you want me to put Love down?" she says to Alma.

Alma shakes her head. "No, Mom. We've got her. You can go. Enjoy your Saturday night."

Lee-Anne nods. "Okay, well, I just took the last loaf out of the oven. I made you all a little snack. The bread is wheat-, dairy-, and sugar-free. It's made from sprouted grains, mainly barley, quinoa, amaranth, and buckwheat. Buckwheat is gluten-free. It's also known as kasha and is very good for you." She gives us a rundown of the health benefits, which is something she always does. Most of the time, her food ends up in the compost, but you gotta give it to her for trying. I'm sure some of her habits will eventually rub off on someone.

"Thanks, Mom. Sounds great. We appreciate it," Alma tells her.

Lee-Anne says her goodbyes and leaves.

"Oh my goodness. Is she trying to punish us?" I scoff.

Alma chuckles. "You know how she is."

"I think it sounds really good. I'll take it home if you're not going to eat it," Cat says.

"That's because you eat ice for a living," I tease.

Cat throws a pillow at me. "I do not. I just eat a plant-based diet."

"I guess if I made as much money as you do off the way I looked, maybe I would, too." I pause and shake my head. "Nope, not even then."

Alma, Amos, and Cat laugh.

"Well, in my defense," Cat says, "I have to be careful. I'm geriatric as far as models go. I want to hold off doing ads for laundry detergent as long as I can. Pretty soon, the only jobs I'll get will be in mom roles. They won't want me on the runway."

"Not true," Alma says.

"Unfortunately, it is," Cat says. "It's fine, though. It's the life of a model. I'm like ten years older than most of the girls on the runway with me. I've had a good run."

"That's ridiculous. You're the hottest woman I know," I tell her.

She laughs. "Thanks, Quinn."

"I still don't think I could give up all the yummy food to look like you, though," I say.

Cat furrows her brow. "First of all, you're drop-dead gorgeous. All three of you." She shoots a wink at Amos.

"And secondly, you get used to it. Your taste buds change when your diet is plant-based."

"I'll take your word for it." I grin.

Amos addresses Alma. "Do you want me to do Love's routine tonight so you can hang out?"

"Yeah, that'd be nice. Thank you. She's so wound up, you're going to have to read her books for like an hour." Alma lifts her brows as she purses her lips.

Amos chuckles. "I don't mind."

"Okay, call me up when she's ready to be tucked in," she tells him.

He walks over to Alma and leans down to give her a sweet kiss. "Will do. Have fun. See you later, ladies."

Love gives us all hugs and takes Amos's hand as he leads her upstairs.

"It's probably going to be like two hours of book reading. She's hyper today." Alma laughs.

"Must be the bark bread. Gives her super energy," I say.

"Yeah, that must be it," Alma says, her lips tilting up at the corners.

I look at Cat. "So how's everything with you and Stephen?"

Cat's married to Leo's older brother, and by all accounts, she's not very happily married.

She waves her hand through the air. "My life is boring. What we need to be talking about is you. What's going on with you and Ollie?"

242 / ELLIE WADE

"Have you spoken to him since you laid it all out?" Alma asks.

"Nope."

Cat holds up her hands. "Wait. Back up. I'm behind. Catch me up. What happened?"

I go over the whole ordeal again, telling Cat everything that Alma already knows. Talking about it hurts because it goes against my whole avoidance strategy, but I also know it's good for me to vent. I'll never get over it if I don't address it, face it, accept it. But that's the thing—I have no interest in doing any of those because I'm still waiting. For him.

When I finish, Cat gives me a sad smile.

"It still breaks my heart that he thinks he let Leo down," Alma says.

"I know," I say.

"Leo would never want Ollie to carry this guilt. Leo loved him," Cat says.

I nod. "I told him that."

"Ollie's such a great guy," Cat states.

"He is," Alma agrees. "He'll come around. I know he will. He just has to come to the conclusion on his own and make peace with his own demons. I saw the way you two were together, and I know he loves you."

"He does. I truly believe that, but he puts so much pressure on himself to save everyone, and I feel like he might be willing to sacrifice his own happiness to do so. He's convinced himself that it's the only way." I blow out a breath.

"Before you," Alma says. "Now that he's fallen for you, he'll realize that he needs to modify his thinking, and he will. It takes time to reframe everything he thought he knew. You entered his life and turned it upside down by showing him what it felt like to be in love for the first time. He needs to work through that and figure out how to make it all fit into his life. As carefree as he always seems, he's never been one to act on impulse. He overthinks everything."

"He's his own worst enemy." I frown.

"Aren't we all?" Cat's question is rhetorical. "It's crazy how most of us are kinder to a stranger than we are to ourselves. Self-sabotage is all too common."

"I really love him." My eyes fill with tears. "I don't know what I'm going to do if he doesn't come back to me."

"He'll make his way back. Just give him time." Alma squeezes my hand.

I'm trying. God knows I'm trying.

Each day that passes without contact from Ollie breaks my heart a little more. I hope he comes back to me sooner than later. If he waits too long, he's going to find a girl with a shattered heart. I'll be a fragment of the person he knew, and by then, it won't matter anyway.

CHAPTER 29

OLLIE

MY TRUCK IS so big and bulky. It feels as if I'm driving a giant yacht around the streets of Ann Arbor. Michigan winters are beautiful, but I miss my bike. Unfortunately, Michigan winters are also long, so I'll have to drive this massive vehicle around for a good five months.

I'm on my way to visit Clementine at the rehab facility. I go see her once a week and sit in on a group with her. She seems to be doing well, and I'm so proud of her. She could leave at any time, but she stays because she wants to get better. That determination in her gives me hope that she'll make it.

She has to make it.

This facility is one of the good ones, and they try to create a welcoming environment, but it still feels cold to me. Granted, rehab centers aren't my favorite places. I've spent way too much time visiting people in places like this.

The chill that engulfs me evaporates the moment I see Clem and her bright smile. Happiness radiates from her. She runs up to me and throws her arms around me in a big hug.

She's going to make it.

"You look fantastic, Clem."

"I feel fantastic."

"I can't tell you how proud I am that you're putting in the work and fighting for yourself."

"Thanks. I wouldn't be here without you."

"Are we going to your group?"

She shakes her head. "No, I just want to visit today, if that's okay."

"Works for me."

She leads us over to a set of comfortable chairs in the corner of one of the living areas.

"Tell me everything. What am I missing?" She pins me with her stare.

"Not much." I chuckle.

"How's Saki?"

"Spoiled and beautiful as ever."

She sighs. "I miss her."

"She misses you."

"How's group? Any newbies?"

I nod. "Yeah, we've gotten a few more members. Sharon and Marty miss you. They told me to tell you hi."

She laughs. "No, they didn't."

"Okay, Marty didn't, but Sharon did. She's been happy lately."

"Sharon happy? I don't believe it. If she's isn't bitching, she isn't Sharon."

"Well, she's dating someone...from work."

"No!" Clementine gasps. "Who would date her? She's god-awful boring."

"Well, it just goes to show you there's someone for everyone. He's a new hire named Stan."

Clementine scoffs. "Of course he's named Stan. Sharon and Stan. Sounds about right."

"He's an accountant, and apparently, it was love at first sight. They did it in the copy room."

She throws her head back in laughter. "I can't believe that number one, anyone would *do* Sharon, to begin with. But number two, that she shared that bit of information. Marty must've been judging her like crazy."

"Would he be Marty if he wasn't? But yeah...she shared way too many details, in my opinion. I don't know which is worse, Sharon in love or Sharon complaining."

"Nothing is worse than Sharon complaining," Clem states.

"You can't say that until you've heard how Stan took her from behind in front of the copy machine."

Clementine laughs so hard that tears roll down her cheeks. "Oh my God! I'm missing so much. I would give anything to have heard that story firsthand. Seriously, Marty's big head must've been near exploding."

"It's okay. All the drama will be there when you're ready to come home."

She wipes the tears of laughter from her cheeks, "I'm real close. I feel ready now, but I want to stay for a while longer just to make sure. I think I've hit some sort of a breakthrough here. I'm seeing my future with more hope than I ever have."

"I'm so happy for you, Clem, and so proud. So very proud." I lean in and place a hand on her knee.

"Thanks," she says.

"So how's Quinn?"

I've managed to sidestep any conversation about Quinn every time I've been here. I know Clem knows that I'm avoiding the conversation, and she's been gracious enough to allow me to, but her question comes with more authority this time.

"I'm figuring it out," I tell her.

It's the truth. I've done little but think about Quinn and our future this past month. Quinn was right in that she's the love of my life. She's my great love, and there will be no other. I didn't make it a lifetime without any real commitment because I'm normal, however. This thing with Quinn has made me realize I have issues I've never dealt with. I think I spend my life helping others so I don't have to face myself.

I've been seeing a therapist this past month to work through my own shit because I never have. I threw myself into bikes and life, and buried the feelings and insecurities that came with my addiction by convincing

248 / ELLIE WADE

myself I was healed. Yet avoidance isn't healthy, and the things that one's avoiding will surface in the end.

The truth is, I want Quinn back more than I want my next breath. She's all I want and all I think about. But she didn't deserve what I did to her, to begin with, so I'm sure as shit not going back to her until I know that I'll never cast her aside like that again.

"Ollie," Clementine chastises.

"I know. I'll get her back. I just had some shit I had to work through. You know as well as I do that nothing's easy with us."

"Yeah, but you're making it harder than it needs to be."

"Maybe, but I'm trying. I'll figure it out."

"You better because she's good for you, and you deserve to be happy."

I nod. "That seems to be the consensus."

"You talk the talk, Ollie, but you need to walk the walk. You're great at giving me advice, but maybe you should take some of that advice and apply it to your life."

Past memories twist my stomach into knots. There's so much loss and pain. I see their faces, those haunted by demons that I couldn't help them escape. The reality, that there was probably little more I could've done to help them, rests just beneath the surface, but it's smothered by the what-ifs. *What if I had called or stopped by more? Were there signs I missed?*

What if?

It's heavy, and it hurts.

It's crucial that I move on or at the very least try to accept it as is. I can second-guess every second of my past, but I'm not going to change the outcome.

"Clem...I am. This time, I am. I'm seeing a therapist and working shit out. Okay?"

"You're seeing a therapist?" Surprise coats her tone.

"Yeah."

"Okay. Well, that makes me happy."

"Well, as long as you're happy." I chuckle.

She claps her hands together. "Okay, so you're going to double your therapy sessions so that you can get your shit together asap because we need to talk Christmas, and Quinn needs to be there."

"She does?"

"She does," Clem deadpans. "Now, what are our plans because we need to make this Christmas really special. Not only will you and Quinn be reunited but we also need to do something incredible for Saki."

"For Saki?" I raise a brow.

"Yeah," Clementine snaps. "You never know when her last holiday will be, so you need to make sure every one is amazing."

"I thought we decided that she had eighteen more years in her?"

"Well, yeah, that's the plan. So the next eighteen years need to be epic."

"Okay." I grin. "Well, I'll brainstorm some ways to give Saki the best Christmas ever. Okay?"

"Don't forget Quinn," she warns.

"Right, and Quinn." I hold out my fist, and Clementine bumps it with hers. "And you keep doing what you're doing because you seem really great."

"I am," she says with a genuine grin. "And I will."

I walk out of the rehab facility feeling lighter than I ever have. I didn't want to admit it to myself, but Clementine's recovery was holding me back from moving forward. I love that girl so much.

I've been dreading *the* call for the past month. The one that informs me that Clementine's gone. It's a constant fear. Losing those I love is always on my mind. It's debilitating.

I know that just because she seems great doesn't mean she's out of the woods forever, but it's enough to allow me to breathe.

It's enough to give me the strength to fight.

CHAPTER 30

QUINN

I STRETCH my arms up over my head and sigh as my back cracks.

"Happy Birthday to me," I say to myself. Turning on my side, I wrap my comforter tighter around my body.

Growing up with a December birthday, December thirteenth to be exact, conditioned me not to make a big deal of the day. Every Christmas, I was met with a "Happy Birthday/Merry Christmas" present from my grandparents and aunts and uncles. I honestly never thought much of it. That's just the way it was.

It wasn't until college, when Alma insisted on making a big deal of my birthday every year, that I realized I should celebrate it despite it being so close to Christmas.

In Alma fashion, she's throwing me a big party

tonight, but I don't feel like celebrating. I miss him so much it hurts...all the freaking time.

Why does it smell like bacon?

I bolt up in bed and sniff the air. It definitely smells like bacon, and seeing that I haven't purchased that meat in a year...it's odd and out of place in my home.

I jump from bed and open my bedroom door, the aroma now stronger.

"Hello?" I call out hesitantly.

There's no response, so I make my way to the kitchen.

I gasp, bringing my hands up to cover my mouth when I find him there.

Ollie turns, a smile crosses his beautiful face. "Happy Birthday, baby."

Wide-eyed, I back out of the kitchen until I feel the couch behind me, and I fall onto it.

What is he doing here? What's happening?

"What are you doing here?" I ask.

"I wanted to surprise you with a birthday breakfast. Alma gave me your spare key."

What does this mean?

A month of suppressed emotions come to the surface at rapid speed, a torrential storm of feelings and hurt I've been avoiding for weeks. Losing control, I bury my face in my hands and cry, full-on back-wrecking sobs.

"Quinn." Ollie is at my side rubbing my back. "I'm so sorry. This was a stupid idea. I don't know. I thought it'd be sweet, but I was wrong. I don't know how to apologize the right way. I'm sorry."

I'm crying so hard that I can't answer. The tears flow freely, carrying a month of pain and sadness with them as they fall. I guess I wasn't avoiding my grief as much as storing it up until it could explode all at once.

My chest aches from my violent tears or the sight of Ollie beneath my roof or both.

It hurts, and I don't know how to make it stop.

Ollie's quiet as I cry. He continues to gently rub my back.

"I'm so sorry," he says.

Eventually, the tears abate, and I catch my breath. Turning to Ollie, I ask, "Why are you here? What does this mean?"

"I came to apologize and to ask if you'd consider taking me back." His blues plead.

"Why?" The question cuts through the hair like a whip.

He presses his lips into a small smile and tucks a strand of tear-soaked hair behind my ear. "Because I love you, Quinn. I love you so much. You're everything. My light. My comfort. My future. You are my happily ever after."

As much as I've wanted to hear these words fall from his lips, I'm scared—hesitant to believe them.

I'm not sure what to say because I'm having a hard time processing everything I'm feeling. Hearing Ollie say that he loves me is everything I've ever wanted, but now a fear resides just beneath the surface of my skin, acting as armor and making it impossible for the words to penetrate my terrified heart.

Ollie taps his thumb against my chin. "I know you're scared. I hurt you. I'd be afraid to trust me, too. You need to know that I wanted to run after you the second you left my house that day. I wanted to tell you that every-thing you said was true because it is. Yet, it was crucial for me to know that I would never put you through that again and never cast you aside, and I didn't trust myself at that moment. I knew I needed help. You are every-thing to me, Quinn. I'm completely, a hundred percent in love with you. I love you so fucking much it physically pains me. The thought of a life without you is unimagin-able. So I had to do the work."

Bits and pieces of my armor chip away with each word he speaks.

"I was fucked up, and the fact is I've been fucked up my whole adult life. I never fully dealt with everything all those years ago, and it was important that I did before pursuing you again. I wanted to come back to you when I was as whole as I could be and confident in the fact that no matter what life throws at me, I'll keep you at my side. I did a shit ton of soul-searching. I went to therapy... a lot. I talked it out with Saki."

I fight off the urge to smile at his last sentence. He smiles down at me, big and happy and free. I see the change in him, and my heart soars.

"But there was one problem. I wasn't whole because

I need you to be complete..." His words bring on another round of tears. Yet this time, they're happy tears. They fall softer and carry so much promise—for tomorrow, and the next day, and every day from here on out—days I'll be spending with Ollie.

He shakes his head. "I'm not perfect, and I never will be. There will be issues in my future. There will be heartache or loss. But I can promise that as long as you want me, I'll be at your side, and we'll face it together. If that's what you want."

His voice drops with hesitancy.

I close my eyes and send a prayer of thanks into the universe. Opening my eyes, I take Ollie's face in my hands and pull his forehead to mine. "I want you. All of you. The sad you. The happy you. The messed-up you. The strong you. The kind you. Just...you."

"I don't know what I did to deserve you, Quinn," he admits.

"I feel the same because being loved by you is the greatest feeling in the world," I tell him before my lips press against his.

The kiss is soft and uncertain at first as our souls find one another and connect once more. Each second his lips are on mine releases the remaining pieces of fear still clinging to my heart until only love remains—pure, intense, crazy love for this man.

Lips still connected, Ollie picks me up and leads me to my room. He places me on my bed, where we stay for the rest of the day making love. We catch up on each other's lives over the past month, then kiss until our lips hurt, and make love again. It's hands down the best birthday of my entire life.

Twenty-eight is going to be my year.

———

At some point after the day of marathon birthday sex, I must have dozed off. I wake up in Ollie's arms. Though content, my stomach and head ache.

"Hey, beautiful," he whispers and kisses my head.

"I'm so hungry and thirsty. I need coffee, food, and a shower. In that order."

"Well, I think it's safe to say that your breakfast that's been sitting out for hours is no longer good, but I do believe I spotted a box of Cocoa Krispies." He kisses my head. "Wait here, and I'll return with coffee and Quinn's signature breakfast. Sound good?"

"Sounds perfect."

He stands, not even attempting to cover his naked body, and I lay against my pillow with a contented sigh.

Moments later, Ollie returns with goodies in hand as promised.

"Thank you," I say after taking a long sip of coffee.

"When you're done eating, we should get ready to go to your party."

The day's activities made me forget all about my birthday party.

I groan. "I don't want to go. Let's cancel. I'd rather

lie here in bed with you all night. I just got you back. I don't want to share you."

"I don't want to share you either, but Alma's been preparing for your party all week. She has this whole *Hawaii in December* theme going on. So you will be getting lei-ed. Just of a different variety."

"A necklace of flowers is nothing compared to you."

"That may be so, but all your friends are going to be there, and everyone's looking forward to celebrating you."

"Today's been perfect. I don't want to leave this room. I'm afraid I'll walk outside to find that this was all a dream and you didn't come back to me."

He sits down beside me. "It's not a dream, and you never have to worry about me leaving you again. I told you, I came back only when I knew for certain that I was ready to love you the way you deserve to be loved. Completely and without fear."

I nod.

"We have every day of the rest of our forever together." He kisses my head.

"Even that won't be enough."

"We'll make each day count. I promise." He swipes my hair that's fallen across my front to my back and then peppers soft kisses against my shoulder. "Finish your coffee and cereal, and come meet me in the shower."

A wide smile crosses my face. "Well, that, I can get on board with."

CHAPTER 31

OLLIE

QUINN LOOKS like a goddess with her flowy white dress and the pink-and-white-flower lei atop her blond hair like a crown. Alma didn't use the fake leis that can be found at any party shop for cheap. A local florist made each lei from imported orchids. The house smells like a tropical rainforest.

Alma's huge house is full of people to celebrate Quinn. Many of Quinn's sorority sisters from college are here, along with the usual group—Alma, Lee-Anne, Amos, Love, Ethan, and Cat. Quinn's friends who live above the Starbucks are here, too—Cassie, Tannon, Everett, and Asher. There are also some friends from the Lair including the cop who instructs the self defence class, and a few people from Quinn's work.

The big surprise is Quinn's parents and her four

sisters and their families that drove down to celebrate with her. She started crying when she first saw them. I'm glad there were lots of surprises. I felt bad that I let the theme slip earlier, but I knew that Quinn couldn't skip the party.

Quinn wipes her eyes as her father releases her from his embrace.

"So this must be *the Ollie* who we've heard so much about?" Quinn's mother says before opening her arms in invitation. I hug her.

"The very one." Quinn smiles wide, her beautiful greens shine with emotion and pride, making my heart twist a little—in love and in regret for what I've put her through this past month.

Quinn's mother is beautiful, as I knew she would be. She looks like an older version of Quinn. Her four sisters stand behind her parents, shooting me interesting stares. They're all similar-looking with the same face shape and smiles. They have varying shades of eye and hair color, but one can definitely tell they're related. I extend my hand out toward her father and shake his. I can only imagine what his life has been like as the only man in a house full of six women. If her sisters have a fraction of Quinn's spunk, I'm sure the poor guy has a million stories to share from the past thirty years.

Iris and Harper, the older sisters, each have a couple of toddlers in tow, and I can't deny that the kids are adorable. I always thought that Love was the only exception to my *not a fan of kids* philosophy, but these little ones are cute. It's not lost on me that they, too, resemble Quinn.

"So Quinn tells us you work on bikes?" her dad says. "You know, when I first met Quinn's mom, right out of high school, I had just bought a Honda CBX."

"Oh, yeah? That's a good bike. I've restored a few of the original Honda's from the late '70s," I say.

Her dad nods. "Yep. Mine was one of the originals. Great bike. I didn't have it long, though." He shoots a look at his wife. "She hated it."

Quinn's mom scrunches her nose. "Sorry." She looks toward me. "I'm just not a fan."

"It's fine." I grin. "Quinn's told me that you aren't the biggest supporter of motorcycles. I get it. They're dangerous and not for everyone."

"It's great that you like them. For me, personally, I just—" she rambles nervously.

I take her hand in mine and release a laugh. "You don't have to explain. It's cool."

"Okay." She smiles.

I knew Quinn had to come from good people because she's one of the best, but it's nice to see first-hand. Her family is great—kind and warm people.

I chat with Quinn's father a little more about bikes and some of the rebuilds I've done, while Quinn introduces her nieces and nephews to Love, and her sisters and brothers-in-law to everyone else.

It's not long before she returns to me and threads her fingers through mine as if she missed the connection. I'm not ashamed to say that I did.

Alma outdid herself with this party. Everything is perfect, from the decorations to the food and even the people. It's an incredible party for an incredible person.

Quinn has barely let go of my hand the entire night, and although I love feeling her small hand in mine, it breaks my heart a little. She's afraid to let me go. I hate myself for what I put her through this past month, but it was needed to get to our future. I'm just going to have to make it up to her every day from here on out until she's no longer afraid of losing me.

She'll never lose me. A month without Quinn after knowing what life was like with her was enough to make it crystal fucking clear that she's my one and only love. My forever. No one could make me as happy as she does. She's mine. For always.

———

Quinn nuzzles into my chest, and I hold her tighter. I should get up and make breakfast, but I don't want to leave this bed. I'm still coming down from the highs of yesterday. It was emotionally and physically exhausting. I've never had so much sex and done so much socializing in one day. As perfect as the day was, I hope to never repeat it. My body feels like it was hit by a truck.

"Don't leave," Quinn grumbles into my chest, sensing my imminent departure into the kitchen. "I don't need to eat."

"You do. We both do, but I'm too beat to make a big breakfast anyway. I can't keep up with my hot young girlfriend." This causes Quinn to laugh.

"Oh my goodness. Stop." She chuckles. "You can keep up just fine. You proved that on many occasions yesterday."

"Well, yesterday was a record for me."

"Me, too," she says. "We had a month of lost time to make up for."

"True."

"What should we do today?" I ask.

She thinks for a moment. "Well, in the few seconds I was in your living room last night, I noticed that you don't have your tree up yet. I'm thinking we should probably decorate."

"You want to get a tree today?"

"Yeah," she says.

"Why don't we just celebrate at your house and skip the decorating here."

I've never been one to decorate for Christmas. I like the holidays and all, but I just never saw the point of decorating my house. It seemed like a lot of work when I'm the only one here to enjoy the tree.

"Do you want to sell your house?" she asks.

"No."

"So you see yourself living here for a long time?"

"I mean, yeah. My garage is here and my work. It's a big lot, and I love this house. Is there something wrong with my house?" I chuckle.

"No. I love your house, but that's my point. We're going to be here for a while, so we need to make memories here. We won't always have two houses. My house is just a house, but yours is a home. So our experiences should be happening here."

"Alright. I get that. Then we'll decorate. We'll go to the store and get everything we need to make a Christmas wonderland in here, and we'll hit up the tree farm on our way home."

"That sounds perfect," she says, kissing the skin above my heart. "Wait, you don't have any decorations? Have you never decorated?"

"Nope. This will be a first."

"You're almost forty, and you've never had your own Christmas tree?" She leans back and looks at me.

"I'm still thirty-eight for a couple of months. Don't rush me, and no, I never have."

"That's really sad," she says.

"Well, maybe I was waiting for you."

She grins and shakes her head. "A lie, but I'll take it. You know we're going to have a lot of firsts together. Does that scare you?"

"Nope. Not a bit."

"Someday soon, I'll sell my house and move in with you. Does that scare you?"

"Nope."

"Then we'll get married. Scared yet?"

"Nope."

"Then we'll have kids. Terrified?"

"Not even a little."

"There will be days when I'm PMSing, and the kids are running around hitting each other with bats and spilling things and screaming, and the dogs are shitting on the floor. That doesn't scare you a little?"

"No...though, I do question why our kids have access to bats if they're using them as weapons. Maybe we should hold off on buying them bats until they're old enough."

"Okay, we can hold off on bat buying, but seriously, nothing I just said scares you just a little?"

I shake my head. "No. I told you. I'm in. A hundred percent. I want everything you just mentioned. I want you with me under the same roof. I want to be your husband. I want you to have our babies. I want the crying kids and the PMSing wife. Hell, I'll even take the dog shit if you're there with me. I want a life, and I want it with you."

Quinn grins wide. "You say the sweetest things."

"They're true. Every word. I love you, Quinn."

"I love you, too, and I'll never tire of hearing those words from you."

"I'll never tire of saying them."

I wrap my arms around Quinn and run my fingers up and down the skin of her back. I've never been happier in my whole life than I am at this moment because I was completely honest. Nothing Quinn said made my heart beat faster with anxiety. I want it all. With her, I want it all.

"I do have a question," I say.

"Yeah?"

"Why were your younger sisters staring at me all night?"

Quinn giggles. "Because you're hot."

"What?" I scoff.

"I don't know. When they found out I was dating a former addict eleven years my senior, I think they pictured some old man troll or something. They had a lot of reservations about us, and I kept telling them not to pass judgment until they met you. Last night when they finally met you, I don't think the vision they had of you and the real you meshed well. They were in awe."

"That's...interesting and a little weird," I admit.

"A lot weird." Quinn laughs. "But that's them. I told them you were gorgeous. It's their fault they didn't believe me."

"What did the rest of your family think?"

"They loved you. How could they not? You're easy to love."

"So are you."

I kiss the top of her head, so grateful that I'm finally where I'm supposed to be. I'm not sure why it took me so long to get here. I guess it happened in its own time, when it was right.

Everything about us is right. And when it comes to Quinn, I have no doubts.

Only love.

CHAPTER 32

QUINN

WE'RE in my living room the day before Christmas Eve, waiting for Clementine to arrive. Ollie and I have a jam-packed holiday season, and I love it. We're spending Christmas Eve with my family tomorrow and then having an early Christmas dinner with his parents. After dinner with his parents, we'll come back to Ann Arbor, where I'll pop in to see all my friends and drop off presents. I love the holiday. The busier, the better...bring on the merriment.

Clementine left rehab yesterday. Today is the first time we're going to be seeing her.

"I'm nervous," Ollie says.

"Don't be. It will be fine," I reassure him.

I grab a tray of sugar cookies from the kitchen and place it on the table in the living room. Ollie sneaks a peek out my front window when he doesn't think I'm looking. The way he cares so deeply about everyone is adorable.

"She's here," he says.

Walking over to him, I lean up on my tiptoes and give him a kiss. "It's going to be good."

He simply nods.

I open the door to a waiting Clementine.

"Merry Christmas!" I say, pulling her into a hug.

"Merry Christmas to you," she says. "Glad to see you back." She shoots Ollie a knowing look. "I told Ollie that you'd better be back in the picture by the time I got home."

"That's our dark period, and we don't talk about it," I tease. "Let's pretend I've always been in the picture, shall we? Come in."

She hugs Ollie.

"You look good. You feel good?"

"I feel great."

Ollie's entire body visibly relaxes.

I take the gift bags Clementine is holding and put them beneath the tree.

"Why are we meeting here? I wanted to see Saki," Clementine asks, disappointment lines her features.

"It's just better," Ollie says.

Clem wears a confused expression. "But it's not. No offense Quinn. Your house is nice and all, but Saki's not here."

I look at Ollie. "Maybe we should do presents before dinner."

He nods in agreement.

Clementine claps her hands together. "Ooh, I love presents."

"Take a seat and close your eyes. Your present isn't wrapped," he tells her.

"Okay!" She sits on my sofa, and Ollie disappears into my guest bedroom.

"Are your eyes closed?" he calls out.

"Yep!"

He sets Clementine's present on her lap, and she gasps, immediately opening her eyes.

"What?" she cries, tears already rolling down her cheeks. "Oh my gosh." She holds the plump old cat against her chest and buries her face into his gray fur.

The elderly feline is already purring loudly, and it makes my heart happy. I feel like he remembers Clementine. Ollie turns to me, his face so content. The joy in the room is all-encompassing, and I simply breathe it in. There are not enough moments in life when everything is this good.

"I don't understand," Clementine says softly, still holding the cat against her chest.

"Well, it was Quinn's idea," Ollie smiles at me. "He's kind of your welcome home, slash, Christmas present. He can live here until you move out of the dorms next year and get a pet-friendly apartment."

"And since I'm always at Ollie's, you can stay here whenever you want," I add.

"Really? You'd do that for me?" Clem asks.

"Of course! The house is here and empty most of the time. There's no reason the both of you can't stay here as long as you need. I'm just so happy that he was still at the shelter when we went back there yesterday." I grin.

"Yeah, Quinn came up with the idea, then we were totally worried that we'd go back and he'd be adopted," Ollie says.

Clem shakes her head. "No, I told you. He would've died in that shelter. No one adopts the old ones."

"Maybe he was just waiting for you," I say.

Clementine smiles brighter at the sentiment and nods her head. "I think so."

"Plus, we have everything you need. Food and water dishes, food, toys, a bed, a litter box, and one of those big cat tower things. It's all in the guest bedroom." I reach down and pet the top of the cat's head. He purrs louder and leans into my touch.

"This is the best gift anyone has ever given me. Thank you so much, Quinn. Thank you, Ollie. I don't know how to thank you enough."

"Just be happy. That's all I want for you," Ollie tells her.

We watch Clementine play with her new cat for a few minutes. It's awesome. Giving someone a perfect gift is one of the best feelings there is.

"Are you guys ready to eat?" I ask.

"Sure." Clementine places the cat on the floor. He stretches out and licks his paw like he owns the place, already completely comfortable in his new surroundings. "What's for dinner?"

I hold my hands together against my chest, excited. "Well..." I quirk a brow. "We're having chili dogs, curly fries, and root beer floats."

Clem throws her head back in laughter. "No way! That's awesome."

I shrug. "I'm sure it won't be as great as your favorite A & W, but it will be good."

"You guys thought of everything," Clem says.

"Once again, Quinn's idea," Ollie adds.

"See? That's why I told you to get her back." Clem jumps from the sofa and follows me into the kitchen.

We fill our plates with food and sit at the table.

"Did you meet any cool people at the place?" I ask, not sure what to call it. *Rehab? Center?* I don't know what holds a negative connotation or not, so I settle on *the place.*

The hot dog in Clementine's grasp is overflowing with chili. It's running down her hand and dripping onto her plate. "Yeah, there were definitely a lot of cool people who I consider friends, but I don't see myself staying in touch with them. It makes me nervous, you know? Having friends who are addicts. Not everyone is as serious about sobriety as me, and I'm afraid of hanging out with one of my new friends in the real world, having them slip, and bringing me down with them. So I think they were just meant to be my friends while I was there.

But now? I want to make friends who don't have my same vices."

"I get that," Ollie says. "It's scary making relationships with people who could impact your life in a negative way, but at the same time, it's nice to have someone in your corner who knows what you're going through and can support you."

"That's why I have you." She grins to him, mouth full of fries.

"Alright. I'm just saying if you were really close with someone who was serious about staying clean. Some friendships are worth the risk." Ollie dips a french fry in ketchup and pops it in his mouth.

Clem shakes her head, twirling her straw in the cup of root beer and ice cream. "Nope. They were nice to have in that setting, but I want a clean start. I don't want to be reminded of the way I felt when I first went in there."

"Okay. Makes sense," Ollie agrees.

"So what have I missed since I've been gone?" she asks.

"Not much. The first month was pretty depressing, and then we got back together, and it's been unicorns and rainbows since." I grin.

"Good. That makes me happy. Are you doing the whole family thing for the holidays?" she asks.

"Yeah. Ollie met my family a couple of weeks ago at my birthday party, but we're going to spend the day with them tomorrow. Then I'm meeting his parents on Christmas."

"Things are getting serious. I like it." Clem bobs from side to side in her chair. "It's been a long time coming. I never thought this one would settle down." She hitches her thumb toward Ollie.

"You've known me for like a year." Ollie scoffs and shakes his head, a grin on his face.

"Well, for me...that year felt like an eternity," Clementine says. "You know, I'm actually looking forward to seeing this new Sharon now that she's getting some. I still can't picture it."

"Ooh, who's Sharon?" I ask.

"This total downer in our meetings. She complains more than anyone I know, but Ollie told me that she's getting laid regularly now and is like this whole new person."

"You know, the meetings have the word anonymous in them for a reason," Ollie teases.

Clem rolls her eyes. "Fine, we'll call her...Beth...no, Nancy since she's a negative Nancy. So anyway...*Nancy* is one of those people..."

Clementine fills me in on the best Sharon/Nancy stories, and we laugh until our sides ache. She also has some musings about a Marty, who we're calling Brad, that are equally as hilarious.

She's different, Clementine. It's visible. It's as if a weight has been lifted off her shoulders. There was always a barrier between us, and I never thought it was a personal thing but more of a sadness that Clementine had to communicate through. All that is gone. She's almost a different person or at least a much happier version of herself.

I'm so relieved. I know there will be others in our future who break Ollie's heart, but I'm glad it's not Clementine, at least not now. Ollie deserves a break.

"You never did tell us what you're naming your cat," I say.

"Oh." Clem's eyes light up, and she looks at Ollie. "I'm naming him Hale. Like the Kawasaki saved you and became Saki's namesake. You saved me."

Ollie presses his lips into a line and smiles at Clem.

Tears fill my eyes.

I swallow the lump of emotion in my throat. "It's a perfect name."

Simply perfect.

CHAPTER 33

QUINN

"MERRY CHRISTMAS," Ollie's voice invades my sleepy haze, and his lips press against mine.

"Morning breath," I grumble.

"I love your morning breath," he says.

"That's gross." I turn my face, pressing it into the pillow as my body protests the act of waking up. Ollie and I got home late last night after spending Christmas Eve up in Mt. Pleasant with my family. It was a long day of family fun, the best kind of day—but exhausting nonetheless.

"Gross but true, and I have a special Christmas breakfast just for you...and apparently, a rhyme." He releases a deep chuckle, laughing at himself.

I look up toward Ollie, my interest piqued. "A special breakfast?"

"Of course. Do you expect anything less?"

I eagerly sit up and scoot back against the bed frame. Good food is my kryptonite and is one of the few things that will get me out of bed at such an early hour. Ollie, wearing nothing but boxers, would definitely be one of those few things, and this morning, I have both.

He sets the wooden tray on my lap.

"This is a maple and pecan French toast bake that my mom made for us every Christmas morning. It's tradition. She only made it the one day a year, so it was always so special."

"I love that. I can't wait to meet your mom today." I take a bite of the sugary bread with glazed pecans and groan. "So good," I say through a mouthful of food. I stab my fork into another piece. "I really need to step up my game as far as cooking. I know I haven't done it much, but I swear, I'm a great cook."

"I believe you." He sits beside me with another tray and a bowl full of scrambled eggs.

As if on cue, Saki jumps onto the bed and starts purring like a little motorboat. Ollie sets the bowl of eggs on the bed for her. "Merry Christmas, beautiful," he says to the cat, and it makes me smile.

He has such a kind heart. I love him so much. I lean my head to the side and rest it on his arm as I chew the delicious breakfast he's made for me. We eat in silence for a few minutes.

There's something special about the happiest of moments that reside within the silence of life. For me, it's how I know Ollie is the one. Just being together in this space brings me utter joy. No words, no actions...just us, together causes a calm that I've never felt to blanket me in warmth. I'd rather do nothing with Ollie than everything with someone else.

We finish eating, and I sip from a mug of warm coffee with peppermint creamer.

"Santa came, you know." An excited mischief lines Ollie's words.

"Santa? I love him!"

I hop from bed, carrying my tray of dishes to the kitchen. Ollie follows me to the living room, where the tree sparkles, emitting a magical glow around the room. I've always loved Christmas morning. When I'm ninety years old and need a walker to get to my Christmas tree, I'll still find it all enchanting.

More presents are beneath the tree than were there last night. I circle my arms around Ollie and lean my face against his chest. The fact that he's had presents hidden away just so he could put them under the tree after I fell asleep on Christmas Eve is the cutest thing I've seen. This—and all the equally sweet little gestures that Ollie does on a daily basis—is why I know he's going to make a great husband and father someday.

"You are so sweet. I love you."

"I love you, too." He kisses the top of my head and holds me tighter.

We sit cross-legged on the rug in front of the tree and hand each other our gifts, starting with our stockings. I had no idea what to expect going into this holiday. Some guys aren't good at gift giving. I've been in relationships where my partner made me give him a list because he didn't have a single idea. To be a good gift giver, one really has to know their significant other well.

Ollie knows me. He listens when I talk. Proof lies in every single gift, from my favorites snacks to a sweater I saw another girl wearing at a restaurant the other day. I had mentioned I liked it.

I giggle, holding the gray sweater out. "Oh, my gosh. Are you serious? How'd you know where to get it?" It's going to look amazing with a pair of skinny jeans and ankle boots.

He wears a look of contentment. "I asked the girl where she got it."

"When?"

"When you went to the bathroom. She thought it was sweet and sent me the link."

I hug the sweater to my chest. "Um, it is sweet. Thank you. I love it. I'm going to wear it to your parents' today."

Not able to wait any longer to give him his main gift, I hand him the large box.

"Wow, Quinn." He stares at the gift. "This is incredible."

I clasp my hand together in front of my chest and grin contently. "I'm so glad you like it!"

He opens the box and pulls out the black helmet. "This is too much."

"Please." I scoff. "So I did a lot of research, and

apparently, this one is the best of the best. I read all the reviews and the studies done on it. It's the safest rated helmet I could find. It has a dual-layer liner that absorbs shock better than any other helmet on the market. Plus, it has two upper air intake vents to keep you cool even when it's super hot out. The lens is fog-resistant, and it's just really cute."

"I wouldn't say cute."

"Fine, sexy."

"Okay." He chuckles. "I can do sexy."

"Yes, you can." I lift a brow.

"Come here." Ollie pulls me onto his lap, kissing me. "Thank you, Quinn."

"You're welcome," I say, thrilled that my gift went over so well.

Ollie reaches toward the tree and pulls out a small package. "I have one more for you."

"Ooo, little ones are always the best." I rip the silver wrapping from the package, and a Tiffany blue box greets me. Inside is a silver necklace with a single star hanging from it. It's simple and beautiful, something I could wear every day. Ollie knows how much I love the stars. We've spent several nights lying beneath them as I've talked his ear off retelling of the stories that live in the stars and constellations. "It's perfect," I say quietly, emotion lining my voice. "Absolutely perfect."

———

"Quinn! It's so lovely to finally meet you." Ollie's mother, Christine, pulls me into a hug. "I can't tell you how much I've been looking forward to today."

"It's so nice to meet you." I immediately love Ollie's mom. She's one of those people you can tell is good, sweet, and kind—the type of person who would do anything for anyone.

I greet Ollie's dad, and he seems cool, too. He's much quieter than Christine but nice.

Mr. Hale takes the gifts we brought to the living room while Ollie and I follow his mom into the kitchen.

"I know it's past breakfast, but I hope you brought your appetites. I thought we could sneak in breakfast, or we'll call it brunch before our main meal." She pulls a big ceramic dish from the oven and places it atop a hot pad on the table. "So," she addresses me, "this is a maple, pecan French toast bake that I made for Ollie every single Christmas morning."

I eye Ollie. He looks at me, his lips pressed into a grin.

"It looks amazing," I exclaim, unable to tell her I already had it a few hours ago. "I can't wait to try it."

"Quinn loves to eat," Ollie says to his mother.

"Oh, good! Me too. I love to cook as well. It makes me feel good serving others. You know?" Christine says.

"Well, that bit of you has definitely rubbed off on your son. He cooks for me every day, and breakfast is his specialty."

She places a hand to her heart. "I love to hear that. Breakfast has always been my favorite meal, too."

"Apparently, Quinn is a good cook, too, Mom. I just haven't seen it yet," he teases.

"Hey!" I protest, filling my glass with orange juice. "I can cook," I tell his mom, taking another bite of the French toast bake. It's just as good as Ollie's from earlier. "My mother made sure all of her girls could. I just never get the opportunity because this one"—I hitch my thumb toward Ollie—"always beats me to the punch. He spoils me."

"That warms my heart, truly. I always knew Ollie would be a great provider. I had my doubts that I'd ever see it. I mean, he's been a grown man for a long time, yet you're the first girl he's ever brought to meet us. I was beginning to lose hope."

"Mom," Ollie chastises. Lifting his hands, he rubs his temples.

"I'm not trying to be mean. I'm just saying he's our only boy, and I was starting to worry if I'd ever get to see him happy and settled down...and maybe with a *family*." She puts emphasis on the last word.

I press my lips together to stifle a laugh.

"Mother." Ollie's voice is monotone, unamused. "We haven't been dating long. Let's just turn the heat down on this pressure cooker. You don't want to scare Quinn away when you're just meeting her. Yeah?"

She raises her hands in surrender. "You're right. I'm

sorry. You know that I worry is all. I want you to be happy."

"I am," he reassures her. "Let's just enjoy the day without planning out our entire future."

"Okay. Okay," she agrees.

We chat over the déjà vu breakfast casserole. Christine is hilarious and makes me feel completely comfortable. Someday when our mothers meet, they're going to love each other. Thank God Ollie's parents are cool. I mean, I'd love him regardless, but it's a bonus that his parents are so nice. I've had many friends divulge horrible in-law stories, so I'm grateful that I'll never be in that situation.

Ollie leaves me in the kitchen with his mother. His dad needs help hanging a new shelf that he got Christine for Christmas.

I wash the glasses we used for brunch.

"Oh, honey. I can do these later," Christine says.

"I don't mind," I tell her. "Plus, you cooked, so we clean. That's the rule, right?"

"Not usually in this house." She chuckles. "But I won't argue with that logic."

I put the last glass on the rack and turn to Christine. "I just want you to know that Ollie may not be ready to admit it quite yet, but he and I are forever. Someday, we'll be married with children, and I promise I'll cherish him every day for the rest of my life. No one will ever love him as much as I do. I know he'll be happy."

Tears fill Christine's eyes. "I don't doubt it for a

second. And he already is—happy—maybe truly for the first time in his adult life, and we have you to thank for that."

She pulls me into a hug. "Thank you for loving my boy. You are this momma's wish come true."

I hug her back.

"Well...he's mine."

OLLIE

Everything about Quinn is so *soft*—her hair, her skin. Do all women have such silky skin, or is it unique to her? I've never stopped to think about it, truthfully. I've never held a woman while she slept just to run my fingertips across the silky softness of her body and admire its qualities.

I hardly recognize myself anymore. I'm definitely not the person I was a year ago.

I'm in love.

I guess love changes shit. It has for me.

I was slow to buy into the whole happily-ever-after philosophy. I suppose I was just waiting for her. *The one. My one.*

Marriage and kids were never on my radar. Until now.

Now, I want it all, as long as it's with her. I love our

life together. It's like I've been taking shallow breaths for my entire existence...just getting by. But with her, I can finally breathe.

Deep.

Full.

Life-sustaining breaths and it feels so good.

It's crazy that a year ago, we were at Love's third birthday party practically eye-fucking awkwardly across the table. *Is eye-fucking a thing?* Anyway, it was weird, and now it's not. Tomorrow is Love's fourth birthday party, and I'll be walking into the party hand in hand with Quinn. No awkwardness. Just us, together, as we should be.

Life is brilliant.

Slowly, I pull my arm out from beneath Quinn, careful not to wake her, and roll out of bed. I put on some boxers before sneaking out of the bedroom and closing the door quietly behind me. I've always been a morning person while Quinn is not. It works out, though, and gives me time to make breakfast.

Before I do anything, I feed Saki. She's been my first priority every morning for twenty-one years. Normally, she's rubbing against my ankle and purring loudly the moment I emerge from bed.

"Saki girl," I call out as I dish the can of wet food into her bowl.

I toss the empty can into the recycle bin, dropping my gaze to where the bowl sits, full with food, without a purring three-legged cat devouring every piece. *Something's wrong.*

"Saki," I say again.

Scanning the space, I make my way to the living room. If she's not at the foot of my bed, I can always find her in the oversized chair next to the sofa.

She's there. Curled into her sleeping position. Motionless.

"No." The word comes out with a gasp.

Hesitantly, I reach down to feel her. She's cold and firm...and gone.

Clutching my stomach, I step back until the wall of the living room halts my descent. Hunching over, choking down a sob, I slide to the floor.

I pull my legs in, and my forehead falls to my knees. The tears come. There's no stopping them. She was twenty-one, which is longer than most cats get to live, and she had a happy life, but it doesn't change how much her loss hurts. The ache in my chest is unlike anything I've ever felt. It's debilitating.

I haven't known a day in my entire adult life without her. She's been by my side through it all. Loyal and loving. She loved me when I didn't love myself. She loved me when my parents were ashamed to look at me. She's seen me at my worst, my best, and every moment between...and loved me through it all. Animals are like that. Their love is unconditional. It's why their loss is so grave.

She saved me, my Saki girl. She will hold a special place in my heart forever.

"Babe," Quinn calls for me. "What are you...?" Her voice trails off when she sees me. "Oh my gosh. What happened?"

I lift my face and look up at her. "Saki's gone."

"Oh no." She falls to her knees beside me. Wrapping her arms around my back, she cries with me. "I'm so sorry."

I nod. "Me, too."

———

Today sucked. For starting out with so much promise, it fell downhill fast. I made a casket for Saki, wrapped her in her favorite blanket and held a funeral for her. It was just me, Quinn, and Clem, and really wasn't much of a service just a couple of words and some tears.

The house is quiet without her. She always had a larger-than-life personality, and her absence has left a gaping hole in my life. It will get easier over time, but right now, it just sucks. There's no denying it.

Quinn's been shooting worried stares my way all day while walking on eggshells around me. I can't really blame her, given that the last time something traumatic happened—and Clem checking herself into a rehab facility isn't even that traumatic—I lost it. I pushed her away and had an early midlife crisis. Things are different now. Just as Quinn said, I want to hold on to her during the rough patches. Together is the only way I want to be. I'm done going through life alone.

Reruns of *The Office* play on the TV, but neither one of us is really watching. I turn from the television to find Quinn looking at me with concern. She quickly twists back toward the show.

"Quinn." I can't help but smile. "Look at me."

She does.

"I'm okay. I promise." I squeeze her knee.

"Are you sure? You don't have to be. I'm just scared for you."

"I'm sad. I miss her. But you and I are good. Okay?" I reassure the doubts I know she's feeling.

She releases a breath, relief visible on her face. "Okay." She smiles and scoots in closer to me, leaning her head on my arm. "I love you."

"I love you, too, babe."

After a while, Quinn says, "You gave her a great life."

"Yeah. She was happy."

"She lived such a long time and was healthy her whole life." Quinn threads her fingers through mine and squeezes my hand.

"That's a blessing really. You know? That she went in her sleep and wasn't sick and had only good years."

"It is," Quinn agrees.

"It's just going to be hard for a while. I barely remember a life without her. She's been with me through everything. She was the best therapist I ever had." I release a chuckle, thinking about how much I've said for Saki's ears only over the years.

"Animals are special that way. I'm so glad you had her."

"Yeah. I know it sounds silly, but a part of me feels like she lived so long because she was waiting for me to find happiness. She was waiting for me to start a life with you."

Quinn drapes her arm over my chest, pulling me into a hug. "I don't think that sounds silly at all."

CHAPTER 35

QUINN

"We are family!" I sing at the top of my lungs.

Alma stands at my side, the most gorgeous bride I've ever seen, her arm wrapped around my back. I hold Love against my waist as Cat stands on the other side of me, her hold connects me to the circle of women.

Alma's mother Lee-Anne, some friends from The Lair, and even Amos's mother joins the circle as we belt out the lyrics to Sister's Sledge's "We are Family."

"I got all my sisters with me!" I bounce Love against my hip, and she laughs in her cute, little four-year-old giggly way that turns my heart to mush every time. I just adore her.

Weddings are the best. I've always loved them, but this one takes the cake.

Alma and Amos borrowed this gorgeous home of almost mansion proportions on Lake Michigan. We've spent the past several days hanging out, eating delicious food, being pampered, and laughing until our sides ached. It's been so special. The whole thing has been a true experience that I'll never forget.

One of the greatest parts was being able to stand up as the maid of honor for my best friend. I wasn't in attendance at Alma's first wedding. No one was except the officiant and photographer. She and Leo were so in love and cocooned in their love bubble that they wanted it to be just them. I mean, I get it. I feel that way about Ollie. Someday, I hope to marry, and I know I'll be tempted to run away with him and get married without all the fanfare, but I won't. I want my favorite people in the world with me when I promise my eternal, unconditional love to Ollie. It just seems more special that way.

Today was that—special. The backdrop of the Caribbean blue waters of Lake Michigan and the gentle breeze and waves made it simply breathtaking.

My absolute favorite part was seeing Alma utterly happy and at peace, finally. She, Amos, and Love make a beautiful family of three of the most amazing people I know.

The song ends, and I guide Love to the floor. Her princess tulle skirt flies out like a parachute as she nears the ground.

Lee-Anne approaches Alma. "It's getting late. I think I'm going to call it a night. I'll get Love tucked in and settled in my room."

"Okay, thanks, Mom." Alma hugs Lee-Anne, and

then she and Amos bend down to shower Love with affection.

I look around and find Ollie chatting with Ethan by the bar. Ethan holds a bottle of beer in his grasp while Ollie holds what I know to be a club soda. It's his go-to nonalcoholic drink for social situations.

The first few notes of Elvis's "Can't Help Falling in Love" play.

I extend my hand toward Ollie. "I love this song."

He excuses himself from Ethan and takes my hand in his. We walk a few steps to the dance floor on the huge deck overlooking the water.

Circling my arms around his neck, I lean against his chest. He holds me close and kisses the top of my head.

There have been no issues since we got back together on my birthday over six months ago. Every day with Ollie has been incredible. He's had some setbacks with a couple of people in NA and a big emotional blow with the loss of Saki, but it hasn't changed our relationship. It's only made us stronger.

I no longer live in fear that some tragedy is going to steal him from me. Going into this relationship with Ollie, with Leo as my only frame of reference, I was terrified of a relapse but learned quickly that wasn't the demon that ever had a chance of taking him from me. Instead, I realized that all the things I love about Ollie—his mind, heart, and compassion—were the same things that had the power to force him away. He cares so deeply about those in his life and carries misplaced guilt when things go wrong. He's been punishing himself for things that were never his fault. He finally sees that and has worked to change his response.

He's finally putting his, and by extension—my—happiness first.

I know, deep in my soul, that he's my forever.

Perhaps, I've always known.

"Did you have a good day?" he asks.

I lift my face from his chest and stare up into his beautiful blues. "The best. You?"

"Yeah. It was wonderful." He pauses. "I felt him here today."

"Who? Leo?"

Ollie dips his chin. "Yeah, I know it sounds weird, but I did. You know the feeling you get when someone is staring at you, and you look around, and sure enough, someone is? It was like that. But it was *him* that I felt, and he was happy."

"I believe it. I think he's happy and free, wherever he is, and I think he wants his family on earth to be happy. I mean, that's what true love is. Right? Loving someone so much that their happiness is the most important thing to you?"

"Yeah. He did love her above all else."

"He sure did, and he loved you, too." I smile up at Ollie.

"Well, then he'll be pleased to know that I'm good."

"Yes, you are." I press my lips against his.

A couple more slow songs play, the telltale sign that

the night is winding down. Alma and Amos retreat to the master bedroom, their own little honeymoon suite.

"Are you tired?" Ollie asks me.

"No."

"Good because I have something I want to show you." He grins—playful and sweet—and my heart clenches at the sight of his handsome face. I've never found anyone as gorgeous as I find Ollie, and I never will.

"I'm intrigued." I purse my lips.

Ollie takes my hand, and we walk down the wooden steps that lead from the house, over the sand dunes and down to the beach.

"It's such a beautiful night. I thought we could take a moonlit stroll on the beach," he says, toeing off his leather dress shoes and socks.

"I love that idea." I kick off my heels.

The water hits my feet, causing goose bumps, and I shiver. Lake Michigan is still cold in June. Ollie pulls me against his side, and we move in silence along the beach where the water meets the dry sand. The stars are bright, the night is dark, and the waves lap against the ground in a soft melody.

The fresh air cleanses my lungs and my spirit with each inhale.

A light catches my eye up ahead, and I squint to make it out. "What's that?"

"I'm not sure. Let's check it out."

We close the distance between us and the mysterious lights. I sigh, my hand to my chest, when I see the path of candles leading to a blanket on the beach. For a moment, I wonder if we've happened on someone else's surprise until I see the telescope set up on the blanket.

I gasp. "You did this?"

Ollie stares down, taking in my reaction, a content smile on his face. He nods.

"Oh my gosh. This is beautiful!" I follow the path of candles until my feet hit the plush blanket. There's a small wooden table set up on the corner of the blanket with a bottle of champagne in an ice bucket, two champagne flutes, and a plate of chocolate-covered strawberries.

"This is so sweet. I can't believe you did this? How did you do this without me noticing?"

His shoulders rise in a shrug, "I had a little help."

The area is lit up in a soft glow from the candles, and it's incredibly romantic.

"Remember the big power outage all those years ago?" he asks.

I smile. "Yeah. Alma's birthday."

He nods. "You talked about stars, the big dipper, the little dipper, and bears and gods."

I bite my lip, the corners of my lips tilting up at the memory. "I remember."

"Looking back, I think I fell in love with you that day. I didn't realize it at the time, but something changed. Prior to that, I'd been attracted to you because...you're gorgeous, but that was the first night I really craved...more."

I lift my arm and cup his face in my palm. "You never told me that."

"Yeah, well...anyway." He takes hold of my hips. "I loved that night and listening to you talk with so much fascination about the stars and their legends. So I researched some constellations, myself."

"You did?" I smile wide. "Which one?"

"Do you know the legend of Cassiopeia?" he asks.

I do, as Cassiopeia is one of the largest constellations in the Northern sky, but I want to hear Ollie's version.

"Tell me," I say.

"Well..." Ollie releases my sides and points up toward the sky. "First, you find the north star, and then look in the opposite direction of the big dipper, and you'll see a group of stars that appear to make an 'M.' Do you see it?"

My belly flutters with giddiness, knowing that Ollie learned about this to show me. "I do."

We look at the constellation for a moment as Ollie points out the different parts of what is meant to be Cassiopeia sitting on a throne.

"If you want to see it more closely." He motions toward the telescope. I find it in the telescope viewfinder as Ollie tells me the story.

"So I was researching constellations about love—"

I cut him off with a squeal. "Oh my gosh. This is

seriously the best. Okay, sorry for interrupting. Keep going."

Ollie chuckles. "As I said, I was researching about love and came across this story. To be honest, the beginning of the story isn't relatable to us because Cassiopeia was quite a horrible person. She was mean, selfish, and very vain...which obviously isn't you, at all."

"Good to know." I chuckle.

"So we'll just skip to the end of the legend because the beginning isn't romantic. I mean, at one point, she sacrifices her own daughter. Anyway, fast-forward over all the crazy shit."

Knowing the story, I'd agree that Cassiopeia wasn't the best of people. "Okay, sounds good." I laugh. "Tell me the good part."

"Okay, well, Cassiopeia pissed off the goddess Hera by telling her that she was more beautiful than Hera. So Hera tied her up in her throne and threw her into the sky."

"Romantic," I tease.

"Just wait...I'm getting to it. So Cassiopeia's husband, Cepheus, came home from a long day of chariot racing to find out that his wife was now in the stars, and he was beside himself in grief. He was so miserable and heartsick, unable to fathom living without his wife. So he went to his buddy Zeus, who, as you know, was the king of the gods. He cried and begged Zeus to be reunited with his wife. Zeus decided to show mercy on his friend, so he flung Cepheus into the sky next to his wife, and their love exploded. Now, to this day, Cassiopeia and her husband Cepheus can be seen as two of the brightest constellations in the Northern sky, clinging to each other in the stars for all eternity, more in love than ever."

"Aw." I giggle. "I love it."

I throw my arms around Ollie and hug him tight.

"I love that you learned that story for me."

"It was the best comparison I could come up with because I never want to live without you..." He lowers to the ground on one knee, and I cover my mouth with a gasp. "Quinn, now that I know what life with you is like, I can never go back to living one without you. You are the greatest, most wonderful part of my life. You make every day an adventure. You love me unconditionally and make me so happy...happier than I knew was possible. I love you more than anyone in this world, and I want to spend the rest of my life making you happy. You are the bright star that exploded into my life, demanding to be seen. You pushed past my walls and boundaries to reach me. Our love story rivals the greatest love stories of all time because no one has loved another person as much as I love you." He reaches inside his suit jacket and pulls out a little square box. Opening it toward me, he reveals a beautiful diamond ring.

Tears flow down my face.

"Do you remember that night when we saw the shooting star?"

I nod.

"You told me to make a wish, and I did. The wish just came to me, on instinct, and I made it. On that shooting star, I wished for you. At the time, I didn't even know what that meant or why you were the only thing that came to my mind in that second. But you were. I wished for you, Quinn. It wasn't our time then, but it's finally our time now. I'm asking you to make my wish come true and be mine forever. Let's write our own love story in the stars greater than all the rest. Quinn Kirkpatrick, will you marry me?"

"Yes! Oh my gosh, yes!" I fall onto Ollie's bent knee, tackling him with a hug. I press my mouth to his and kiss him over and over again. It's a blur of tears and kisses and so much happiness I want to scream.

We kiss until my lips hurt.

"Do you want the ring?" he asks, his smile against my lips.

I pull back. "Of course." I hold out my hand.

Ollie retrieves the fallen ring box from the side of the blanket and pulls out the engagement ring. It slides onto my finger in a perfect fit.

The ring is stunning. It looks like a two-carat cushion-cut diamond in a halo setting. Small diamonds that look like shining stars circle the platinum band. It's sexy, classic, and modern at the same time. It's perfect.

I kiss him again, unable to stop my tears from falling.

"You know that shooting star?" I ask.

"Yeah."

"I wished for you, too."

CHAPTER 36

OLLIE

QUINN FEEDS me a chocolate-covered strawberry and takes a bite of one herself before climbing back under the blanket with me.

We lie on our backs facing the night sky. The sounds of nature and gentle waves surround us. I'm glad I brought extra blankets because it's chilly by the water at night, but it's cozy beneath the blanket with Quinn.

"See that one right there, and that one...see how it makes an arrow?" Quinn points up toward the sky.

"Yeah."

"That's Sagittarius, my birth zodiac sign. It's an arrow. It's best seen in the Michigan skies in the summer months. Supposedly, Sagittarians are optimistic, hilarious, fair-minded, honest, and smart. We are fun and spontaneous and have lots of friends. We're also super chatty...the best conversationalists out of all the signs."

"Sounds like you." I chuckle.

"You're an Aquarius, which is actually one of the signs most compatible with me, obviously."

"Obviously."

"We can't see your constellation tonight. Aquarius is best seen up here in like October-ish. But an Aquarian is the most humanitarian sign. You're a thinker who wants to change the world. You're independent, intelligent, unique, and idealistic."

"Do you think that's me?" I ask.

"Absolutely. Are you kidding? You're all about helping people. That totally describes you."

"Well, okay. As long as we're compatible." I kiss her temple.

"Oh, we're very compatible."

I swipe her hair away from her face. "Did you really wish for me that night?"

"Yes." She playfully hits my chest. "I'm telling the truth. I did."

"That's kind of crazy. Right?"

"Or just fate."

"Maybe."

"There's no maybe about it. We're meant to be together, and since that night, our path has been written in the stars. We just had to wait a little bit." She kisses me softly. "I love my ring, by the way. It's perfect."

"Good. I'm glad. I thought it looked like you."

She holds her hand in front of her face, admiring her ring. "Just like me."

"I'm serious when I say you make me happier than I ever thought I could be. I don't know what I did to deserve you, Quinn, but I'm going to spend the rest of my life making sure you know how much I cherish you."

"I feel the same way."

We slip out of our clothes and toss them out of the blanket.

Quinn straddles my hips. Sliding atop me, she takes me in inch by inch until we're completely connected. We make slow, sweet love beneath the stars, knowing that we're in this crazy, beautiful life together. Forever.

For a moment, I think that it'd be cool if another shooting star presented itself tonight, but I realize it wouldn't matter. I already made my wish, and she came true.

Quinn is everything I need in this life, and what comes next is just a bonus.

———

Hushed whispers wake me from slumber. I lie bare against Quinn's naked body beneath a blanket. The sun shines brightly behind us, heating our surroundings. I squint as the sounds of the water lapping gently against the beach sing a song luring me from sleep.

It takes me a moment to register the bright colors before me. Coming into focus are two elderly women in neon track suits out for their morning stroll along the beach. Only, they've stopped and stand at the foot of the blanket, peering down toward us.

I clear my throat and pull the blanket up, making sure it's covering Quinn. "Good morning."

"Appears so," one woman says.

"Good morning to you, handsome," the other adds.

I sense Quinn waking beside me, and she covers her face with the blanket, completely disappearing from view.

"Well, have a good day," I offer, urging the women to continue by us.

"You too," the one in the bright pink tracksuit says.

They walk on by, the woman in neon yellow says to her friend. "You don't see that every day. Have you and Earl ever made love on the beach?"

I slink beneath the blanket with Quinn, not wanting to hear the details of Earl and pink tracksuit lady's love-making history. Quinn giggles, and I laugh along with her.

"Awkward." She chuckles.

"Very. We should probably get dressed. I'm sure there'll be more people walking along the beach soon."

She splays her hands against my chest. "Ugh. I don't want to. This is heaven. The best night of my life."

I kiss her lips. "Same."

"I can't believe we're engaged," she exclaims, kissing me once more.

"I feel like I've been waiting my whole life for you, Quinn Kirkpatrick."

"Soon to be Quinn Hale." She snuggles against me. "I love you so much, Ollie."

"I love you more."

"I don't know if that's possible, but since you picked out the most beautiful engagement ring in the world, I'll let you claim it for now."

I kiss her nose. "You're too kind."

"It is one of my many attributes."

Her soft skin is against mine, and our legs are wrapped together.

"I don't want this night to end," she says. "It's been so perfect. I want to lie beneath this blanket in our happy place forever."

"Quinn." My voice turns serious. "Anywhere with you is my happy place, and we have a lifetime to explore them all. Every moment from here on out is part of our forever, and it's going to be great. The magic isn't going to end when we step out from this blanket. It's only going to get better. We have a forever of perfect moments to cherish."

She presses her lips to mine.

"Plus, you can show everyone your ring and tell them the good news over breakfast."

Quinn releases a shrill sound that's a mix between a laugh and a squeal. "Oh, so true. Fine...we can get dressed."

"If we must," I tease.

I retrieve our clothing. Limbs flail beneath the

blanket in a heap of laughter and awkwardness as we get dressed, at least enough to cover all the important parts.

Tossing the blanket to the side, I hop up and extend a hand to Quinn.

Her bridesmaid dress is pulled to the side. Her left arm is pulled through the strap intended for her right, and the side of the dress is bunched at her front. The loose curls she wore yesterday have been replaced by her classic early morning lion's mane, and streaks of mascara trail down her cheeks.

I can't help but smile. "You're one beautiful hot mess."

She laughs with a shrug. "And you're just hot. How is that fair?"

I extend my hand, threading my fingers through hers. "Come on. I'll come back for everything else later."

We walk along the beach toward the house where everyone's probably still sound asleep.

"The water's so serene right now," Quinn says.

I follow her gaze and agree. There's barely a ripple until it meets the sand. The sun from the east shines down, creating little sparkling diamonds along the quiet surface.

"It's gorgeous. Almost too quiet." My last thought is a challenge.

"No," Quinn protests. "It's freezing."

Bending, I circle my arms around her thighs and hoist her over my shoulder. She laughs and kicks.

Smacking my back with her hands, she yells, "Don't you dare, Oliver Hale."

"It's too late. It's already in motion."

"No! No! No!" Quinn squeals as I run through the frigid water, creating waves of our own.

When I'm waist deep, I throw her through the air. She screams as she hits the water. She jumps up from beneath the water with a gasp. "Oh my God. It's so cold. I'm going to kill you."

She runs toward me.

"You'll get used to it." I laugh as she splashes me with water. "It's refreshing, right?"

"No. It's freezing."

She circles my neck with her arms, and I lift her. Hiking up her long dress, she wraps her legs around my waist. "I can't believe you did that." She laughs.

"I promised you adventure."

"Should I have specified *warm* adventure?" She lifts a brow.

"A life of adventure lies in the unpredictable cracks of life, in the unplanned moments."

Her wet lips kiss mine. "I'll take it all."

"Good."

"Can we plan a warm bath together after this moment, though? Because you know, marriage is also about compromise."

"I can get on board with that," I say against her lips.

I kiss my fiancée, her warm body against mine in the cold water creating the perfect balance. I suppose that's what life is all about, balance. The cold with the hot. The good with the bad. The happy with the sad. It's all going to be there throughout our lives. I can try with all that I am, but I'll never keep all the heartache away. I'll never be able to make every day perfect and magical.

My life with Quinn is going to be amazing and full of love and laughter. But in the moments it's not, I'll have her by my side to get through it all. For me, that's true love. It's finding the person who makes the good days deliriously blissful and the hard times bearable. It's finding the person who loves me unconditionally through it all, just as I love her.

It's answered wishes.

It's laughter, passion, friendship, and love.

It's Quinn.

My one and only.

She's my happily ever after, and I'm going to cherish every single moment of it.

EPILOGUE

OLLIE

ONE YEAR LATER

Every single day I wake up, and my chest aches...with love. I'm so fucking grateful for my life and for her—my Quinn. She and I are living a life I never dreamed of, sharing a love I never knew was possible. Everyone always talks about *the love of their life*, but truthfully, I never truly got it.

I get it now.

My love for Quinn is the greatest, most amazing feeling that has led me to the most incredible experiences. I can barely remember my life before her, and I suppose it's because my life with her shines so brightly—it's all I can see.

At this moment, my chest aches more than it ever

has because she is, without a doubt, the most beautiful bride to ever exist. She takes my breath away.

Walking down the aisle, she is simply stunning. She's wearing an ivory A-line princess V-neck dress. The bodice and train have an overlay of intricate lace and beading. It's classic, traditional, and sexy as fuck.

I know these terms to describe a wedding dress, along with every flower in her bouquet, from the coral pink peonies to the white Alfred Carriere roses because Quinn has been planning this wedding every single day since the moment I slipped that ring on her finger a year ago.

Planning her wedding was a lifelong calling of hers that I didn't even know she had, and she took it very seriously. It was adorable, but thankfully, we only have to get married once.

The theme is a classic, rustic barn wedding. I'm certain she's had her father cleaning out the large barns on his property for the past twelve months. One holds the ceremony while the larger one is for the reception. Everything looks straight out of a magazine. Ropes of flowers hang from the large wooden beams. Romantic candles light the space.

I see Quinn in every detail, and it's all simply beautiful. Yet the most stunning part of the wedding is her.

She wears her hair up in a fancy updo of curls. Her makeup is subtle, just enough to accent her stunning features, and I know she did that for me. I've always found her more beautiful just the way she is.

Clementine stands to my side in a form-fitting tuxedo as my best woman. She holds our little gray pittie puppy with cerulean eyes named Blue in her arms. Quinn and I still volunteer at the shelter with Clementine, and although we were going to wait until after the wedding to get another pet, it was love at first sight with Blue.

And now...he's wearing a bowtie...and is our official ring bearer. *Because of course he is.*

Alma is Quinn's matron of honor, and her four sisters are her bridesmaids. Love and Quinn's two nieces are our flower girls.

Quinn has planned every detail out to perfection. I hope it's everything she's dreamed about because I can't imagine anything more perfect.

Her father gives his blessing and kisses her on the cheek before placing her hand in mine.

She stands facing me, and I can't stop smiling. "You are so beautiful," I whisper.

"So are you." She smiles back.

The minister says all the things, and I repeat the words where I'm supposed to, but it's all a blur. It's hard to focus on anything else when Quinn's standing before me, promising to be mine forever.

I am one lucky man, and I'll never take that for granted.

———

"In Da Club" by 50 Cent pounds through the speakers. Quinn and a circle of her girlfriends squat low toward the ground, bouncing their booties in the air.

"There's college Quinn." Alma chuckles beside me.

"Sure is." I smile wide.

"I'm so happy for you, Ollie. You two are perfect together."

"Thanks." I wrap my arm around Alma's back, and she leans in for a hug. "Where's Love?"

Alma scans the barn and chuckles. "Dancing behind Quinn, of course, and apparently learning how to dance just like her." Sure enough, Love is imitating Quinn's dance moves. "She had better not ask to play 50 Cent anytime soon. I'm not ready for the Disney soundtracks era to be over."

"I'm sure she'll be back on the Disney train tomorrow." I shoot her a smile. "I have a surprise for Quinn, but Love will love it, too. Make sure to follow us out."

I join Quinn on the dance floor. She grinds up against my leg, and I laugh. "Hey, I have a surprise for you."

She stops dancing and squints toward me. "Your face looks mischievous. Is this a good surprise?"

"Aren't they all?"

"Uh, no. Some surprises are not good, my love. Especially on a day that I've been planning for so long."

I take her hand in mine. "You're going to love it, and I guarantee you that no other elegant, rustic barn wedding will have what I'm about to show you."

"Oh, no. What did you do, Ollie?" She looks hesitant.

"You'll see." I pull her outside, and we walk around the barn.

She starts laughing when she sees her surprise in the field.

"You are crazy." She laughs.

"And you love it."

"That, I do." She pulls me into a kiss.

A large white castle bouncy house and a huge white inflatable waterslide have been set up in the field.

"I'm all about the bouncy house," she says. "But I am not going down that waterslide in my dress."

"You only live once, babe." I shoot her a wink.

"Can I go in the bouncy house?" Love asks.

"Of course, Lovie. Lead the way," I tell her.

A group of us climb into the castle bouncy house and start jumping into the air. The space is filled with laughter. People in their best attire are toppling over and falling to the floor of the inflatable castle, landing in all sorts of compromising positions. It's awesome. I face Quinn and hold her hands in mine, and we bounce up and down. Her curls fall around her face as she laughs.

"Great choice for our rustic wedding, right?" I ask.

"Yeah." She chuckles. "Perfect."

A line of our friends and family wait outside the bouncy house for their turn.

"Come on." I help Quinn out of the castle. "We should lead the way for the waterslide."

"Ollie." She lets out a sigh. "But...my dress. It's going to be all wet."

"You don't have to do it if you don't want," I say in all seriousness. "Or we can wait until the very end or tomorrow when you're out of your dress."

Quinn looks up toward the tall waterslide and releases a sigh. "No." She shakes her head. "I signed up for a life of adventure. Let's go."

"Are you sure?" I quirk a brow.

"Yeah, all the big stuff—the cake cutting, and dancing, and pictures are done with. Let's do this." She grins.

"Oh, there will be pictures." I chuckle as I lead her toward the stairs of the waterslide.

We climb up the steps until we reach the top. There are two slides, side by side. Water rushes out the tops of both slides and speeds down to the waiting pool below.

"You wanna race?" she asks, positioning herself in front of one of the slides.

I step in front of the other. "Of course."

"Okay, count," she says.

I nod. "On three. One. Two. Three."

We jump onto the slides. Quinn screams beside me as we fly down the slick surface. My entire body submerges beneath the water at the bottom before I shoot back up to find Quinn, drenched and laughing.

She throws her arms around my neck, and I hold her to me. "Who won?"

"I'm pretty sure it was a tie." I press my lips to hers.

"I think so." She kisses me again. "Thank you for

choosing me," she says, her tone more serious. "I love you so much, Gorgeous."

"Thank you for choosing me, Little One, and I love you more."

She smiles. "Let's go again."

QUINN

EIGHT YEARS LATER

"Hey baby, bring Momma the shovel," I say to my little Leo, our two-year-old bundle of energy. Leo holds the plastic sand shovel in his pudgy little grasp and walks it over to me. "Thank you. Are you still working on your castle?"

He nods.

"Okay. Make sure to put more sand in the bucket so we can make it even bigger. Momma's gonna work on the moat so your boat can get to the castle."

I dig the shovel into the white sand of our favorite beach in Hawaii.

Ollie and I spent our honeymoon here and fell in love with the island. We've come back twice every year since. Hawaii has become our home away from home. We'll never leave Michigan because our families and favorite people are there. It's our home, but we definitely look forward to our tropical paradise visits.

I look toward the ocean and cheer, clapping my

hands. Our oldest daughter, Maisie at seven years old is up on her surfboard, riding a wave toward the shore. The next wave surfaces, and Ollie and our daughter, Maddie, stand together on the board, surfing the wave. Maddie hasn't been able to get up on her own yet, but she's close.

The girls were born just a year apart. Maisie has my personality and Ollie's looks, whereas Madelyn looks just like me but is a hundred percent Ollie in personality. And then baby Leo, who is our *blessing*, also known as our unplanned baby, is a perfect mixture of the two of us in both appearance and personality.

We thought our family was complete with the two girls, but Leo came along unexpectedly, and now I don't know what we'd do without him. Our family is perfect.

Maddie squeals as she and Ollie ride the surfboard toward shore. Ollie's laughter can be heard over the crashing of the waves, and it makes my heart soar.

It's all come full circle. When I first met Ollie, he reminded me of a surfer, and here he is as the hottest forty-eight-year-old I've seen making surfing look easy while building cherished memories with our children.

I've loved Oliver Hale since I was nineteen years old. He's always been irresistibly attractive to me. I loved him as my friend, boyfriend, fiancé, and then my husband. But he has never been more beautiful to me than he is as the father to our children. He's the best husband I could've ever asked for, and somehow, an even more incredible father.

We've been married for eight years, and I still find myself loving him more every day.

I will love him until the day I die, and even after that, for he's my forever.

He's given me a life of love and adventure—so much more than I knew to wish for. And yet it all came true anyway.

Every wish.

The ones I knew, and the ones I didn't.

All because he loves me.

ACKNOWLEDGMENTS

I want to thank my readers so very much. Thank you for reading my stories and loving my words! I wouldn't be living this dream without you. Thank you from the bottom of my heart!

To my beta readers and proofreaders—Gala, Suzanne, Amy, Kylie, and Kim—You all are so awesome. Seriously, each of you is a gift, and you have helped me in invaluable, different ways. I love you all so much. XOXO

To my cover artist, Letitia Hasser from RBA Designs —Thank you! Your work inspires me. You are a true artist, and I am so grateful to work with you. People do judge a book by its cover, so thank you for making mine *gorgeous*! XO

To my editor, Jenny Sims from Editing4Indies— Finding you was a true gift, one that I hope to always have on this journey. Thank you for always fitting me in! I am so grateful for you and everything you have done to make this book the best it can be. XOXO

To my proofreader, Kylie Ryan from Final Cut Editing—You are the best! I don't know what I'd do without you! Thank you for everything you do for me! Love you!

Lastly, to my loyal readers—I love you! Thank you for reaching out, reviewing, and sharing your book recs with your friends. There are seriously great people in this book community, and I am humbled by your support. Your messages breathe life into my writing and keep me going on this journey. Truly, thank you! Because of you, indie authors get their stories out. Thank you for supporting all authors and the great stories they write.

You can connect with me on several places, and I would love to hear from you.

Join my readers group: www.facebook.com/groups/wadeswarriorsforthehea

Find me on Facebook: www.facebook.com/EllieWadeAuthor

Find me on Instagram: www.instagram.com/authorelliewade

Visit my website: www.elliewade.com

Remember, the greatest gift you can give an author is a review. If you feel so inclined, please leave a review on the various retailer sites. It doesn't have to be fancy. A couple of sentences would be awesome!

I could honestly write a whole book about everyone in this world whom I am thankful for. I am blessed in so many ways, and I am beyond grateful for this beautiful life. XOXO

Forever,
Ellie <3

Other Titles by Ellie Wade

The Flawed Heart Series

Finding London

Keeping London

Loving London

Eternally London

Taming Georgia

The Choices Series

A Beautiful Kind of Love

A Forever Kind of Love

A Grateful Kind of Love

Stand-alones

Fragment

Chasing Memories

Forever Baby

A Hundred Ways to Love

ABOUT THE AUTHOR

Ellie Wade resides in southeast Michigan with her husband, three children, and three dogs. She has a master's in education from Eastern Michigan University, and she is a huge University of Michigan sports fan. She loves the beauty of her home state, especially the lakes and the gorgeous autumn weather. When she is not writing, she is reading, snuggling up with her kids, or spending time with family and friends. She loves traveling and exploring new places with her family.